tomorrow**never**knows

To Diana for, well, everything

tomorrow**never**knows

the silverchair story

jeff apter

COULOMB
COMMUNICATIONS

Published by:

COULOMB
COMMUNICATIONS

PO Box 751
Port Melbourne 3207

National Library of Australia Cataloguing-in-Publication entry:

Apter, Jeff, 1961–
    Tomorrow never knows: the Silverchair story.

    ISBN 0 9580737 2 4.

    1. Silverchair (Musical group). 2. Rock groups – Australia.
    3. Rock Music – Australia – 1991–2000. 4. Rock music –
    Australia – 2001–2010. I. Title.

    781.660994

Every effort has been made to acknowledge the source of all photographs reproduced
in this book. If any acknowledgements have been omitted, please contact the publisher
and these will be rectified in subsequent editions.

Contents

Acknowledgements

To Silvia Kwon, for reminding me that I could actually do this; John Watson, Melissa Chenery and all at Eleven for being way more accommodating than they had to be; Stephanie Holt for making sense of it all; Diana Gonsalves for digging deep; Elissa Blake and Darren Gover for coping with a temperamental author-under-development; David Fricke, Robert Hambling, Nick Launay, John O'Donnell, Van Dyke Parks, Craig Mathieson, Tobin Finnane, Peter McNair and Tracee Hutchison for going on the record (at length); Rob Hirst for giving it the once over; Guy McEwan at the State Theatre for the backstage pass; the Silver-families for checking the facts; and www.chairpage.com for their bottomless archive; and, of course, Daniel Johns, Ben Gillies and Chris Joannou (aka Silverchair) for revisiting the past — and for making the music in the first place.

Comments and quotes that appear in the text, unless otherwise noted, were derived from interviews conducted by the author with the following people: Daniel Johns, Chris Joannou, Ben Gillies, Tobin Finnane, John Watson, John O'Donnell, Nick Launay, David Fricke, Elissa Blake, Van Dyke Parks, Robert Hambling, Tracee Hutchison, Peter McNair, Craig Mathieson, Paul Mac and David Bottrill.

Anthem for the Year 2003

*'A lot of bands can't duplicate what they do on record.
I think Silverchair can.'*

—Daniel Johns

Daniel Johns has every reason to be nervous. It is April 10, 2003 and the blond Silverchair singer/songwriter/frontman is backstage at Sydney's State Theatre. The band is due on stage in an hour. It's a cramped backstage area for such an opulent theatre, but Johns doesn't want too many people hanging about anyway. The room has been cleared of family and friends and well-wishers.

Backstage with Johns are his bandmates and long-time buddies from Newcastle, bassist Ben Gillies and drummer Chris Joannou, plus the other two members of Silverchair's touring party, keyboardists/singers Julian Hamilton and Stuart Hunter, and the band's long-time crew — production manager Bailey Holloway and lighting man Hugh Taranto. The band's manager, John Watson, and tour manager, Melissa Chenery, are drifting in and out, checking that all is ready for the show and updating the band as to when they're due on stage. The mood is slightly tense. Johns — hardly a man you'd describe as talkative — is quietly fidgeting with his guitar strap and staring at the wall. It's been a tough struggle to get to this strange crossroad in his career — a comeback at the age of 24.

The past two years have been the highest and lowest of Johns's turbulent life. He wrote, recorded and co-produced the band's fourth long-player, *Diorama*, the most challenging album of their career and after a self-imposed two-year break, he and the band had made a small-scale live return at the Big Day Out, in January 2002, but Johns didn't regard the shows too highly. 'Festivals are like infomercials,' he said at the time. What Johns desired was a venue such as this one, typically the site for sit-down shows and, a few months earlier, the setting for a brilliant three-night stand by Brian Wilson, the reclusive Beach Boy legend. *Diorama*, an often-elegant album of orchestral rock & roll, wasn't suited to the steamy heave of the moshpit. It was more a record for quiet consideration — even if the State Theatre's huge chandeliers posed a glittery distraction.

During those Big Day Out shows, Johns had been feeling the pain. His joints had started aching and he was depending on a mixed bag of painkillers to get him through the band's short sets. The pain he was feeling was intense and debilitating. Within weeks of the Big Day Out shows, he could barely move. His joints had stiffened, and he needed a cane to walk the few metres to answer his door. He spent a lot of time at his parents' home, very close to his house at Merewether, on the NSW north coast. As time passed he virtually relocated to their home. He could barely move. One day his brother, Heath, was seated next to him on the couch. When Heath shifted his weight, Daniel cried out in pain.

Johns had previously been diagnosed with Parvo Virus and this had triggered reactive arthritis. Johns is among the 8 per cent of the population predisposed towards this condition. His bout had begun when he was mixing *Diorama* in November 2001, when he came down with a condition very similar to chronic fatigue syndrome. Weakened, he woke up one morning and couldn't move his leg. 'Then it moved to my pelvis, my back,' he told me. 'I pumped myself full of painkillers for the Big Day Out. I can hardly remember being on stage.'

For Johns, much of 2002 had been a blur. The band managed to premiere *Diorama* on April 1 with a 'Live at the Wireless' set at radio station Triple J, then with an extended appearance on Channel 10's *Rove Live*. Three concerts in New Zealand rounded off the week. But Johns's pain was increasing. He wasn't keen to use prescription drugs as a crutch, as he'd done a few years earlier when suffering from an eating disorder, and by the middle of 2002 he'd spent several days in hospital due to intense pain. His muscles deteriorated and there was nothing supporting his joints; he was virtually crippled. The band cancelled all overseas promotion for their new album, and it quickly slipped out of the charts.

Johns had always had an interest in things alternative — from rock & roll to medicine — so he booked himself into a naturopathic treatment centre in Los Angeles just before the ARIA award ceremony in October 2002. He'd tried several conventional treatments, but these had actually increased the pain he was feeling. Twice a week he would meet with a specialist for tests and treatment recommendations. Then he would front for treatment, usually with his fiancée, singer/actress Natalie Imbruglia. To say the treatments were intense would be a serious understatement.

A typical day of treatment ran like this: acupuncture for 45 minutes; oxygen chamber for an hour; physio for an hour and a half; and, finally, a treatment 'which breaks all the hardened fluid in my joints — you feel like all the bones are exploding in your legs.' Johns would limp out of the treatment with tears in his eyes and another day of the same to look forward to. To speed up the process, he was swallowing roughly 80 pills a day to help transport all the nutrients into his bloodstream.

In the middle of this therapy bootcamp, Johns had flown back to Sydney for a one-off ARIA appearance on October 15 at the Sydney Superdome, where the band collected five gongs, including those for Best Album and Best Group. More importantly, he, Gillies and Joannou, along with pianist Paul Mac and Julian Hamilton, the musical all-rounder from Sydney band Prop, tore into a live version of *Diorama*'s first single, 'The Greatest View'. As the song built to its anthemic, deeply melodic conclusion, the crowd of six thousand — jaded music-biz types and diehard punters alike — jumped out of their chairs, applauding madly. It was the night's peak. Silverchair went away winners, and Daniel Johns's recovery had begun. As for *Diorama,* it raced back up the Australian charts. With some Sunday news-magazine cover stories and a special Silverchair episode of *Rove Live*, it stayed there through Christmas and the first few months of 2003.

'It seemed a good way to test the waters,' Johns told me at the time of their ARIA one-off. 'We got asked to play and I said, "I don't know if I can," but I decided it was a good thing to try. It was only two weeks out of the treatment time, anyway.' Still, six months passed after the ARIAs before the band made their proper live return.

Johns returned to the city of angels after the ARIAs, staying there through late October and November, and then parts of January and February, to continue his treatment. Gillies went home to Newcastle to surf and learn to dance the salsa with his ballerina girlfriend, Hayley Alexander. Joannou, meanwhile, retreated to the NSW Central Coast, where he shares a comfortable coastal spread with his girlfriend Sarah McLeod, frontwoman of ARIA-winning rock band the Superjesus. The three old schoolfriends see little of each other nowadays. Their lives have changed hugely since they used to bang out songs in the Gillies family garage after school at the nearby Newcastle High. They are now wealthy 20-somethings whose faces — especially Johns's — are regular features in both gossip rags and the credible music press. They understand this is the downside of being in Australia's biggest rock band, but the off-stage attention isn't something they enjoy.

The band finally got back together to rehearse in Newcastle in February 2003. By then, Johns was itching to get back on stage; not because he loved the touring life — he hated it — but because he had a point to prove. 'A lot of bands I see live can't duplicate what they do on record,' he told me. 'I think Silverchair can do live what they do on record. Just before the Big Day Out [2002] we rehearsed all the [*Diorama*] songs — "Tuna in the Brine", "Across the Night", "Luv Your Life" — and it sounded great. I didn't expect it to work but somehow we made it work.'

Backstage at the State Theatre, the adrenalin pumping through the sold-out crowd of two thousand is almost seeping through the walls. The band haven't staged their own headlining tour since December 1999. They've only played live eleven times since then — and six of those gigs were truncated Big Day Out 'infomercials'. Johns, Gillies and Joannou can sense their own anxiety and the crowd's eagerness to experience these new songs, which were released a year ago, almost to the day. Can they still cut it live? How will the crowd react to the epic sweep of *Diorama*'s songs, which are a long way from the band's early rockin' fury? How many punters will expect to hear

'Tomorrow', the anthem that made them stars back in 1994? Have they become — at 24 — a Generation X nostalgia act?

Manager Watson pokes his head around the door. 'It's time,' he tells the band. The house lights dim and a roar lights up the room. The band shuffle on-stage in the dark and plug in. Golden sounds fill the theatre — it sounds great and feels even better.

Silverchair are back in the building.

Bibliography

'Making of Diorama: The Resurrection of Daniel Johns' Australian *Rolling Stone* June 2002; 'The Uneasy Chair' Australian *Rolling Stone* September 2002; 'Silverchair's Greater View' Australian *Rolling Stone* April 2003

1

Innocent Criminals

'When you're that age you don't make music to get laid or to make money or to see your photo on the cover of a magazine. You make music because you like the noise you make when you bang on your guitar. All great music is born from that.'

—John Watson

Silverchair are Australia's most popular rock band of the past ten years. Each of their four albums —*Frogstomp* (1995), *Freak Show* (1997), *Neon Ballroom* (1999) and *Diorama* (2002) — has debuted at Number One on the Australian charts, and they have shifted, in total, over six million copies worldwide. The band's fanbase stretches from their hometown, Newcastle, to most parts of the globe. In a golden run between 1994 and the end of 1999, they had twelve consecutive Top 40 singles in Australia, making them the most successful local chart performers of the '90s. They've also won enough Australian Recording Industry Association Awards (ARIAs) to fill several mantelpieces.

They're an ambitious band who in this short stretch have grown from punked-up grunge-keteers to a trio that's more than happy to bring in an orchestra when needed. But there's more to Silverchair's success than great songs, powerful recordings, frenetic shows and a diehard following that accepts every creative step the band take, no matter how radical. Their singer/guitarist and key songwriter, Daniel Johns, has lived through any number of personal crises. He's endured a life-threatening eating disorder, crippling arthritis, chronic depression and the heavy emotional baggage that comes with a life lived reluctantly in the public eye. What he's drawn from these hardships is a batch of passionate, deeply felt songs that have connected with an audience that understands what it feels like to be an outsider.

More than once, the band has been a press release away from chucking it all in — as they freely admit. But the trio has endured and prospered, striking out for new musical territory with their most recent album, *Diorama*.

In the background, savvy management has ensured that the trio hasn't suffered from overexposure, the kiss of death at a time in rock & roll when a band gains veteran status if they make it past their first album. The timing of Silverchair's rise was perfect, too: they surfaced as the grunge wave broke — and being all of 15 at the time, they had an irresistible hook for the music media. And, impressively, their audience hung about, even when the band found that grunge no longer filled any holes in their souls. It didn't hurt, of course, that their lead singer was blond, blue-eyed and in desperate need of a hug.

Silverchair's rise followed one of rock's worst flat spots. It's no small irony that one of the world's biggest bands of the 1980s and early 1990s was named Dire Straits. Contemporary music was in a baggy-suited, headband-wearing state of transition, and Mark Knopfler's spruced-up mob of former UK pub rockers ruled the airwaves and the small screen.

A cursory run through the ten top singles of 1991 and 1992 reveals plenty about the dire state of music in that post-punk, pre-grunge, pre-Silverchair time. The 'Grease Mega-Mix' was 1991's best seller, with Daryl Braithwaite's slick 'The Horses' and Bryan Adams's even slicker '(Everything I Do) I Do It for You' not far behind. Pop diva Cher and supermodel-chaser Rod Stewart were selling large amounts of records, as was straitlaced songbird Mariah Carey.

The following twelve months weren't much better. Billy Ray Cyrus, the linedancing cowboy, sat at Number One with 'Achy Breaky Heart', while Julian Lennon's treacly 'Saltwater' also made the list of the ten best sellers. Watered-down soul-sters Simply Red and the Australian cast recording of *Jesus Christ Superstar* shifted serious units.

Bored punters started looking towards England, especially Manchester, where such bands as the Happy Mondays and the Stone Roses were gulping Ecstasy and doing their bit to knock down the wall that separated rock and dance. But their music was rarely heard on commercial radio in Australia — if it was played at all, it was during the graveyard shift when advertisers didn't really care about the playlist. In the main, this new British music was relegated to specialist stations such as the Sydney-based youth network Triple J and Melbourne community station 3RRR. Mainstream Australia was being force-fed the tarted-up pub rock of the Baby Animals or the lung-straining bluster of Jimmy Barnes, whose unstoppable covers album, *Soul Deep*, was such a no-brainer that the man himself admitted 'a monkey could sing these songs and they'd still be hits.'

Yet during the 1980s, the very same Jimmy Barnes had been at the forefront of a distinctive style of Australian rock & roll — Oz rock, in shorthand — which had made an enormous impact. Cold Chisel, Rose Tattoo, the Angels and Midnight Oil had endured apprenticeships served in such sweaty dives as Sydney's Stagedoor Tavern, the Bondi

Lifesaver and Melbourne's Bombay Rock. They emerged from this to make powerful, important records such as Cold Chisel's *East* and Midnight Oil's *10, 9, 8, 7, 6, 5, 4, 3, 2, 1*.

Oz rock crowds were male-dominated. They were up for big nights of drinking and sex, or fighting, if the ladies weren't keen. And these bands — the Oils, the Chisels, the Tatts — supplied the soundtrack to thousands of their gritty, beer-stained evenings. Though the bands were diverse in style, there were common threads: a blazing guitar riff and a ball-tearing vocal to keep the crowds keen, and if the lyrics could connect to Aussie themes, well, all the better. The publicans were happy, because the punters drank. The bands got work.

The introduction of Australian quotas on radio meant that local bands were receiving healthy airplay, which quickly led to record sales. In April 1981, Oz rock reached a very public early peak when Cold Chisel caused havoc at the *Countdown* Awards, smashing the set (even though they were miming). Within a month, their album *East* had sold over 200,000 copies. Unlike what was to follow, Oz rock was a locally based sensation that was more about sweat and hard yards than image and good grooming. All was good.

However Oz rock was fading by the late 1980s. Venues were closing, bands were splitting or losing their crowd-pulling appeal. The Angels and Midnight Oil started looking Stateside for a larger audience, which meant their Australian followers started looking elsewhere for new bands to love. The credible, punk-influenced Australian underground bands that had emerged during the Oz rock phase — Brisbane's Go-Betweens and the Saints, Perth's the Triffids, the Nick Cave-led Birthday Party — had all left town, either to develop and prosper overseas or crash and burn, citing the usual inner-band politics.

But as the 90s began, there were ripples of change in the mainstream, both in Australia and overseas. Funky Californian punks the Red Hot Chili Peppers hit big, really big, in 1992 with their junkies' requiem, 'Under the Bridge', and its parent album, *Blood Sugar Sex Magik*, which reached Number One in Australia during November 1991 and hung about the charts for 61 weeks. American college rockers REM had crossed over into the mainstream in 1991 with their *Out of Time* album and its breakout hit single, 'Losing My Religion' — without sacrificing any of their garage-rock sensibilities or singer Michael Stipe's intriguing weirdness. And at the Number Seven spot on 1992's best-selling album chart was the album that started the musical and cultural revolution known as 'alternative': Nirvana's *Nevermind*.

So what was Australia's contribution while alternative music was starting to make an impression on the charts? Nothing much, just such safe local acts as 1927, Wendy Matthews and the Rockmelons, playing music designed, as one critic put it at the time, 'for people who don't like music'. Still stuck in the 1980s, most labels were trying to hunt down the next Noiseworks. Offering a more polished, American-influenced variation of Oz rock, this band were favourite sons of the beer barns. Noiseworks' first two albums, a self-titled effort from 1987 and 1988's *Touch*, sold almost 400,000 copies. But such new signings as Bang the Drum, Wildland, 21 Guns and Big Storm all fell flat, in part because the musical tide was shifting away from the slick, over-produced pop-rock that made Noiseworks stars.

Occasionally, underground bands like punkish popsters Ratcat broke through with a hit, but their success was as brief as the songs they sang. Meanwhile, at the major record labels, Artist and Repertoire (A&R) talent-spotters such as Sony's

John Watson, Polydor's Craig Kamber and Ra's Todd Wagstaff
were on the lookout for Australian bands that packed the same
anti-everything attitude and pure rock & roll clout as Nirvana.
'Alternative' bands such as You Am I (signed to Ra Records, a
part of the Warner Records empire) and stoner rockers
Tumbleweed (who had their self-titled debut distributed by
Festival Records, before signing with Polydor Records) were
seen as the bands to shake up the mainstream. But their sales
didn't make much of an impression on the Top 40.

None of this mattered much in Merewether, the sleepy
coastal suburb that is one stunning coastal vista away from
Newcastle, the second-largest city in New South Wales.
Newcastle had been founded in 1804 as a colony for the
First Fleet's worst convicts, and in the shadows of WWI it
became home to one of BHP's major steelworks. It was a city
of industry, Australia's answer to British industrial cities such
as Manchester, only warmer. For much of the century it
flourished, a rough and tumble place where rugby league
ruled and beer was the drink of choice. Its beachside neighbour, Merewether, slumbered quietly. But work in the
steeltown and its surrounds started to slacken off. The region
was hard hit by unemployment, which ran somewhere near
30 per cent by the early 1990s. Merewether supplied its share
of those out of work.

Silverchair's Daniel Johns was asked in 1996 about growing up in the area. 'One half of Newcastle is real industrial,
and the other half is all beach and stuff,' he explained. 'It's a
reasonably small town [Merewether]. People basically leave us
alone, but some call us long-haired louts.' Those name-callers
didn't know that these 'long haired louts' would soon become
Merewether's most famous exports and the answer to an
A&R guy's prayers.

Daniel Johns was born in Newcastle on April 22, 1979. His Silverchair partners, Ben Gillies and Chris Joannou, were born on October 24 and November 10, 1979, respectively. Johns was the first of three children for his parents, Greg, who ran a fruit stall in Newcastle, and Julie. Ben was the second child for David Gillies, a plumber, and his wife Annette. Joannou was one of three kids; he had an older sister as well as a twin sister. David and Sue Joannou operated a dry-cleaning franchise. It was all in keeping with the blue-collar mindset of the area and its people: unpretentious, dedicated, dreaming of maybe, one day, wiping off the mortgage and not having to work so damned hard.

Gillies and Joannou first met in kindergarten. In grade three at primary school they met Daniel Johns. Initially, the boys' common bonds were simple and very much a product of their environment: they loved music, bodyboarding and surfing. But none of them were really soaking up the music of the 1980s. Despite the name-checking of Newcastle's Star Hotel in their immortal shouter of the same name, Cold Chisel and Oz rock meant little to the Merewether three. 'I never got into the pub rock scene, it didn't appeal to me,' Johns said in March 1999. Ben Gillies can remember hearing Cold Chisel on the radio 'but not really liking it'.

Instead, as Johns revealed much later, it was their parents' record collections that got them interested in music. These were collections big on the type of bands — Deep Purple, Led Zeppelin, et al — that fancied loud guitars and crashing drums and wailing vocals; the perfect soundtrack to pot and pacifism. Johns's father, in particular, was a huge hard-rock fan, with a serious collection of Deep Purple vinyl. 'Mum and Dad were really into the whole hippie thing,' Johns told *Rolling Stone*, 'so I grew up listening to Hendrix, Deep Purple, Black Sabbath, Cat Stevens and John Lennon.'

Growing up, Johns's favourite albums included *Deep Purple in Rock* ('the first rock album I ever bought'), *Led Zeppelin IV* ('one of the first records I heard, along with Sabbath and Deep Purple') and Midnight Oil's *10, 9, 8, 7, 6, 5, 4, 3, 2, 1* ('the first Australian album I got, when I was about 10 or 11'). Speaking with Craig Mathieson for his 1996 book, *Hi Fi Days*, Johns confessed his deep-felt love for Deep Purple. 'I wanted to be Ritchie Blackmore,' he admitted.

A lot of early Silverchair history replays the responses of 15-year-olds who aren't sure their time in the sun will last much longer than their first hit. They said what they pleased and stretched the truth when required; they thought it all a bit of a laugh. Johns once boasted that his father was a big fan of Tool and Helmet, hard-rock bands from the 1990s that Johns junior happened to love and hoped to emulate. It's highly unlikely Greg Johns played their music in the car — but the claim did make Johns's pretty damned normal upbringing sound much cooler in the pages of the music press.

The boys' parents — especially their fathers — had dabbled in bands when they were younger. Gillies's father played rhythm guitar and his mother played piano. Joannou's father played bass, as his son was soon to do. Much later, Johns's brother, Heath, would start his own band with more than a little help from his successful sibling. Music was definitely in all their bloodlines.

Gillies, Johns and Joannou had grown up within a few blocks of each other in Merewether. While Johns was lost in his Ritchie Blackmore dreams, Gillies — who'd bought his first drum kit for $75, aged 8, after deciding the drummer in the school band was 'so cool' — was locked away in his bedroom, repeatedly playing John Bonham's memorable, monolithic drum solo from the Led Zeppelin film, *The Song Remains the Same*. Gillies was hypnotised by the awesome power of the man they called Bonzo. (Gillies ended up selling that first kit for $300. It now resides, battered and bruised, in the music room of a Newcastle primary school.)

With a schoolfriend helping out on keyboards, Johns and Gillies, then aged 9, had formed a rap outfit, the Silly Men. Their repertoire included rhymes about Welshmen and a leg of beef, with 'The Elephant Rap' being the highpoint of their set. 'An elephant was walking down the street,' the pair would shout, 'And his feet were tapping to the beat / His ears were flapping and his toes were, too / And he was doing a rap, just for you / Elephant Rap! Doing the Elephant Rap!' (Years later, Gillies and Johns would still bust out these rhymes in the back of the bus when the tedium of touring became too much for them.)

While Gillies was drumming with the school band, the 'Marching Koalas', Johns and Joannou had taken trumpet lessons, but they weren't inspired by the instrument. (Although Johns once made a passing reference to taking violin lessons, you can put that down to Silverchair myth-making.) Gillies had been drumming for several years by the time Johns received his first guitar: 'I got this little electric guitar for $80 or something for a birthday present,' Johns said in February 1996, 'It was called the Rock Axe. It looked kind of like a Strat[ocaster], but it was really small. And it was all white. I thought it was good at the time, because I could just turn up the amp and go "Yeah!"'

In Gillies's parents' garage, he and Johns started jamming enthusiastically. Johns had taken a year's worth of classical guitar training, so there was some finesse amidst the racket the two were making. As he told *Guitar School* magazine in February 1996:

This guy, he just taught me all the main chords and stuff. And after a year, I thought, I can't be bothered having lessons. So I just decided to figure out my own stuff. I never wanted to play all those fast guitar solos. I just thought, I'll be like Pete Townshend of the Who. I'll do what he does and play powerful chords and stuff.

Johns and Gillies worked through a variety of band names: the Witchdoctors, Nine Point Nine on the Richter Scale, Short Elvis. Short Elvis lasted all of one show — playing Elvis covers, naturally. Then it was back to the garage. Johns fronted for rehearsals trailing his trusty 60-watt Fender amp; Gillies pounded his tattered drum kit with all the gusto his skinny frame could muster. It was fun; they were making a noise. It was a good outlet for whatever frustrations they had at school, even though both seemed pretty well adjusted, if not overly inspired by the education system.

In 1991, the two 12-year-olds played their debut school concert. They were now called the Innocent Criminals. Silverchair legend has it that Johns, exhibiting the same kind of diffidence then that made him question rock & roll's value many years later, spent the entire show singing while facing the back of the stage. He couldn't meet the eyes of the few students who'd gathered to check them out. Gillies, however, has a different recollection of the show. 'I think that's been overexaggerated,' he told me. 'I think he was just looking away, a bit.' What Johns didn't know was that his father, Greg, was watching proudly from the back of the hall, invited by Newcastle High School principal Peter McNair. 'I never really wanted to be a singer,' Johns said in a 1996 interview. 'I just wanted to play guitar. Then one day we had a gig and we still didn't have a singer. None of us wanted to sing. But I ended up doing it, and from then on I've been the singer.'

Around this time, Johns and Gillies started jamming with another schoolmate, Tobin Finnane, also playing guitar. 'I got talking with Daniel and Ben,' Finnane recalls. 'They wanted to get the band going.' The Gillies home had always been the drop-in centre for the boys, including Joannou, who was yet to join the band. It was on the way to school, so they always stopped in. 'You'd eat all the biscuits and keep going,' Joannou remembers, laughing. Now the band gathered there not just to eat biscuits but to jam, first in the lounge room, then in Gillies's bedroom and, finally, in the garage (aka The Loft). Gillies's parents were supportive, although his mother would occasionally poke her head in and tell them to turn the volume down.

One day, a Gillies family friend dropped in, at the request of Annette Gillies, to show the boys how a bass worked. As Gillies recalls, he played along with the band, using the most simple bass lines possible, and Johns, Gillies and Finnane were thrilled. 'We went "Wow! How cool did that sound?" Then we went on a mission to find a bass player.' Johns and Gillies asked a few schoolmates, but most were keener on playing drums or guitar. But they knew that the father of their good buddy Joannou owned a bass — a copy of a Hofner, no less, just like Paul McCartney played when the Beatles took over the world. Surely the bass couldn't be that hard to master? After all, it had two less strings than their own guitars. They approached their friend, encouraging him to learn how to play. Within days Joannou started jamming with them at Gillies's home.

If volume is any indication of quality, by 1992 the four-piece Innocent Criminals were on their way; Gillies recalls how 'it just seemed to get louder and louder.' They entered a few local talent comps, playing Black Sabbath and Pearl Jam covers plus a few originals that Gillies, Finnane and Johns were thrashing out in The Loft. But then Finnane announced that his parents were leaving Merewether to live in England for a year. Keen to keep the band together, the Finnane and Joannou families struck up a deal: Tobin could live at Chris's house for a year. But at the last minute, Finnane changed his mind. 'I didn't think I'd get the experience again of travelling overseas,' he now says.

At this time, the Innocent Criminals were two pairs of tight buddies: Johns and Gillies; Finnane and Joannou. When Finnane left, the remaining three were unsure what to do next — split the band or kick on as a trio? But they felt that they'd gotten this far, so why not keep going? When Gillies and Johns made the proposal to their fast-improving bassman, Joannou was all for it.

While overseas, Finnane asked if he could rejoin them on his return to Australia. They wrote Finnane a letter telling him of their plans to continue as a trio. 'They made it clear it wasn't going to happen,' he told me, of his hopes to rejoin the band. 'I was a bit pissed off by the way it was handled.' Given the band's rapid rise, it's not surprising that by January 1996 Finnane was downplaying their first album — on which he received a thank-you — and telling the Australian tabloids that 'I just don't like the music. It's not very good.' Asked about this in 2003, Gillies figures that Finnane is still holding 'an eight-year grudge'. Finnane, who went on to complete an Honours degree in music at the Newcastle Conservatorium and now teaches and plays guitar for a living, still feels slighted by his one-time bandmates: 'I see them around but we don't talk to each other. The vibe's not the greatest.'

The Innocent Criminals played their first professional show at a Newcastle street fair. 'We got 10 dollars each to play,' Johns recalled, with a fair dash of teen spirit:

> We got up there and played Deep Purple, Led Zeppelin
> and Black Sabbath songs. Actually, we ended up getting
> bounced. This old guy complained because it was too loud.
> He came over and said, 'If you don't stop playing, I'm call-
> ing the cops.' So we had to stop playing. But we didn't care,
> we still got paid.

'They were absolutely dreadful,' the complaining resident told
the *Newcastle Herald*, 'The music was amplified, it was loud
and it was really bad.'

Gradually, the three were expanding on the rock albums
that littered their parents' collections. Meanwhile, in America, a
change had come. The unlikely rock & roll epicentre was now
Washington State — especially the city of Seattle. Here bands
such as Mother Love Bone (soon to morph into Pearl Jam), Tad
(fronted by a 300-pound lunatic going by the name of Tad
Doyle), Mudhoney, Soundgarden, Alice in Chains and, cru-
cially, Nirvana, were annexing sludgy post-Sabbath riffs to
lyrics that howled with disgust at how music had lost its way
and its meaning, and had become all spandex, no spleen.

Unlike their party-hearty, coke-sniffing predecessors from
the 1980s, the drug of choice for many of these grunge bands
was heroin (a drug that would eventually kill Love Bone's
singer, Andrew Wood, Alice in Chains's Layne Staley and,
indirectly, Nirvana's Kurt Cobain). Hence their inward-look-
ing lyrics about dysfunctional lives, encapsulated in such
anthems as Nirvana's 'Smells Like Teen Spirit', Pearl Jam's
'Alive' and the entire *Dirt* album from Alice in Chains. Girl-
hungry Mötley Crüe they weren't.

Collectively, this surly, seemingly noncommercial style of
rock was labelled 'grunge'. Unlike such '80s rock heroes as
Van Halen's 'Diamond' David Lee Roth, vocalists like Pearl

Jam's Eddie Vedder sang to the floor (or their shoes) and wore flannel. Guitar solos were a no-go zone. 'Selling out' to the mainstream ranked with speaking ill of Iggy Pop and the Stooges, the godparents of punk rock, whose furious riffology had left its mark on grunge. The links between 1970s punk rock and grunge were strong. When rock biographer Victor Bockris wrote that punk 'nurtured the seeds of working-class rebellion, with a punk philosophy that was anti-superstar and anti-establishment', he may as well have been writing about grunge.

By 1991, Pearl Jam's *Ten* and Nirvana's epochal *Nevermind*, led by the smash hit single 'Smells Like Teen Spirit', were unavoidable. Nirvana's blitzkrieg of a set at the 1992 Big Day Out, the debut of what would become Australia's annual summer rockfest, inspired thousands to pick up a guitar and scream at the world, among them a slight Jewish kid from Bondi, Ben Lee, who formed his wisecracking band of teen punks, Noise Addict, the following day. But it was the Eddie Vedder-led Pearl Jam that excited Daniel Johns the most. In a November 1995 interview with *Request* magazine, he admitted that his own bottomless vocal growl, a signature sound that made his band's breakthrough hit, 'Tomorrow', so distinctive, was hugely inspired by Vedder. 'He was, like, my hero,' Johns admitted in a rare moment of teen candour. 'And I was going, "Yes, I'm going to try and be like Eddie Vedder."' Johns would find himself playing down that statement many times over the next few years.

Just like the Beatles, Silverchair came from working-class stock, where expectations weren't high. But they were possibly the luckiest teenagers on the planet. Despite the familiar rock mythology in which bands rise up in spite of repression and the pressure to study hard and get regular jobs, the trio's principal at Newcastle High, Peter McNair, gave the band more rhythm than they could ever have imagined. The school prided itself on tolerance and diversity; unlike many high schools, piercings and coloured hair weren't frowned on, and creativity was encouraged. According to McNair — who took up his post the year Johns, Gillies, Finnane and Joannou started high school — the unofficial school motto among the 1300 students was 'It's cool to be different.' McNair encouraged them, and other school bands, to play at lunchtime for their schoolmates. (When Silverchair's success escalated, especially around the time of their second album, *Freak Show*, McNair and the band's parents developed a flexible study program for the trio to ensure they could tour overseas and still gain respectable Higher School Certificate results.)

'I was new,' says McNair, still Newcastle High's principal, who good-humouredly boasts of being an early Silverchair adviser/roadie, 'I wanted to get the kids involved.' By charging two dollars admission (which wasn't quite in keeping with Board of Education guidelines), the band raised enough cash to rent some lights and a PA and buy a new amp. The shows were a roaring success. 'I knew there was something special,' McNair recalls of the Innocent Criminals. 'They had a sound that was so raw, so honest. The older kids were jumping around in excitement. Teachers still remember it today.'

Despite their obvious intelligence, school wasn't proving too inspiring for the band. Johns admitted he was 'shit in maths and science' and took art as an elective because 'it's a bludge.' (In 1997, as their Higher School Certificate exam approached, Johns revealed that he chose Marine Studies, 'because I thought I'd go to the beach'; later that year he figured that 'English was my best subject because I was crap at everything else.') A lot of Johns's and Gillies's time was soaked up writing songs, which the three mixed with cover versions in their lunchtime sets and garage jams.

Word of these Innocent Criminals made its way to the local newspaper. In late 1993 it featured a small item on the band, which was noticed by Terry Farrelly, who ran Platinum Studios, located in the Newcastle suburb of Cardiff. Farrelly claimed to be the former drum technician for British rock giants Led Zeppelin, a band much loved by Johns, Joannou and especially Gillies. (Today, however, Joannou isn't so sure of the guy's history: 'Well, he had a Pommie accent,' he laughs. 'He certainly sucked us in.')

Farrelly offered the band cheap studio time. It was their second time in a studio. When Finnane was still in the picture, they'd recorded originals 'How Do You Know?' (sample lyric: 'How do you know where you're going / When you don't know where you are?') and 'I Felt Like It', plus a cover of 'Twist and Shout', in a studio in Mayfield. Farrelly's offer was generous: not only did it let them familiarise themselves with the workings of the studio, but they were able to record basic versions of four songs, including a six-and-a-half-minute long version of 'Tomorrow', which became their first single.

Johns figured the session 'cost about $75. We weren't in there for more than an hour.' In a historical footnote, ever since these Silverchair recordings, bands have been hiring Platinum Studios hoping some of the magic will rub off on them. As their manager, John Watson told me, 'We've heard of young bands recording there, in the false belief that it's where the band recorded *Frogstomp*.'

Of the four demo tracks, 'Tomorrow' was the obvious standout. The other three — which included 'Never Knew Your Powers' and 'Won't You Be Mine', a take on the Cult's hit 'Wild Flower' — were quickly discarded by the band.

Watson, describes them as 'much more Guns 'n' Roses-influenced' songs, which 'didn't really fit alongside the alterna-rock/Sabbath influenced stuff'.

'Tomorrow' had started to come together in a Gillies bedroom jam, at a time when a session consisted of playing their favourite records, jamming on a riff that they heard and liked, and seeing where their song went from there. As Gillies recalls: 'We were jamming and Daniel sang the line "You wait 'til tomorrow" and I went "Man, that's a cool line." He didn't really like it, but I managed to convince him. Then we sat down with a couple of acoustic guitars and wrote the verse and the chorus and the pre-chorus.'

'We just had a jam,' Johns said, 'and I came up with the riff to the chorus. Ben liked it but I didn't really like it. He kept ringing me, saying "We should make something out of this." I was saying "Nah, nah." But finally we made it into a song.' It was a smart move. While the song would provide its share of nightmares in the years to follow, without 'Tomorrow', Silverchair might still be jamming in the Gillies garage.

In early 1994, a neighbour of the Johns family, Sarah Lawson, noticed that *nomad*, the music program on multi-cultural TV network SBS, was promoting a music competition called Pick Me. Lawson had a big influence on Johns's musical taste: 'Every band I get into is from her,' Johns said in 1996. 'If I like it I would just go and find the CD or steal her CD.' The competition's organisers were in search of the best demo recording by an unsigned Australian band, and one of the prizes was a day's recording at Triple J's Sydney studio, as well as the chance to make a video for the song.

Lawson told the band, who got about as excited as diffident 15-year-olds can become. They submitted the tape of their Platinum Studio session accompanied by a statement —

in 25 words or less, as the rules insisted — as to what made the band so special: 'We're not hip-hop or rap,' the three wrote. 'We're rock!'

Out of the 800 entries, 'Tomorrow' was the song that caught the ear of competition judge Robert Hambling, an SBS freelancer and expatriate British video director who'd moved to Australia in 1988, after having worked on films including *Greystoke: The Legend of Tarzan* and *Pink Floyd's The Wall*. Hambling was destined for a long history with the band, as an archivist, video maker and insider. 'I sat at home listening to demo after demo after demo,' he told me. 'Basically, I came up with Silverchair, or the Innocent Criminals as they were then, which hit me like a brick.'

Among the entries Hambling was sorting through were such eccentricities as the Von Trapp Family Crisis, who were a favourite of *nomad*'s producer, Tracee Hutchison, a former Triple J DJ. Hutchison was torn. She knew that 'Tomorrow' was a strong song, but she was also keenly aware of the need to select an act in keeping with the SBS multicultural charter. And she knew that the program was in line for the axe. 'I was merely being mindful of what I hoped Pick Me might achieve for the longevity of a popular music program on SBS TV,' she reflects, adding, 'You know, keep it on air.' Hambling described the Von Trapps as 'a Melbourne-based goof band; good but wild and wacky'. Another entrant was a solo artist calling himself Fishhead, who cut up samples from TV shows *The Fugitive* and *Star Trek*. Much of the rest was unremarkable.

No wonder Hambling was sold on the Innocent Criminals:

'Tomorrow' had all those things you want out of a great song. Memorable lyrics, a really good hook. And there was no denying their connection to the Seattle sound. But it never went through my head that they were borrowing; it was just what they were listening to. And my point at the time was that if you're going to pick a competition based on the best entry, this is it, it doesn't get any better than this. Three very young kids, living in Newcastle, playing out of their bedroom — what else do you want?

'If anything,' Hutchison now says:

> it was the fact that "Tomorrow" was much more musically accessible than where *nomad* sat most weeks that made me think hard about making it the winner. It was destined to be a mainstream hit and there was nothing mainstream about *nomad*.

Hambling persevered:

> They still weren't convinced. I thought I was going nuts. So I went around to Nick Launay's [Hambling's record-producer neighbour and friend]. He thought it was good, so I asked him to do one of his magic edits on it. By then he thought it was brilliant, so I knew I wasn't mad.

Finally a consensus was reached and 'Tomorrow' was declared the winner.

During the competition judging, Hambling had called the number supplied with the Innocent Criminals entry to advise them they were on the shortlist. Unaware, at the time, of their ages, he spoke with Johns's mother. Even though she told him Daniel was at school, he was convinced she was the singer's wife or girlfriend, because the song sounded so mature. Then Hambling called the Johns household to announce that the Innocent Criminals were the winners. The call was answered by Daniel, who was told they'd won the right to record

'Tomorrow' at Triple J and have *nomad* direct their video. 'We didn't, like, go spastic or anything,' Johns recalled of the news, 'but we were pretty happy.'

When the band convened in Gillies's garage, however, they could barely contain their excitement. According to Joannou:

> Daniel was over at my house — after school, we'd go past my house and we'd always come in, have a drink, and then go home — and, like, Daniel's mum was at my house and she ran out and said, "They won! They won!" We were just crazy, running around, going so berserk. It was so exciting.

Gillies remembers 'running around my house and yelling at the top of my voice. Then I remember thinking, "Fuck, how long is this going to last?"'

This wasn't the last competition they would win. Three weeks after their *nomad* video screened, the band cleaned up at the annual Youthrock awards, a school band competition held at Campsie in western Sydney. They were the pick of 40 bands, winning a day's recording at a Sydney studio and $1500 worth of musical gear for their school. In the audience was John Woodruff, who was keen to manage the band. (He would later guide Savage Garden to huge international success.) The year before, when Finnane was still in the Innocent Criminals, they had won the Encouragement Award at the same event. But whereas Youthrock was a small-scale, teen-band comp, *nomad* would bring the band national attention.

Hutchison subsequently called Johns, asking him if the song could be cut down from six to a more serviceable four minutes. She was hoping that her then husband, producer Tim Whitten, could do the edit, although that ultimately didn't happen, and she asked Launay (who had done a rough edit on the demo version on his home equipment) to produce the song.

Launay was excited to be asked. He and Hambling had already played their rough edit of 'Tomorrow' to their many record company contacts and none seemed too impressed. 'We got an amazing "So what?"' Hambling recalls. They had started nurturing plans to release the song themselves if they couldn't get a label interested in the band. One label it seems Launay and Hambling didn't visit was the huge multinational Sony. John Watson — soon to be a key player in Silverchair's rise and working at that time in Sony's A&R department, the first port of call for anyone pitching a new band — insists that being 'a huge Oils and INXS fan' he would have agreed to meet with Launay.

On the eve of recording 'Tomorrow', however, Launay fell sick and the production job went to Triple J's in-house producer, Phil McKellar. (A year later, returning from some production work in America, Launay heard 'Tomorrow' on an in-flight music channel. By then it was a multiplatinum hit. Launay thought the song sounded familiar but couldn't quite place it, or this band named Silverchair. It turned out that the rough edit of 'Tomorrow' was still sitting on his machine at home.)

McKellar recorded the song in one day at Triple J's Sydney studio, incorporating some of Launay's ideas, and bringing in extra equipment of his own for the band to use. Hambling — now incredibly passionate about the band, and professionally involved because of the *nomad* competition —'baby sat' the session. The only real hold-up was that Chris Joannou had to hire a serviceable bass, with Hambling's help, to replace his Dad's 'shitty' four-string. While Platinum Studio may have been a shoebox with microphones, the band's recording experience helped them make a smooth transition to the sophisticated Triple J facility. The way Gillies saw it, 'This was just on a more grand scale.'

Once the recording was ready, Hambling and Hutchison travelled north to join up with the band. 'It was just me, Chris, Ben, Daniel, their three mums and the cameraman from SBS,' Hambling recalled, neglecting to mention that Hutchison also made the trip. Hambling directed the moody video, which included footage of the streets of Merewether, hardly the rock & roll capital of the universe, and a jail cell in the old Newcastle police station. The video set *nomad* back $2000. (A typical US video budget at the time was US$200,000.) 'The only special effect was that we screwed a light bulb into a cord and pushed — it was all very George Lucas and R2D2,' Hambling recalls. After the shoot, Hutchison interviewed the band in front of Newcastle landmark Fort Scratchley.

A little after 8 pm on Thursday, June 16, 1994, during what turned out to be its final episode, *nomad* announced that the Innocent Criminals had won the Pick Me competition. They screened the video and aired the interview with the band. No one knew it at the time, but Australian music history was being created.

It was almost three years since Nirvana's 'Smells Like Teen Spirit' had broken out all over, and local music-business tastemakers were still searching for an Australian answer to the grunge phenomenon. Sydney act Ratcat had had some chart success with a guitar- and hook-heavy sound, but frontman Simon Day didn't wield Kurt Cobain's couldn't-give-a-fuck charisma or his dysfunctional menace. Instead, he wore striped tops and was just way too cute. Ratcat's 1991 album, *Blind Love*, raced to Number One in the local charts. Their 1992 LP, *Insideout*, sank like a stone. But Johns not only had an unreasonably sonorous voice to echo the sound of Seattle, he was also enigmatic, sullen and serious. There was something going on here.

After the *nomad* announcement, Triple J staffers had circulated the 'Tomorrow' video to record-company contacts who they thought would 'get' the band. Enough interest was building in the Innocent Criminals to entice Sydney-based record company talent-spotters to check them out — including many of the tastemakers who had rejected the song played to them by Hambling and Launay a few weeks earlier. The Innocent Criminals were the complete package; this new band from Newcastle not only rocked like heathens, they also had a growling lead singer whose dirty blond hair and razor-blade riffs had scenesters whispering about 'the new Kurt Cobain'. And young girls swooned when he sang.

Meanwhile, Johns's mother, Julie, was booking the band's shows and dealing with these money men with the caution you'd expect from the parent of a talented 15-year-old. The three sets of parents were keeping close tabs on their sons as the opportunists started to circle.

Ex rock & roll journalist John O'Donnell and Sony's John Watson had a copy of the video, even though neither had seen the *nomad* broadcast. The pair, both in their early 30s, were sharing an office at Sony's Sydney base. O'Donnell was only a week into his job with Murmur Records, a boutique 'development' label established in June. A former plumber raised in Sydney's western suburbs, O'Donnell had left his post as founding editor of *Juice* magazine (and an editorial post at *Rolling Stone* before that) after Watson recommended him for the Murmur job. Watson, a former musician (he was in a band called the Spliffs, no less), record-shop worker, journalist and manager of Sydney indie band the Whippersnappers, was then Sony's Director of A&R and

International Marketing, a global role which would soon help Silverchair's overseas progress no end. Their backgrounds were ideal for developing a band such as this: they understood how the media machine operated and were aware of how it could chew up an overexposed act.

Both also knew that the lifespan of record-company staff could be dangerously short. Murmur had been set up by Sony after much procrastination as a base to release the new, cutting-edge music that the major-label suits had noticed making a mark on the charts. The label had been named by O'Donnell in a nod to his favourite REM record. 'The perception of Sony from the outside wasn't great — it was Margaret Urlich and Rick Price,' recalls O'Donnell, naming two very bland mainstream pop acts, 'That image scared young rock bands off.' O'Donnell and Watson, by contrast, were deeply into the loud flannel-clad bands coming out of America. 'We were listening to all the things they were listening to,' says O'Donnell of the Innocent Criminals, 'from Pearl Jam to Nirvana to Screaming Trees and Soundgarden, as well as Sabbath and all that stuff they'd grown up around. We were genuine fans of that music.'

Sony's generosity only stretched so far: O'Donnell needed a hit to make his new job safe. And Watson was a determined man; previously, in his A&R role, he'd tried to sign hot new bands You Am I and Powderfinger, but because of the corporate rigidity of Sony he couldn't offer these bands the flexible deals they needed — both signed with other labels and went on to become two of the country's biggest alternative rock acts. Watson and O'Donnell were both impressed with the Innocent Criminals. They were exactly what Murmur needed to get started: a cool rock act — and a homegrown one, no less. And Sony boss Denis Handlin had granted O'Donnell, as head of Murmur, the flexibility to break the company rules; he could offer bands record deals that didn't stitch them up for life.

As Watson recalled in an interview in 1997:

> As A&R manager, I had certain criteria in my head. Silverchair [or the Innocent Criminals, as they were at the time] had it all: with them, all the pieces of the puzzle fit: they played great, had catchy songs, good attitudes and they were fresh, charismatic — and they looked good. They remind me of why I got into the music business in the first place. When you're that age you don't make music to get laid or to make money or to see your photo on the cover of a magazine. You make music because you like the noise you make when you bang on your guitar. All great music is born from that.

And as Watson pointed out to me in 2003, his and O'Donnell's interest in Silverchair was very much a collaboration: 'The process of signing them truly was a joint effort — neither of us made a move without consulting the other.' O'Donnell calls their working relationship a 'tag team'.

O'Donnell had a key move to make — he called Julie Johns to find out when the band was next playing. She told them there was a gig on the following Tuesday, but a contingent from Michael Gudinski's Mushroom label, home to such successful Australian acts as Paul Kelly and Kylie Minogue, had already made enquiries, as had EMI. Gudinski had seen the Innocent Criminals play at Youthrock in 1993. Curiously enough, it was the older songs on the Platinum Studio demo tape that interested Mushroom, rather than 'Tomorrow' — they thought the now-discarded 'Won't You Be Mine' was the perfect first single. O'Donnell and Watson were stuck, because a big wheel from Sony's international division was in Sydney on that same night, and they had to toe the corporate line, thereby missing the Criminals show.

Mushroom, however, made the gig and met with the band and their parents. It looked as though O'Donnell and Watson had missed their chance. But O'Donnell called Johns's mother again and urged them not to sign with anyone else. Not yet, anyway.

On June 24, 1994, the Innocent Criminals played Newcastle's Jewell's Tavern. Because the band were under the legal drinking age, they had to set up and play in the bistro and stay in the band room between sets. O'Donnell and Watson — and some bored bikers who kept yelling for the band to play 'Born to Be Wild' — checked out the show, which included early takes on originals 'Acid Rain', 'Stoned' and 'Pure Massacre', as well as Pearl Jam, Hendrix, Kiss and Black Sabbath covers. There may have been only a dozen people in the room — and a few of those were keener on the rugby league game on the pub TV — but the two record company execs were so impressed that O'Donnell remembers being 'totally speechless. It was like seeing the Beatles at the Cavern before they became stars.' As Watson remembers, 'It was literally the only time I've been to a show where you go, "This can't be happening." I vividly recall driving home and saying to John, "If I ever leave to manage a band, this is the one."'

On the drive back to Sydney they started formulating a career plan for the band, one that would be sensitive to their ages rather than use them as a marketing device. As O'Donnell told me, it was a strategy that would ensure 'they would still be going strong when they were 20 and beyond.' This would prove decisive when the trio's parents sat down to figure out which label would be right for their sons.

Both Mushroom and Murmur made offers to the Innocent Criminals. Mushroom were keen to capitalise on the 'teen rockers' appeal of the band. They loved the band name — which Johns, Joannou and Gillies were tiring of — and planned for them to play concerts in front of a banner that screamed out 'Innocent Criminals'. Mushroom also offered just a little more money up-front, but Murmur's more cautious plan appealed to the band, as did the coolness of O'Donnell and Watson, who won the trio over by slipping them rare Pearl Jam live CDs. And, coming from good working-class stock, O'Donnell talked rugby league with John's father, which helped sweeten the deal.

'I remember riding our bikes to school one day,' says Joannou, 'and I said to the other two guys, "I like the two John guys the best," and we all agreed.' According to Gillies:

> They just did it so much more smartly. Mushroom's whole sell wasn't very good. They wanted to put out 'Won't You Be Mine', but the other guys said, 'No, "Tomorrow" is the one.' They were just much cooler. I think if we'd signed with Mushroom it would have been all over after 'Won't You Be Mine'.

The band signed to Murmur, originally for just one album (although by December 1994 the deal had been extended to three albums). Silverchair became their second signing, joining up just a week after Perth alt-rockers Ammonia, who despite some chart success locally and some whiffs of interest in America, folded after two albums. The advance paid to the Innocent Criminals — which they would have to recoup through record sales — was modest, less than $100,000, which included the recording budget of their first album. They could afford some new gear and not much more.

Murmur might have offered the band less money than other majors but they also allowed them more creative elbow room. As Johns explained at the time, 'We knew if we just signed straight to a big label [Mushroom] they'd really want to promote us. There'd be all this advertising and shit.' How to deal with all this 'advertising and shit' was a key part of the Murmur deal. O'Donnell and Watson didn't want to over-hype the band or position them incorrectly. They knew the band were still too green for such serious music press as *Rolling Stone* and *Juice*, but neither did they want the three to be seen as some kind of teen pin-ups, grinning from the pages of *Girlfriend* magazine. So their first step was to score the band some coverage in the free music press, where the band could build credibility and gain the right kind of buzz.

O'Donnell and Watson had drilled what they called an 'anti-marketing strategy' into the heads of their young charges. They stressed that all publicity should focus on the band's music; Watson was aware the media could turn them into 'a teeny-bopper band, which would have given them a short shelf-life'. O'Donnell comments, 'Our thing with them was, you are a real band and from a marketing sense it's almost negative that you are so young. We wanted to work around that and make sure that didn't hurt their career.' Watson was also concerned about the so-called 'Ratcat syndrome' in which a band explodes and implodes within the course of a couple of years.

This 'cool at all costs' mantra clearly made sense to Johns; he repeated it frequently during interviews:

If we did teen press and things like that, we would be getting the wrong kind of audience. We're not going for the same people that listen to Bon Jovi. We just wanted to reach the alternative press, street press, fanzines, guitar mags and stuff like that. We really didn't do anything like *Rolling Stone* until after people already had an idea of who we were or what we are like.

The band toasted their signing with a legendary gig on October 22 at Sydney's Vulcan Hotel, a venue Joannou remembers being 'about as big as my kitchen'. They were supporting alt-rock acts Nancy Vandal and the Popgun Assassins, but the house was full for the support act. It was so full, in fact, that the stage collapsed due to the crush. 'People were crowd-surfing, hanging onto the roof,' says Joannou. 'It was just madness.' The cover shot for their 'Pure Massacre' single was taken from that gig; it proves Joannou was right on the money.

By August 1994, calls started coming in to *Request Fest*, a listener-driven Triple J program, asking for 'Tomorrow', which had initially been played on Richard Kingsmill's *Oz Music Show*. This heavy, lyrically naive anthem was striking all the right kind of chords, even if Triple J's music director, Arnold Frolows, wasn't so sure about the song. 'When it came in,' he told Sydney's *Daily Telegraph* in 1995, 'we didn't think that much of it. It wasn't like we thought, "Oh God, this is a hit."'

At the same time, the trio were having some doubts about the name Innocent Criminals, as were Watson and O'Donnell. As Johns said in September 1994, the band had 'started to get sick of it and we found it a bit of a kids' name. We wanted something a bit more mature so people didn't think of us as kids.' 'We thought it was a really bad name,' says O'Donnell, 'it threw too much light on the fact that they were a teenage band.' The band's parents, however, liked the tag and thought, quite justifiably, that a lot of goodwill and recognition had built around it after the Youthrock and *nomad* wins. During one of their now regular meetings at Hornsby

RSL — a mid-way point between the Sydney base of Watson, O'Donnell and the band's booking agent, Owen Orford, and the Merewether home of the Silver-parents — the idea for a name change was put forward. Despite the resistance of their parents, the band's casting vote meant they were now operating as Silverchair.

The story of the Innocent Criminal's evolution into Silverchair is deeply entrenched in local rock & roll mythology (and, yes, until 2002 that was a lower case 's', because, as Johns explained to Triple J announcer Richard Kingsmill, an upper case 'S' 'just looked spastic'). The band's standard line at the time was that the new name came one night when the band had gathered at Gillies' parents' home to make calls to Triple J's *Request Fest*. Johns wanted to hear You Am I's 'Berlin Chair', while Gillies opted for Nirvana's 'Sliver' and suggested they ask for 'Sliverchair'. Joannou transcribed this incorrectly, and the name Silverchair — or 'silverchair' — was born. It sounded a whole lot better than some of the other names on the shortlist, which included Grunt Truck and Warm Fish Milkshake, so the name stuck.

But John Watson, looking back in 2002, had a different recollection: 'It was from the C.S. Lewis Narnia books.' *The Silver Chair* was written by Lewis in 1953, one of seven books in the Narnia series. 'We had literally hundreds of names on a list,' Watson continued. '"Silverchair" came from a catalogue in the Johns household. At that stage, nothing was dismissed as a potential band name, and through a process of attrition, that's the one that stayed.' And the book title's similarity to the two songs the band loved didn't hurt the choice of name, either.

So the band now had a name and a following, but no new music to share with their hungry audience. 'Tomorrow' was slated for an official release on September 16. The band played a Sony music conference in Sydney on August 19, then returned to Triple J studios, again with producer Phil McKellar, to cut the tracks 'Stoned', 'Blind' and 'Acid Rain'. It was a memorable session for the Sydney-based producer. Johns was 'just like any other kid standing there in Doc Martens, until he opened his mouth,' said McKellar, 'When he did, I just went, "My God, this kid can sing." Just because he was from Newcastle didn't mean it wasn't the real thing.'

Along with 'Tomorrow', these songs made up the band's debut release, a four-track EP priced at $9.95, three bucks more than a regular single. But this was part of the marketing plan of O'Donnell and Watson — keep it low-key, make the songs the focus, don't oversell the band. As O'Donnell read it, 'We thought if we stopped some young girl buying the record and making it a teen-based thing, great. As it turned out, it didn't hurt sales at all.' Or as Watson commented in 1996:

> I always like the way Midnight Oil handled their career. And one of the things they did well was that, in between albums, they kept it low-key — very low-key — so that when they came back, people were hungry to hear more about them again.

When Silvermania really broke out, O'Donnell even bought up all photos of the band in circulation, buried them in his bottom drawer and shut down all publicity until the eve of their debut-LP release. He was trying to shield the band from overexposure, a sure-fire killer in an environment where credibility is as significant as catchy hooks. At times Murmur even banned photographers from live shows.

As noted in Watson and O'Donnell's (handwritten) marketing plan, the original goal was to sell 6000 copies of 'Tomorrow'; that way both band and label would be on track to recoup Murmur's (that is, Sony's) minimal investment. Yet an almost indefinable quality about 'Tomorrow' connected with a lot more than 6000 punters. Despite some clumsy high-school poetry from Johns — 'there is no bathroom and there is no sink / the water out of the tap is very hard to drink' — the song's stop-start rhythms and Johns's growling vocal, which packed an unclear but quite palpable discontent, hit paydirt. And in keeping with the early '90s ethos, Johns's guitar growled like a wounded beast. It was a song born of the grunge sound, bound to send moshpits into convulsions.

So what was Johns so angry about? It was nothing personal. The song was inspired, like many of his early songs, by what he witnessed on the evening news:

> I saw something on telly. There was this poor guy taking a rich guy through a hotel to experience the losses of those less fortunate than him. The rich guy is complaining because he just wants to get out and the poor guy is saying you have to wait until tomorrow to get out. That's one of our least serious songs but it still has meaning to it.

What life experiences did a relatively well-adjusted 15-year-old kid have to draw from, anyway?

Meanwhile, the calls kept coming in to Triple J and the Silverchair buzz was gathering momentum. But the band were about to understand that popularity comes with just as many lows as highs. In October 1994 a mysterious letter appeared in Melbourne's free 'street press' magazine *Beat*. A female writer bragged how, along with her girlfriends, she'd snuck Silverchair back to her house and 'took something away from these innocent boys that they'll never be able to give any other girl'. Gillies replied by stating: 'That's the biggest load of crap.' They weren't old enough to drive or drink, they didn't even shave, for God's sake, but already Silverchair were the object of female fantasies. All this did was make Watson and O'Donnell even more wary about the band's dealings with the media.

In November 1994, Silvermania became official, when 'Tomorrow' reached Number One on the Top 40 singles chart, going gold the next week and staying on top for six weeks. Gillies was getting ready for school when his mother got off the telephone. 'She said '"Tomorrow' has been number one for six weeks." My first thought was, Fuck, what's going on here? That was really fucking weird.'

By December 'Tomorrow' had sold 180,000 copies, 30 times more than the Murmur marketing plan goal. This obviously excited the suits, but O'Donnell and Watson were concerned whether the public would give the band the chance to prove themselves more than some faddish, one-hit grunge wonder. They thoroughly understood the fickle nature of rock & roll.

Daniel Johns's expectations had been even lower, as he explained at the time:

> We expected it to sell about 2000. And then when it started going up a bit, we're going, 'Oh my God, ha ha ha!' Then when it got to 15,000, we're going, 'Hope it doesn't sell any more, we don't want it to sell any more.' When it went to Number One, we were kind of spewing. They're going 'Congratulations', and we're going, 'Everyone's going to expect every record to go to Number One.'

Gillies, Johns and Joannou were already well aware of the 'tall poppy' syndrome, and their tight group of schoolmates objected at the first sign of rampaging ego. 'As soon as you said something acknowledging yourself, someone would come out and cut you down,' Joannou said. 'So we cut ourselves down. We were always thinking twice.'

In keeping with the anti-rock attitude of grunge, the band didn't want to be stars. Eddie Vedder of Pearl Jam had declared that uncool, and many bands — Silverchair included — treated his every mumble as gospel. 'We don't want to be very big at all,' Johns said. 'We don't want to be known as the band who think they're rock stars.' At a time when multinationals were offering the band crazy amounts of money to play corporate shows (up to $250,000, according to one report), the band opted to do a show at Avalon in Sydney for the Surfrider Foundation. They each received a new surfboard and wetsuit as payment. But nothing could stop the band's momentum. By the end of 1994, 'Tomorrow' was the ninth-highest-selling single of the year and hit Number 5 on the tastemaking Triple J Hottest 100 chart. The band then signed on for their first Big Day Out. The madness had begun.

Bibliography

'Record Collection' Australian *Rolling Stone* March 1999; 'Director's Chair' *Newcastle Herald* 21/12/2002; *Australian Chart Book: 1970–1992* compiled by David Kent; 'Rock 'n' Roll High School' *Guitar School* February 1996; Craig Mathieson. *Hi Fi Days: The Future of Australian Rock* 1996; 'Teen rock idol who never was' The *Sunday Telegraph* 21/01/1996; 'How agony stopped the music' *Newcastle Herald* 08/06/2002; Victor Bockris. *Keith Richards: The Unauthorised Biography* Omnibus Press, 2002; 'silverchair: Sonic Youth' *Request* November 1995; 'silverchair's Seat of Learning' *Daily Telegraph* 20/11/97; 'School's Out, Rocks Off' *Sydney Morning Herald* 28/11/97; 'silverchair enjoys success despite adult criticism' *The Daily Egyptian* 08/12/1995; 'Here Today, Here Tomorrow' *The Aquarian Weekly* 17/01/1996; 'silverchair in L.A.' *OOR Magazine* January 1997 ; 'Star Check' *Sydney Morning Herald* 05/05/1995; 'Teen Spirit — Tomorrow Belongs to silverchair' *Daily Telegraph Mirror* 29/07/1995; 'Interview with silverchair' *The Buzz* magazine September 1994; 'Days in the Sun' Australian *Rolling Stone* February 1997; *Beat* magazine October 1994; 'silverchair Speak Out!' *Smash Hits* January 1995; 'silverchair — Three lads in the fishbowl' *Chart* April 1999

2

Frogstomping All over the World

*'A shirtless loon shimmies up a light pole overlooking the
heaving moshpit. He dangles from his perch, poised to
execute what looks like the ultimate stage dive — four
storeys down. Fortunately, security gets to him first as
silverchair, to their wry amusement, are rushed off the stage.'*

—Rolling Stone

Australia needed the Big Day Out. For twenty years promoters had tried to establish a workable festival of local and
overseas bands, but nothing stuck. One of the earliest and
best-known attempts was the anything-goes Sunbury Festival,
held on Melbourne's outskirts in the early 1970s. It was an
acid-, dope- and beer-drenched sweatfest headlined in 1972
by '60s pop idol Billy Thorpe, who'd reinvented himself as a
wild-maned hippie with an electric guitar.

A festival veteran, Thorpe had also appeared at the
Odyssey Festival, held at Wallacia, on Sydney's outskirts, in
1971. It was another well-intentioned debacle, as he recalled
in his ripping yarn of a 1998 memoir, *Most People I Know*.
Fried on LSD, Thorpe recalls drifting into a slow blues 'ripped
to my toe tips. My guitar felt like it was made of rubber with
my fingers growing out of it.' Festivals like these — and their
1980s variants, such as Narara, which managed to entice the
Pretenders, Simple Minds and the Talking Heads to a muddy

bog two hours north of Sydney, next to the site of Old Sydney Town — were fuelled by idealism, dope and distant dreams of Woodstock. In keeping with a local music industry still in development, rock festivals were amateurish at best, anarchic at worst.

Ken Lees and Vivian West were Sydney-based promoters heavily into alternative music. They were well connected, with good taste and ambition, in a cool-school, indie-cred kind of way. Since the late 1980s, they'd enticed such well-regarded international acts as Billy Bragg, They Might Be Giants and the Violent Femmes to tour Australia. On January 25, 1992, the Australia Day long weekend, they staged their first Big Day Out. The event was closely based on Lollapalooza, the US alternative-rock roadshow established by promoters Marc Geiger and Don Muller. Lollapalooza crisscrossed America between 1991 and 1997, mixing such cutting-edge acts as Beck, Smashing Pumpkins, Soundgarden and Jane's Addiction with political activism and exotic food not found in your typical strip mall. All this stimulation was held outdoors, spread over several stages. For punters, Lollapalooza offered the chance to get seriously rocked *and* join Greenpeace, all on the one day. For bands that made the bill, the exposure guaranteed strong record sales and some well-paid shows.

'As a promoter I've always tried to do things that were interesting,' West said on the day of the inaugural Big Day Out. 'I get bored with just putting together the same old bills.' To drive home his aversion to the 'same old bills', the debut Big Day Out was a musical smorgasbord. Sandwiched between indigenous rockers Yothu Yindi and student favourites the Violent Femmes, was Nirvana, whose second album, *Nevermind*, was about to explode in the US and then all over the world. Playing before 9000 mad-for-it punters in

Sydney's Hordern Pavilion, their set, as described by *Rolling Stone* magazine was: 'blistering, intense and wildly received, with the moshpit drenched in water and a frenzy of stage divers. They brooded and threatened rather than rocked, and culminated with the animalistic trashing of their equipment to the delight of the devoted audience.' The verdict was unanimous: the Big Day Out was a hit.

There were attempts to bring Lollapalooza to Australia, but that notion was discarded as the Big Day Out just kept getting bigger. In 1993 the Big Day Out went national. In 1994, the top five acts on the bill — Soundgarden, the Cruel Sea, Björk, Smashing Pumpkins and Urge Overkill — saw their albums in the Top 10 within two weeks of the event. Major labels found this commercial knock-on effect very attractive, and lobbied Lees and West to get their bands on the bill. And for local acts with just a whiff of ambition, a spot on any of the four main outdoor stages guaranteed some decent record sales and a leg-up for their career. It was also confirmation that they'd been accepted by the alterna-rock movement, which had started to break down barriers between mainstream and independent music in the early 1990s. 'It's the spirit of the event that counts,' promoter West said in 1994, 'so audiences are open to seeing all bands on the bill.'

Well, yes, but there was really only one band that had 'must see' written all over them at the Big Day Out 1995: Silverchair. They'd ended 1994 with a platinum-selling Number One single and a follow-up, the grinding 'Pure Massacre', that had debuted at Number 2 three days after their first Big Day Out show. The buzz surrounding the band's appearance almost matched Nirvana's three years earlier.

The band had been signed up at a bargain price — shades of the Beatles 1964 Australian tour — when O'Donnell approached West in late 1994. He had met with the promoter for an hour, slipping him a pre-release copy of the 'Tomorrow' EP and talking up the band. West checked out the chaos at the band's Vulcan show in Sydney and was sold. 'He got it straight away,' says O'Donnell. 'They got the band for next to nothing and it created all this excitement. We needed the band to play the right kind of shows — and with other credible bands.' In keeping with Watson and O'Donnell's softly-softly strategy for the band, at the Sydney Big Day Out, Silverchair were booked for a mid-afternoon spot on the outdoor Skate Stage, a hundred metres away from the main stage inside the Hordern Pavilion. At a stretch, five thousand punters could see the band. Instead, fifteen thousand sun- and beer-drenched fans tried to squeeze in, sardine style, to check out this new band of baggy-shorted, T-shirted teen hotshots. This first Big Day Out appearance not only made clear just how popular the band were, it also proved to the often hard-to-please alternative rock audience that the band could really play.

David Fricke, a senior editor from American *Rolling Stone*, was in Australia to attend the Big Day Out and see how it stacked up against America's Lollapalooza. Every band Fricke encountered who had played the Big Day Out had praised it, so he was keen to get a taste for himself. Still, he couldn't quite believe what he witnessed when Silverchair hit the stage:

> Tsunami-force waves of crowd surfers repeatedly roll towards the stage, damn near crushing the packs of defiant, cheering teenage girls pressed against the security barrier. Several enterprising fans, determined to get a better view, scramble up a drainpipe to the roof of an adjacent building, breaking the pipe and yanking part of it off the wall in the process.

Then a shirtless loon bored with rooftop slamdancing shimmies up a light pole overlooking the heaving moshpit. He dangles from his perch with one hand and a huge doofus grin on his face, poised to execute what looks like the ultimate stage dive — four storeys down. Fortunately, security gets to him first as silverchair, to their wry amusement, are rushed off the stage.

(In Melbourne, punters actually dived off nearby rooftops into the huge moshpit and trampolined on the tarpaulin hanging over the band.)

It was 3 pm when Silverchair exited the stage. Still to play at Big Day Out was Hole, fronted by Courtney Love, the widow of Nirvana's Kurt Cobain, and Offspring, the Californian punk band that had recently run roughshod over the charts with their hit album *Smash*. But it was Silverchair that everyone was talking about. Fricke again: 'Johns sings with a full-blooded voice that belies his age. The madhouse atmosphere is not a Pavlovian reaction to overnight success; the Seattle-fried crunch of 'Stoned' and 'Pure Massacre' is truly potent stuff.'

The mouthy Love was in the midst of a drug-fuelled mourning period for the husband who'd shot himself in their Seattle garage the year before. Yet she was sufficiently aware to notice the attention directed towards the Novocastrian trio. In typical Love fashion, she decided to bring Silverchair down a notch or two. 'So this young guy from Silverchair looks like my dead husband, Kurt, and sings like Eddie Vedder,' she drawled during her set. 'How lame.' She repeated this observation a few nights later at her band's show at Sydney nightspot Selinas. Whatever her intention, Love's comments showed that, almost against his will, Daniel Johns and Silverchair were leaving their mark on the rock world beyond Australia. Even an insult meant that they were definitely on the cool radar. (Four years later, in St Louis, Love and Silverchair again crossed paths. Only this time, she was topless. As Joannou tells it, 'She passed Daniel in the hallway, stopped, and said, "Are you doing heroin?" He said "No." She said "Good, because that's so '95."')

Other international acts at the 1995 Big Day Out paid Silverchair more respect than Courtney Love. Brit rockers the Cult called them up onstage in Perth during the final date of the festival and declared them 'Australia's finest'. Backstage, the Cult had given them penknives as gifts. Silverchair responded by donning wigs and dancing on-stage, badly, as the Cult riffed on.

But it was all becoming a bit much for the 15-year-olds of Silverchair. Johns had summed up the mixed emotions they felt about their success when he introduced the mosh-inducing 'Tomorrow' at the Sydney Big Day Out: 'This one is called "Cat's Scrotum",' he mumbled. Gillies and Joannou didn't say a word.

Another American in the mass at the Sydney show was David Massey, the Vice President of A&R with Epic Records, a subsidiary of Sony Music. Given that Murmur was part of the giant Sony group, Massey had an option to release Silverchair's music in North America. He was smitten by the band, and especially by Johns, and promptly agreed to release *Frogstomp*:

> He's 15 years old, he's got blond hair but he's nothing like Kurt [Cobain]. He's a bright, young surfer kid. They have their own identity.

> What impressed me most about them live was how well
> they actually played, how much presence they had on stage,
> and how developed their sound is for their age. The audi-
> ence response was pretty rapturous and it made me realise
> there wasn't the tiniest issue of novelty.

Well, maybe not, but any A&R guy worth his corporate credit
card could spot the obvious appeal of the band — they were
young, a little wild, had some great songs, and their ages gave
journalists an angle. Silverchair had something for everyone.

'We were learning a lot of things then,' Joannou figures,
recalling their Big Day Out experiences. 'We just loved to
play and didn't care about anything else. It was very surreal,
wandering around, being part of this big circus.'

It was a crazy time for the trio. They were caught up in a
whirlwind of manic shows, and they were also about to travel
overseas for the first time, where Silvermania would be cra-
zier still. Even going to Sydney had been a big event for these
three small-town teenagers — now they were venturing into
the largest rock & roll marketplace in the world.

While Big Day Out madness was happening all around
them, the band were keen to prove they weren't two-hit
wonders — and Watson and O'Donnell needed to prove their
new stars didn't have a short expiry date. During December
1994 and January 1995, the band spent nine days with South
African-born, Australian-based producer Kevin 'Caveman'
Shirley in Sydney, recording what would become *Frogstomp*,
their debut album.

Shirley had worked the desk for some well-regarded but
small-selling Australian bands, including power-riffers the
Dubrovniks, and had engineered the Baby Animals's 1991
debut album, which reached Number One in Australia and

sold 300,000 copies, but he was an unknown quantity as a producer. Watson, however, was keen to have Shirley produce the album, in part on the strength of some demos he'd produced for the Poor, a poor-man's AC/DC Sony had signed in 1994. ('They were fucking great, sonically.') And O'Donnell liked Shirley's work with the Dubrovniks. Although many at Sony thought this a risky choice, it turned out to be another smart move by the two Johns.

Shirley was known widely as a true 'rock dog'. A gradually emptying bottle of Jack Daniel's sat on the desk throughout every session he worked on. It was a sight that didn't rest well with Silverchair's parents, still the band's surrogate managers, who came into the studio each afternoon to check out their boys' progress. But Shirley's reputation wasn't fully deserved. A single parent, he brought his son Josh, who was on school holidays, into most sessions, and although 'he did have a drink each day,' as O'Donnell recalls, 'he was totally tied in.'

A fast worker, Shirley did his best to get the teen trio interested in the workings of the studio and the recording process, even if their short attention spans usually got the better of them. His approach in the studio was smart. Rather than the traditional method of recording rhythm tracks first, then adding guitars and vocals, he worked song by song. By the end of each day, one, sometimes two songs were ready for playback. He understood that these guys were teenagers; he'd let them crash about the studio corridors while he set up takes. Joannou laughs at the memory. 'We were just having fun. He was perfect; he'd call us in and say, "Right, we need you now." We'd go in, do it and then see what other stuff there was to break.'

They spent four days in Festival Studios in Pyrmont recording the basic instrument tracks, and another five days recording overdubs and Johns's vocal parts. Capturing those world-weary vocals — so unsettling from a teenager, and such a major part of the band's sound — was the most difficult part of the recording. On the first day, thanks to studio inexperience and a lack of proper vocal training, Johns simply ran out of voice. Then he caught a cold, which meant he had to return a fortnight later to finish five tracks. In an effort to get Johns motivated, Gillies and Joannou decorated his vocal booth with *Playboy* and *Penthouse* centrefolds and then rattled around the studio's corridors on equipment trolleys, just like 15-year-olds are expected to.

'He has the best sounds — drum-wise, everything-wise,' Joannou said in 1995, of recording with Shirley. 'He's great to work with and he's got a good brain. He mainly made things a bit longer or shorter.' The views the band were expressing about Shirley changed at the time of their second album's release, with indirect accusations that he was a control freak. But those close to the band believe the boys were blowing smoke in an effort to blame the inevitable Seattle/grunge comparisons on something — or someone — other than their songs. When asked about *Frogstomp* in 2003, Johns was very proud of the album:

> Kevin did a really good job. We were so young and inexperienced at the time that we probably needed somebody who could take control of the recording side of things and that's exactly what he did.

> A year or two after we made *Frogstomp* I really didn't like it, because it pigeonholed us and felt restricting. But that wasn't Kevin's fault — it had more to do with the songs and some of the stuff that happened around the album.

These days some of the songs on *Frogstomp* make me wince, but overall I think it's a fun record.

Frogstomp was wrapped for around $40,000. What wasn't absorbed by studio rental costs was mostly spent on Shirley's fee, travel expenses and accommodation. It was a relatively low-budget effort that would recoup its investment many times over, and then some. 'We did the album pretty quick,' Joannou comments, 'because we didn't have a lot of time. You know how people say it takes, like, three months to do an album? That's a load of crap. You can do it in 10 days — piece of cake.' (By the time of *Diorama*, their fourth album, they'd be spending months in the studio.)

'The alarming thing is that the guys sound as mature as they do,' Shirley said in 1996:

> You can definitely hear the influences. But they weren't embarrassed about showing those influences.

> I think the age card is a funny one. George Harrison was 16 when he joined the Beatles. Michael Jackson was going a long time before that age. It's nothing unusual in the history of rock & roll.

Frogstomp — named after a Floyd Newman song Johns spotted on a Stax-Volt singles compilation in Watson's record collection — was released in Australia on March 27, 1995, debuting at Number One in the album charts and staying in the top spot for three weeks. It was the first debut album by an Australian act to chart at Number One in its first week. By April 10, it had been certified platinum (70,000 copies sold). By May it had sold more than 100,000 copies, principally on the strength of Triple J airplay and live shows. It was only at the end of the year, under pressure from Sony executives, that Watson and O'Donnell agreed to a week's worth of TV advertising — and only if they could produce what amounted to an 'anti ad'. According to O'Donnell, 'We just didn't want to be greedy.'

For a trio of 15-year-olds still finding their own rock & roll voice, *Frogstomp* was a remarkably solid, if hugely derivative album. More than anything else, it was an album of its time, propelled by what would be recognised as the sound of Silverchair: Johns's full-throated roar and serrated riffs (check out 'Pure Massacre'), Joannou's fat, fuzzy basslines (best heard in 'Israel's Son') and Gillies's muscular tub-thumping (everywhere). They worked from the definitive grunge template as perfected by Soundgarden, Nirvana and Pearl Jam: quiet verses followed by loud choruses and a sound as thick as sludge. However, Johns's old-beyond-his-years growl and the melodies that broke through the sonic murk were distinctive.

Johns, who still insisted that he drew most of his lyrical ideas from watching television, whipped up a batch of songs dominated by death, violence and powerhouse rock riffs. 'Faultline', for starters, was written about the Newcastle earthquake of December 1989, which killed thirteen people. 'I just saw on the news that a guy's brother was killed, so I wrote lyrics about it three years later when I remembered it in a dream,' Johns explained.

Of the rest of *Frogstomp*, 'Shade' was a howling power ballad, 'Leave Me Out' wielded a simple 'back off' message and 'Cicada' was pure teen angst (with guitars). The sombre, surprisingly restrained 'Suicidal Dream' was the album's most disturbing track. Johns calmly sang the lyric 'I fantasise about my death / I'll kill myself by holding my breath' as if it were just another pop song. 'It's not about me,' Johns insisted. 'It's about teenage suicide and the ideas people have. I don't try and write lyrics about me.' Regardless of where Johns's lyrics came, *Frogstomp* connected with more record-buying teenagers than the band or their label could ever have imagined. And despite attracting such condescending tags as 'Nirvana in Pyjamas', 'silverhighchair' and 'Not Soundgarden, Kindergarten', most critics treated the album with respect. Writing in the *Sydney Morning Herald*, buzzkilling journalist Shane Danielsen called it 'an impressive debut', noting their 'ability to pile layers of punishing noise atop a tune worth humming'. Australian *Rolling Stone* gushed that 'silverchair make a noise like they're here to stay,' concluding, with only the faintest hint of condescension, that 'this is eminently moshable stuff, guaranteed to cause carnage in lounge rooms across the country.'

While they mightn't have a sound to call their own, Silverchair had grabbed hold of the grunge zeitgeist with all six hands, even down to the fine detail of wearing the right T-shirts — including for locals You Am I and Ammonia, and US bands Ministry, Helmet and the Offspring — in band photos. Some wear their influences on their sleeve — Silverchair wore them on their skinny, hairless chests.

The band were big winners in the annual Australian *Rolling Stone* Reader's Poll awards, published in April 1995, winning Artist of the Year, Best New Band, Best Hard Rock Band and Brightest Hope. 'Tomorrow' picked up Best Single, while the obligatory nay-sayers also gave them the tag Hype of the Year. But Silverchair were getting used to their critics.

The band readily admitted the influence of Pearl Jam on their runaway hit of a single 'Tomorrow', but began to play down the long-term impact of the multiplatinum grungers. 'When you hear the album, it doesn't sound anything like that,'

Joannou assured writer Mel Toltz. 'That was early,' Johns threw in. 'That was on the first EP. At that time we were very strongly influenced by Pearl Jam. That's all we ever listened to. And then we started listening to Soundgarden and Helmet and stopped listening to Pearl Jam.' A defensive tone crept into his diatribe: 'Because we were just starting out, we didn't know.'

Even as 15-year-olds, the trio were already developing a rock-solid defence to the tall-poppy syndrome that is such an intrinsic part of Australian culture. 'People give us shit,' Johns said. 'It's good in some ways. It stops you from getting a big head if you know like millions and millions of people hate you. And if people hate you, it makes you want to keep going, 'cause you want to prove them wrong.'

Ben Lee, the teen hipster from Noise Addict, was a very public critic. His band had emerged at the same time as Silverchair, but whereas the Newcastle three were immediately embraced by the mainstream, Lee's outfit stayed resolutely in the margins, maintaining their indie cred and the coolest possible connections (their second-ever gig was opening for New York art-rockers Sonic Youth). Lee's scorn for Silverchair was clear when he told *Rolling Stone* magazine: 'There's no way they're ever going to live this down. They'll always be "the kids from silverchair". Those kids, they don't know what they're letting themselves in for.'

On April 12, 'Israel's Son' was released, the third single from *Frogstomp*. But it was a limited release, for three weeks only. This was another Watson and O'Donnell move to control the exposure of the band, in the face of an alterna-rock-hungry public that couldn't get enough of them. And still the song bruised the Top 10, peaking at Number 11. The Sony-employed pair were now acting as caretaker managers for the band, along with the boys' parents, especially Julie Johns. But what Silverchair really needed was someone to take on the management job full time.

In August 1995, the worst-kept secret in the local rock biz was revealed: Watson decided he was ready to look after the band full time, quitting his A&R position with Sony. Watson had been planning his move since March. Despite a few expressions of interest — John Woodruff, who'd checked them out when they'd won Youthrock '94, was the highest profile manager keen on the band — there was no other logical contender for the job. The deal was sealed over a few lunches with the trio's parents. 'It was just a question of when I was going to jump ship.'

As for the band themselves, they were happy enough about Watson taking over, but as Gillies put it, 'We so weren't thinking about it; we didn't give a shit.' Speaking with rock scribe Stuart Coupe in his Music Industry News & Gossip column in Sydney's *Drum Media*, Watson explained:

> After more than four years at Sony Music this has been a very difficult decision to make. However, things have finally reached the point where silverchair really do need full-time management rather than part-time career guidance which John O'Donnell and I have been trying to provide since the band signed to Murmur last year.
>
> The support I had from the band, their parents and everyone at the record company has been tremendous and I am excited at now being able to focus 100 per cent on helping silverchair achieve the international success they deserve.

Around the time Watson took over management of the band, murmurs of Silverchair interest emerged in America. It came from a variety of sources.

'The Big Backyard' was a government-subsidised initiative that produced half-hour radio-ready programs of new Australian music burnt onto CD, and distributed via embassies and diplomatic posts to more than 750 radio stations in 100-plus countries. In an effort to get the band's US label, Epic, excited about the act, Watson bought the Big Backyard mailing list and fired off a Murmur mailout. It included a letter from the program suggesting stations check out this new Australian music.

Back in March 1995, a Perth-based fan had mailed over a copy of 'Tomorrow' to a relative who worked at Detroit radio station 89X, which, on March 27 became the first US radio station to playlist the song. Brian Philips, the chief programmer for Atlanta's 99X station, was in Australia on holiday just as 'Tomorrow' fever started to spread. He grabbed a copy of the song everyone was talking about and playlisted it on his return to Atlanta. Within a week, it was one of the top five songs requested by listeners. Chicago's Q101 also added 'Tomorrow' to their playlist; soon Seattle's KNDD did the same, as did Milwaukee's WLUM.

The band had already played three fly-by European dates, in Frankfurt, London and Amsterdam, between March 29 and April 3, which bassist Joannou casually dismissed as 'just a bit of a thing to spread the word that we were a new Australian band'. The amiable Gillies decided London would have been 'legendary if it was warmer and had a beach'. But America was where the serious interest was developing in the band, and as Watson and O'Donnell knew, it was also where the serious money was to be made.

Epic had planned to run with 'Israel's Son' as Silverchair's first US single and have the band tour to coincide with *Frogstomp*'s release late in the year. Now they had to change their plans and lead with 'Tomorrow' — and get the band over for at least a few dates. By June 6, when the single was officially released to radio, David Massey knew he had a phenomenon on his hands. As he told *Rolling Stone* magazine, this wasn't record company spin at work. 'Tomorrow' had been 'getting an amazing response from the public,' he said. 'It comes from the public as opposed to industry hype.'

On June 21, the band played their first American date, in Atlanta (even though a visa hassle in Sydney meant they almost didn't make the trip at all). Although they made a press stopover in Los Angeles, they didn't play shows there. Instead, they opted to do gigs in the cities where radio response to 'Tomorrow' was strongest: Atlanta, Chicago (on June 23) and Detroit (June 24), at the 'birthday bash' for station 89X. It was a smart move by the band's management: make a few splashes and let the ripples spread from there. And by playing radio-sponsored shows, the band were establishing some goodwill. It is one of modern rock & roll's unspoken rules that by playing a free radio show a band becomes entitled to good treatment by station playlist programmers.

Despite the impressive local radio interest, no one could have expected the response at the Atlanta show. The venue, the Roxy, housed 1500 punters at a squeeze. Mid-afternoon, a shocked Watson put in a call to O'Donnell back in Sydney: 'You're not going to believe this, but we're at soundcheck and there's a queue of 150 people going around the corner.' By six o'clock, two hours before the doors were due to open, a line of three thousand hopefuls snaked a kilometre down the street. On a home-video made at the show, Watson can be heard muttering about the out-of-control crowd response.

The mayhem continued throughout the short tour. At their Chicago gig two days later, while the crowd moshed themselves senseless, a female voice shrieked from the balcony, 'Oh my God, they're so cute I can't believe it.' To bring the band back down to earth, when Johns broke a microphone stand during their set, the venue insisted they pay for the damage. The *Chicago Tribune*'s Greg Kot reviewed the show, describing how the band overcame a wobbly start to 'put some wallop behind the insidious melodies of "Tomorrow", "Real [sic] Massacre" and "Israel's Son"':

> There was no denying the savvy sense of dynamics, muscular melodies and tight ensemble playing. All of which suggested that silverchair has the potential to match the impact of some of its influences, if not make Mom and Dad sell off their old Zeppelin albums.

Watson and O'Donnell had suspected the band would draw a strong response, but this was the stuff of which managers dream. By the time of the Chicago show, *Frogstomp*, which had been released less than a week before, had sold five thousand copies, two thousand in Atlanta alone, where it debuted at Number 11 even before it was fully stocked in stores. The following week, sales doubled. As 99X programmer Philips stated: 'It is not in my experience for a band to launch itself into the stratosphere this quickly. This is a very special thing.'

Watson and O'Donnell insisted, just as they did in Australia, that the band would only accommodate the 'right' type of media, even to the extreme of turning down *Time* magazine's request for an interview. Their first US radio interview, with Sean Demory from WNNX, was a useful reminder that, after all, these rock-stars-in-the-making were teenagers. Whereas most bands would have been talking up whatever product they had to sell, Silverchair were talking up rollercoasters, especially those at Magic Mountain, an amusement park in LA. 'That is the best place in the whole world!' Johns gushed. Their exchange touched on everything from seeing hardcore favourites Helmet at Brisbane's Livid Festival (Gillies: 'And that was very legendary.') to in-flight meals, arcade games and the lack of American beaches. It was all good-natured chaos, with the band maintaining their credibility by requesting a Helmet song rather than the track off *Frogstomp* that the DJ had already cued up. 'You don't have to play something off that CD,' Gillies and Johns shouted in unison.

After the Detroit show, the band returned to Europe, playing the Roskilde festival, Denmark's answer to Lollapalooza and the Big Day Out, on June 30. There were more European festival dates in France (where they were almost wiped out by a speeding truck in the middle of the night), Switzerland and England, before returning home in mid July. Back in Australia, they toasted *Frogstomp*'s success with a hometown show on August 12 at the Newcastle Workers Club, at the curiously named Llama Ball. A favourite animal of the teen wonders for a short time, they would name their fan club the Llama Appreciation Society and Johns titled his publishing company Big Fat Llama Music. *Frogstomp*'s liner notes stated 'no llamas were harmed in the making of this album' and encouraged fans to 'support the liberation of the llama nation'. As Watson explained, 'They were 15-year old guys; llamas were funny.'

These llama-lovers were also homecoming heroes.

Meanwhile, Epic wanted a bigger-budget video for 'Tomorrow', so they hired director Mark Pellington, later to become the director of such Hollywood flicks as *The Mothman Prophecies*. MTV soon had the clip in their 'Buzz Bin', on high rotation.

Silverchair's timing couldn't have been better. Nirvana were all over when Cobain killed himself in 1994; grunge giants Pearl Jam were off the road, immersed in a legal battle with Ticketmaster over concert prices; and both the Smashing Pumpkins and Soundgarden had retreated to the studio. American rock lovers wanted something loud and energetic and youthful, and they wanted it now. Silverchair was just the band — and Epic fully understood this. '"Tomorrow" is a stone-cold smash,' Massey said at the time. 'It's a really American sound, it fits in perfectly.' It also didn't hurt that their lead singer was desired by girls and envied by their boyfriends. Even parents loved Silverchair; as New York writer Geoff Stead observed: 'Silverchair's image has received the stamp of approval from the mums and dads of America. They believe the young Australian band is not tainted by the drugs and sex scandals which surround many groups.' 'I'm not a fan of their music,' said Glen Bernard, a parent of four Silverchair fans, 'but my kids love them and it's good, clean fun.'

Timing, business-wise, also helped their American invasion. At this time Epic had no in-house A&R rep (they were wait-ing on a new recruit to shift from Virgin), so they weren't signing many new US acts. This gave priority to such non-American Sony signings as Oasis, Deep Forest, Des'ree and Silverchair — all big sellers in 1995. Usually, American signings are favoured, because a homegrown hit means that Sony won't have to pay a 'matrix royalty' to the country where the act is signed. But in 1995, Sony had no option. On July 10, *Frogstomp* debuted in the Billboard Top 200 at Number 106. By August 7, it was certified gold, having sold half a million copies.

Proving what a listener- and public-driven success this was, *Frogstomp* had been certified platinum on September 11, 1995, well before most reviews of the album appeared.

American *Rolling Stone* wrote that the band 'exude a rugged confidence and an otherworldly grasp of noise rock that belies their tender ages.' Fort Lauderdale's *Sun-Sentinel* newspaper declared that 'Silverchair's music is in a realm of its own.' The *New York Times*' Dmitri Ehrlich wasn't completely sold, but could spot the band's strengths:

> Obviously derivative of Stone Temple Pilots, Nirvana, Pearl Jam and Soundgarden, the group proffers dark musical theatrics with a tossed-off air and a visceral, corrosive texture. Aggressive to a fault, Chris Joannou makes use of intentionally distorted bass line[s] juxtaposed against Mr. Johns' shimmery man-child vocals.

Request magazine's Jim Testa noted that:

> [*Frogstomp*] 'may not be the most original album of the year, but it's certainly one of the most accomplished, displaying a vaunting command of dynamics and tempo changes, and an impeccable grasp of the nihilism and frustrations shared by most young Americans.

Not bad for three Aussie brats still in high school.

Silverchair's first full-scale US tour started in Chicago on September 2, and took in Boston, Washington DC, Atlanta, Los Angeles, San Francisco and Seattle, before ending with a free show on Santa Monica pier on September 17. By that time, *Frogstomp* was Number 9 on the Billboard chart — outselling even Michael Jackson's *HIStory*. No Australian band since INXS had steamrolled the American charts in that way — and it took INXS several years on the road, sleeping in the tour van and eating at diners, to make the slightest impact. Silverchair, however, broke overnight. Despite their 'don't give a shit' attitude, the band were fully aware of their good fortune. As Joannou told me in 2003, 'Watto [Watson] made it very clear how lucky we were that we weren't stuck in a van, trudging around, playing gigs to three people.'

But still the band behaved as you'd expect 15-year-olds to behave. Life on the road with Silverchair was something like a three-way version of *Bill & Ted's Excellent Adventure*. 'They seem oblivious to the silvermania that is sweeping the US,' wrote *Rolling Stone*'s Mel Toltz, who caught up with the band during their American tour. 'Odd remarks and crude comments appear from nowhere and are volleyed back and forth across the room over an imaginary net.'

Curiously enough, this happened even though the band's entourage included their parents. The Silvermums and Silverdads would take turns travelling with their sons. The band agree that the mothers were the strictest; Joannou's father enjoyed the life so much he even grew his hair half-way down his back, just to keep up with his bass-playing offspring. Gillies believes his mother was the strictest of all when it came to band curfews. 'It was just a pain,' he said. 'She managed, for a little while, until I was about 16, to keep the reins on me. She'd make sure I was back by 1.30.' (The mothers did warm to touring, nonetheless. Today the band joke that their parents still ask when they're next touring, so they can join them and shop till they drop.)

In the midst of the madness, on September 7, the band took part in the MTV Music Awards in New York. They performed 'Pure Massacre' and 'Tomorrow', while perched on a stage atop Radio City Music Hall's entrance marquee — between songs they had to crawl back inside through a large window. The three tore through the performance, more bemused than excited by the company of America's A-list of rock stars (including Courtney Love) and such movers and shakers as Sony chief Tommy Mottola, who introduced himself to the band in their dressing room. The only time the trio truly loosened up was when human livewire Taylor Hawkins, then drumming for Alanis Morissette but soon to become a Foo Fighter, introduced himself and wished them luck. Rather than walk the red carpet with the other stars, the band walked around it — their way of staying one step removed from the glitterati. Chris Joannou joked, 'We thought we would've got in trouble if we walked on it.'

Craig Mathieson captured the frenzied atmosphere in *Hi Fi Days*. As 'Pure Massacre' ends:

> Johns coaxes spasms of feedback from his guitar, Gillies (literally) attacks his drums with fervour and Joannou unceremoniously drops his bass. Noise rings from the stage as silverchair walk off. For a few seconds the camera lingers on the abandoned instruments as the white noise fades. The camera cuts to co-host Tabitha Soren, who looks taken aback by silverchair's firestorm and grins nervously before putting everything into perspective with a clarifying comment: 'Whew'.

On September 10, the band supported the Ramones in front of a twenty-thousand strong crowd in Atlanta, at a show, not coincidentally, entitled The Big Day Out. (Station programmer Philips had obviously returned from Australia with more than a Silverchair CD.) Few rock stars outwardly impressed Silverchair, but this was a show that stuck with them for some time. 'They were legends; they were hell men,' Johns declared of the original New York punks.

Silverchair were at the centre of a major buzz, and the album kept selling. And the big names kept gravitating towards the band, with Nirvana bassist Kris Novoselic fronting at their September 15 show at Seattle. 'He was sitting on the side of the stage with his girlfriend,' Johns remembered of his encounter with the lanky man from Nirvana. 'He kept telling us about his toothache. It was so funny.'

Their American tour, however, ended on a bloody note. During their free final show on the Santa Monica Pier, the band experienced technical problems, which slowed down their set. Someone in the surly mob hurled a bottle onstage, which hit Johns on the left side of his head, opening a gaping wound. He kept playing, finishing the show with blood streaming down his face, looking more like one of the Newcastle rugby league Johnses than the softly spoken front-man of Silverchair. As soon as the show ended he went to hospital. It was Johns's first real taste of the downside of fame, even though he laughed about it later on. 'I got stitches and everything and came back and our sound guy was complaining about the PA and shit. It was so funny. It was heaps good fun. Everything went wrong.'

Joannou remembers that show as one of the roughest they'd ever witnessed. 'It was really hardcore. It had one of the craziest mosh circle things I'd ever seen. [In the US, moshpits have a tendency to develop into strange, danger-ous 'circles' of slam-dancers, who look as though they're performing some bizarre ritual dance.] Big dudes were run-ning around slamming their mates; these guys were crazy. They'd whack some guy really hard and then pat him on the back.'

If Santa Monica was a bust, Silverchair's return to Australia was a dazzling high — even better than the Magic Mountain rollercoaster. The annual ARIAs were held on Monday October 2 at Sydney's Darling Harbour. The word doing the rounds was that the 'old guard' of Farnesy, Barnesy and co. were about to be dethroned by three kids from Newcastle. There were other bands at the front of the alt-rock revolution, too, such as Sydney trio You Am I, who'd just released their second and best album, *Hi Fi Way*. Even though Janet Jackson was the guest of honour and mainstream pop star Tina Arena won four gongs, including Best Australian Album for *Don't Ask*, it was Silverchair's night.

The band cleaned up, winning awards for Best New Talent, Best Debut Single, Best Australian Single and Highest Selling Single ('Tomorrow'), as well as Best Debut Album for *Frogstomp*. Typically, rather than come off like a bunch of poseurs and accept the awards themselves, the band sent along Josh Shirley, the 7-year-old son of *Frogstomp*'s producer to collect their pointy statuettes.

But the band weren't just being whimsical. Josh Shirley was the only person, apart from Johns, Gillies and Joannou, to actually play on *Frogstomp*. You can hear him flailing about on the drums just before the start of 'Findaway'. The link was meant to be explained by presenter Meatloaf, but the big guy didn't quite make it to that part of his cue card. The press, who the next day tore a few layers off the band for being smug, were actually missing out on a great story.

It didn't matter to Silverchair, though. They hooked up with You Am I's Tim Rogers to close the night with a tearaway cover of Radio Birdman's 'New Race', having the rockingest time of their life. Rogers was as big a hero to the Silver-trio as Eddie Vedder; Johns had even sported a You Am I T-shirt on an American TV broadcast. 'We only practised for about an hour and thought, "Yeah, that's all right."' Johns said afterwards. 'Shit, it was funny.' The new guard had entered the building, even if they didn't bother stepping onstage to collect their trophies.

The lines between mainstream and so-called 'alternative' acts were blurring, with Silverchair leading the way.

Just as satisfying was the band's success at the 1995 Australian Performing Rights Association (APRA) Songwriter Awards, held on December 12, when Johns and Gillies shared the 'Songwriter of the Year' award. These awards are greatly valued by musicians because they're judged by music-making peers, not the industry players who make the decisions at the ARIAs. Silverchair didn't just have industry approval; their fellow musos thought they were pretty cool, too.

The rest of Silverchair's 1995 was spent in motion. And there were more injuries. During an October 27 gig at the Palace in St Kilda, Johns stage-dived into the crowd. Joannou and Gillies kept playing, while keeping a wary eye on their frontman. When Johns hadn't surfaced after a minute, they started to panic. Local rock & roll legend maintains that when Johns dived, the crowd parted and he hit the deck. The truth, of course, is slightly different. As Joannou told me, 'Daniel stage-dived and then people started to grab his shirt and stuff and he went, "Whoom!", straight to the bottom.' Plucked out of the sweaty mass by security guards, Johns made it back to the stage with his clothes ripped. When his eyes started rolling back in his head, the show was over. (Joannou: 'We went, "Fuck, he's dead!"') Thankfully, there was an off-duty police car outside; they raced Johns to hospital, where he was held for observation. But still the show went on — within two days, Silverchair were playing another (this time incident-free) gig at the same venue.

Their next American tour started on November 25, in San Diego, and continued on to December 18, where they shared the bill at LA's Universal Amphitheatre with Radiohead, Bush and Oasis. They put in a *Saturday Night Live* appearance on

December 9, and four days later played New Jersey's legendary Stone Pony, the club whose place in rock & roll's folklore was secured as the starting point for Bruce Springsteen and his E-Street Band.

Rock writer Stuart Coupe found himself in the eye of the Silverchair storm when he caught an all-ages show in Philadelphia. Backstage, Coupe noted 'how remarkably down-to-earth and relaxed' the band seemed, despite the pressure of photo shoots, interviews and pressing the flesh, which are required to break new albums, especially in America. Nonetheless, the controlling hand of manager Watson was ever-present. 'An interview?' Coupe wrote in Sydney's *Drum Media*. 'Watson says he'll think about it but reckons he doesn't want to do any Australian press for the moment.' Coupe knew that American *Rolling Stone* writer David Fricke had just spent a few days with the band — he was pissed off. Coupe observed, 'It was hard not to think about the situation with INXS when they were just toooo big for the Australian media.'

Coupe met up with Fricke a few nights later, at the band's show in New York's Roseland Ballroom. He asked the respected US scribe how Silverchair stacked up next to Nirvana. 'He tells me that Kurt had a bit more angst and menace,' Coupe wrote, 'but aside from that, silverchair are putting on a show to rival that band.' Right then in the United States, that was more than enough to satisfy an alt-rock crowd short on heroes.

Silverchair closed 1995 with an outdoor New Year's Eve show in Perth. By then, *Frogstomp* had sold a million copies in America (it went on to sell 2,025,000 copies there out of 2,898,000 globally). The band had cleaned up at the ARIAs. Their estimated gross earnings for the year were $6.4 million. They'd rocked Europe, Australia and America, coast to coast.

You want an excellent adventure? It had been the biggest year of these kids' lives. Bill and Ted would be proud.

All of three days separated the band's New Year's Eve show and their opening date of 1996, where they put in a rapturously received set at the inaugural Homebake, an Australians-only rock festival held in Byron Bay, on the NSW north coast. But in January, the band learned — just as Johns had in Santa Monica — that fame's yin can often outweigh its yang. Success really had a funny way of biting them on the arse and bringing them down, just when their outlook was ridiculously bright.

It all started with a *Daily Telegraph* headline, which shouted: 'silverchair shocked. Violence appals us, band says.' Another headline yelled: 'A script for murder'.

On August 11, 1995, in Washington State, 16-year-old Brian Bassett and his friend Nicholaus McDonald had shot Bassett's parents and drowned his 5-year-old brother. When caught, they told police they were playing 'Israel's Son' at the time. Their trial opened on January 18, and both were being tried as adults, which guaranteed far more media coverage than yet another tragic case of American patricide. McDonald's lawyer, Tom Copland, claimed that both his client and Bassett had been driven to kill by the song; he wanted it to be made admissible evidence. He stated that the song was 'almost a script' for the murders. There was even talk of subpoenaing Daniel Johns, who wrote the song.

Naturally, Watson sprang to the band's defence, making an official statement that:

> silverchair do not, have not, and never would condone vio-
> lence of any sort. The band is appalled by this horrific
> crime and they hope that justice will prevail in prosecuting
> whoever is responsible for it. silverchair absolutely rejects any

> allegation that their song is in any way responsible for the
> action of the alleged murderers. It is a matter of public record
> that the song in question is inspired by a television docu-
> mentary about wartime atrocities. The song seeks to criticise
> violence and war by portraying them in all their horror.

Responding to Copland's argument, deputy prosecutor Jerry
Fuller asked 'What does it prove? Does it prove that Bassett hated
his parents? Does it prove he had the motive to kill his parents?
No. All it proves is that it was a song that he played.' The next day,
Judge Mark McCauley ruled that 'Israel's Son' could not be
played during opening statements and reserved judgement on
whether the song could be played at all during the trial.

But the damage was done: suddenly a very green bunch of
16-year-olds from Newcastle were receiving a similar treatment to British metal outfit Judas Priest, who were being
sued in an American court by two families who blamed the
album *Stained Class* for the suicides of their sons. That case
was also dismissed, but the stigma was pervasive. O'Donnell,
Watson and Silverchair's parents had every reason to close
ranks just a little more around their charges.

Speaking eight years down the line, Watson considers this
a pivotal moment for Johns, one that triggered his increased
wariness of the limelight and which would soon turn him
into a virtual recluse. A *Daily Telegraph Mirror* article from
October 1995, headlined 'How a $6m boy gets to school' and
showing Johns, in school uniform, riding his pushbike, only
exacerbated the problem. 'I'm not saying the media caused
the problems which happened later,' says Watson, 'but there is
not a doubt in my mind that they were one of several contributing factors.' O'Donnell agrees: 'I think the "Israel's Son"
thing hit him really hard.' (Johns would have the last laugh

when it came time to vent his anger and write the bitter lyrics for future albums *Freak Show* and *Neon Ballroom*.)

Next move for the band, however, was a US stadium tour with the Red Hot Chili Peppers, rescheduled from the previous November, when Chili Peppers drummer Chad Smith had been injured in a sporting mishap. The two bands connected well; Silverchair got on famously with Smith, the most sociable Chili Pepper, who Joannou described as 'quite a dude'. The shows were huge, including a February 9 stop at New York's Madison Square Garden, the biggest indoor gig in the city that never sleeps. Twenty thousand people turned up. It was almost a year to the day since the band had played Melbourne's inner city Prince of Wales Hotel. Things had changed.

'Playing the Garden was a dream come true for us,' said Johns. 'We used to watch Led Zeppelin's video *The Song Remains the Same* [which was filmed at Madison Square Garden] two times a day, and to play there was mind-blowing.' Gillies was an even more hardcore fan; he'd watch John Bonham's drum blitz, 'Moby Dick', in slow-mo, then he'd flail away on his bedroom kit, copying Bonham's moves. To this day, it's still his favourite rock movie. 'It was this buzz,' he says of the Madison Square Garden show. 'I'm going to play where one of my biggest idols had played.'

One thing in particular had changed for the band: the kind of attention they were receiving from women. During a warm-up show in Los Angeles on February 4, a tiny scarlet-coloured bikini bottom fluttered through the air, landing at the feet of a bewildered Daniel Johns. And on the final night of the tour, February 16, at Long Island's Nassau Coliseum, the band were in for a shock when the Chili Peppers hired two strippers to dance around the stage, topless, while the band played on. The trio's parents observed from side stage, unamused.

'The Red Hot Chili Peppers thought we'd be little arse-holes,' Joannou told the *Sydney Morning Herald* after the tour:

> When a band starts out sleeping in the backs of cars and in $50 hotels, then works their way up to 15,000 [seat] arenas, then they're, like, really good guys. But the guys that get successful really quick are total wankers. The Chili Peppers thought that because our album went pretty good in America quickly, we'd be real little shits. After they got to know us, it was cool.

The fun ended pretty swiftly, because the band was having more trouble with 'Israel's Son'. Their US label had asked them to reshoot the video. Johns claimed that the label thought it too violent. 'I thought, "That is a good clip for us,"' Johns told MTV in February 1996. 'Then someone had to go and have a whinge about it [and] now we've got to change it all because of [a] stupid thing.' According to Chris Joannou, the one image that bothered Sony 'just had a noose hanging off a beam of wood'. 'And a dog in a cage,' Johns added. 'They said it was too violent. It's bad.'

Curiously, in the reworked video, the use of lighting and colours is very reminiscent of Nirvana's 'Smells Like Teen Spirit', while Johns wears what one fan described as a 'grandpa sweater' — exactly the type Kurt Cobain used to fancy. In an even more perverse twist, Johns wears a shirt with the number 27 on it — the age Cobain (and Janis Joplin and Jim Morrison) was when he died. It was becoming clear how Epic was positioning the band for American youth: Nirvana reborn. The band were learning a big lesson about the role mythology played in selling rock & roll records.

By the time the band reached Europe on February 20 for a run of shows in England, France, Germany and Holland, they were already looking ahead to their second album, while defending themselves against assertions they were a grunge band.

'The same fucking people are always comparing us to Pearl Jam and Nirvana,' Gillies told Holland's *Oor* magazine. 'The album [*Frogstomp*] doesn't have a Seattle grunge sound at all.' To which Johns added: 'In a couple of months, after the European tour, we'll start with recordings for a new album. You'll hear jazz, funk and rap. We already have a lot of new songs.' Gillies threw in:

> The next album will be hard and dark. The sound has to be even more fuller and fatter. We can do that now because we have a much bigger budget. Maybe we'll put a more cheerful song on the middle of the album to cheer the listener up. But the rest of the songs are meant to go cry with.

Silverchair returned to Australia after a March 6 show in Cologne, breaking for shows in Japan on April 2 and 3. Again, they cleaned up in the Australian *Rolling Stone* Readers' Poll, winning Best Band, Best Single, for 'Tomorrow', Best Male Singer, Best Hard Rock Band, Best Album Cover and Brightest Hope for 1996.

And Johns was voted Best New Talent in *Guitar World*'s Reader's Poll, rolling Foo Fighter Dave Grohl and Korn. Johns's solo on 'Tomorrow' ruled over such wannabes as Eddie Van Halen and Dave Navarro. As the magazine stated in their editorial, 'We suspected the teenaged phenoms of silverchair were popular, but we didn't know they were immensely popular.' Johns, typically, played down the award. 'I don't really rate that as a solo. Basically, we really don't think that solos are worth doing for our music.'

The band had one more show to close the globetrotting *Frogstomp* tour: an April 9 set on the final day of the Royal Easter Show in Sydney. It was kids' day at the show; it made perfect sense that the prime entertainment for the day was a band of guys who could just as easily have been part of the crowd, shopping for showbags and riding the ghost train.

Twenty thousand fans fronted for the show. Backstage, among the music-business insiders, the whisper was that the band was about to collect $5 million for the publishing rights to *Frogstomp* and their next album. Onstage, the band ripped through a 75-minute set, Gillies performing the ritualistic trashing of his drum kit at the close of 'Israel's Son'. As fireworks lit up the sky, a hundred teens in the moshpit were led away and treated for cuts, scratches and bruises.

Just under 90 gigs and several million sales of *Frogstomp* down the line, Silverchair were the kings of the world. So what next? Just as importantly, could it last?

Bibliography

Random Notes, Australian *Rolling Stone* March 1992; *Sydney Morning Herald* 03/04/1995; 'Boy's Life' American *Rolling Stone* April 1996; Billy Thorpe. *Most People I Know (Think That I'm Crazy)* MacMillan 1998; 'Concert Action Is Up Down Under' *Billboard* 12/11/1994; 'Rocking 'Chair' *The Orange County Register* 18/06/1995; 'Still at School' *Metal Masters* May 1995; 'Introducing the Australian Nirvana: silverchair' *Music News of the World* 08/04/1995; Craig Mathieson. *Hi Fi Days: The Future of Australian Rock* 1996; Australian *Rolling Stone* May 1995; 'silverchair's Excellent Adventure' Australian *Rolling Stone* April 1995; 'Noise Addict & silverchair' Australian *Rolling Stone* 1994 Yearbook; 'Watson to Manage silverchair' *Drum Media* August 1995; *Raw* May 1995; 'silverchair: Face to Face with America' Australian *Rolling Stone* September 1995; 'Youthful Openers silverchair Outbuzz Headliner Hum' *Chicago Tribune* 26/06/1995; Transcript: Radio Interview with Sean Demory, WNNX Atlanta, 21/06/1995; 'Red Hot and Silver' *Daily Telegraph* 15/02/1997; American *Rolling Stone* Online; 'silverchair Stays With Its Style' *Sun-Sentinel* (Fort Lauderdale) 20/10/1995; *The New York Times* 22/10/1995; *Request* October 1995; Transript: Interview on MTV's *Modern Rock Live* 02/02/1997; *Rip It Up* October 1995; 'Songs from the Big Chair' *Drum Media* 11/12/1995; 'Silverchair Shocked. Violence Appals Us, Band Says' *Daily Telegraph* 20/01/96; 'Teen Band silverchair Blamed for Youth's Action. Song "a Script for Triple Murder"' *Daily Telegraph* 19/01/96; 'How a $6M Boy Gets to School' *Daily Telegraph Mirror* 20/10/95; ''chair, Hair and Chili Peppers' *Sydney Morning Herald* 05/04/1996; MTV's *Week in Rock*, February 1996; 'Interview with silverchair' *OOR Magazine* 24/02/1996; 'Reader's Poll' Australian *Rolling Stone* April 1996; 'Teenage Riot' *Guitar World* March 1996

Madness in the Moshpit:

an interview with David Fricke

Renowned American music writer David Fricke joined *Rolling Stone* in 1985 as Music Editor; he's now a Senior Editor. He was the first influential American writer to see Silverchair in action when he caught their legendary set at the 1995 Sydney Big Day Out. He then hit the road with the band when they toured America in the northern winter of 1995, as the band went platinum with 'Tomorrow' and its parent album, *Frogstomp*. Very much a Silverchair advocate, and an Australian music buff, he's tracked the band's career ever since.

What brought you to Australia in 1995?

I went because REM were opening their world tour there. I got there in time for two of their Sydney shows and the Big Day Out was within that 10-day period. Being Music Editor at the time, I was able to give myself special dispensation to stick around for the Big Day Out. I'd never seen one and figuring that we'd given so much coverage to Lollapalooza, and all the festivals that had sprung up in its wake, thought it was worth seeing.

Had you heard much about the Big Day Out through bands you'd interviewed? Did the festival have a buzz overseas?

It had started to get a reputation because of the year Nirvana played there [1992]. And there was a buzz from Australian musicians and writers I knew. I also thought it was worthwhile covering because Hole was playing there, Ministry was playing there, plus all the Australian stuff, which I'd always been interested in. We ended up running a lot of photos and my blow-by-blow account.

What was your awareness of Silverchair at that time?

By that point, John O'Donnell, who I knew through his time at *Rolling Stone* — and who'd given me the heads-up when he started at Murmur with [John] Watson — had started sending me stuff. I'm pretty sure that an early copy of the EP had gotten to me. I was familiar with those songs, particularly 'Tomorrow'.

Other than that, all I knew was that they were real young and that John [O'Donnell] was very excited about them. I'd seen John while I was in Sydney and he was talking them up. By the time I saw him at the Sydney show, everyone was raving about the Melbourne show a few days before, where people were jumping up and down on the roof and all this sort of stuff. Obviously there was a buzz going on. Fortunately, they were [playing] on the day I made the festival.

What are your recollections of the gig?

When the afternoon started, the crowd started lining up to see them — and it was out of control. They were obviously playing in a space too small. I'm sure the fire department would have had objections. People were up on the roof, they were standing at the back — and as for people up in the front, well, you could just imagine the rib cages cracking. It was really packed. It was an amazing buzz. It's really hard these days to get that sense of anticipation at a rock show because we all know how they are; they've evolved into ritual. But this was a band that was way too young to be part of the ritual — and a lot of the crowd were way too young to be jaded.

Did you get a sense of ownership from the crowd?

I definitely got a sense of pride. It was excitement, it was pride, it was anticipation. It was something you definitely didn't get when Hole was on stage, or Ministry. You got it as well when You Am I played the bigger stage later on, although it wasn't as packed. It was something that was shared throughout the entire day; that this was the first major surfacing, nationally, for a lot of those bands, rather than a regional situation. But Silverchair were the one: they'd gone number one, they were so young — and the combination of the novelty and the achievement made them unbeatable.

How did they stack up against other acts on the bill?

They killed me; they absolutely killed me. It wasn't anything special that they did, but they were so good, unselfconscious, and they didn't seem cowed by the fact that they were the hottest thing since the invention of the wheel.

John [O'Donnell] took me backstage briefly before the gig and introduced me to John Watson for the first time, and the three guys were just sitting against a wall, on the floor. They were so, you know, 'whatever'. They were so nonchalant. Meeting me was no big deal — John was going, 'David Fricke, *Rolling Stone*, America, dah, dah, dah,' and they just went, 'Cool.' I wasn't offended; I just figured that these guys have it under control; they didn't give a shit in the best kind of way. They were ready to go out and play.

To them, the playing, the songs, the music, and all the excitement that came back from the crowd was the thing. It wasn't about the fact that some guy from a magazine was there, or the zillion record company people — it wasn't like they were surrounded by friends. They were surrounded by adults. It wasn't worth getting excited about. The real excitement was to get out and play. That's how I read it.

And what about their set: it was quite brief, right?

It was fairly short; it was essentially the first album. I'm not sure how much was finished by that stage. 'Israel's Son' just blew me away — if I remember correctly, that was the last number. In a sense, 'Tomorrow' almost sounded old compared to that and songs like 'Pure Massacre'. It's got that soft/loud dynamic, but it was almost like a ballad compared to 'Massacre' or 'Israel's Son'. Not only was 'Tomorrow' good, and these guys were good and loud and looked great, but they had some serious songs that were worth banging your head to.

Where were you while all the action was happening?

I was standing right to the side of the stage, in the pit, near the corner where Daniel was standing. It was loud; I was right there. If I was any closer I would have been on stage. I was blown away. It was a day of really great stuff — You Am I were great, Spiderbait were great, it was a real blast to see Deniz Tek after being a Radio Birdman fan for twenty years — but Silverchair was the great shock. I came back to New York and didn't stop talking about them.

Did Courtney Love give Daniel the once over?

Certainly at the Sydney Big Day Out, Courtney was rocking and reeling all over the place, so why shouldn't Daniel get a taste? The whole atmosphere backstage was so freewheeling, but, at least in Sydney, they didn't seem to take too much part in it.

What happened next?

Frogstomp came out here in the fall and did its inexorable climb. I went out on the road with them in December '95 — I remember, because it was fucking cold. The record was breaking in a way that deserved a feature story, so I got myself assigned to go out on the road with them for a couple of dates in Canada and then went to Detroit with them.

Had they changed much by this stage?

They were a lot more at ease around me. My previous meeting with them was kind of, 'Hi, huh,' in that teenage, don't-give-a-shit way.

And I have zero problem with that. But once I got out there with them, and knew John [Watson] a bit better — I think he might have told them that I was an OK guy to hang out with — they loosened up. And they were having some fun at my expense. I mean, they were 16 years old. They were laughing and cracking wise and making all kinds of bodily function jokes and stuff like that. It was like going back to high school.

Were their chaperones on the road with them?

The dads were there, and I think, with all due respect, they were a bit looser because the dads were there and not the mums. The dads were enjoying the trip as much as the guys. Although they kept the discipline thing going on, it was more like going on the road with your best friend than being on the road with your mum. It was a different atmosphere. They were actually cool to talk to. The parents did not do interviews, but they all agreed to sit there, all three of them, and do an interview at the hotel in Detroit. They were quite funny. They were all working class guys; their thing was that it was as much fun for them as the guys. In a way they were growing up with their sons all over again. It was like a big camping trip.

Did the dads spend their time warning their sons of the evils of the music industry?

Not as much as you might expect. By that point the mums and dads had been in the thick of it with regards to negotiating a record deal and everything going nuclear in Australia, so they already had some expertise in what was stupid and what wasn't. The one thing I could detect in all three dads was that as goofy as the guys could get, they didn't seem to fear that they [the band] would go running off, picking up hookers and doing drugs. The one thing that was weird for everyone was drinking, because the drinking age here is 21. And in some cases they played clubs that served alcohol. But then again, they'd played pubs in Australia. They'd had a year of that, the only difference here was that it was bigger, there was more of it.

Did the American media focus on the ages of the guys in the band? Was that their key angle?

I think it was less of an issue with people buying the record than those writing about it. In Detroit they were playing to an audience older than them, who were there because they liked the songs and liked the sound. It wasn't Noise Addict or Jimmy Osmond; they didn't look like they were 8 years old. These guys could play; Ben was a thundering drummer, Chris really held the bottom end down well and Daniel could project. He wasn't projecting as well as he would two tours down the line, he didn't have the eyeliner or the devil beard, but he knew how to hold his own on stage. You didn't think about age unless someone brought it up. The only time it became an age thing was when they would moon someone from the bus; then you went, 'Oh yeah, they're 16.'

Was Daniel regularly compared to Kurt Cobain?

You'd read about it, people would talk about it, but personally I didn't give a shit. I'd interviewed Cobain, I'd seen Nirvana and I thought they were two different things. Daniel was young, he was blond and he screamed a lot. It's a grand tradition — look at [the Vines'] Craig Nicholls.

What about their 'Australian-ness' — did media focus on that?

I was interested in them initially because they were Australian and because I've had a long-time love affair with what goes down there musically. But the radio wouldn't announce 'Tomorrow' as 'that song from the Australian band Silverchair'. By the time it hit they were just

Silverchair. It wasn't like they were waving the Australian flag or had wallabies dancing in the videos. They didn't make a big deal about it. Because of their ages they were developing their own personal identities, much less some kind of weirdo nationalism.

One of the truly Australian characteristics about their story was the way they got that record deal. Here, you don't have hip national radio contests that involve young bands with demos. What do we have? *American Idol* [the US version of *Popstars*]. The idea that Triple J could be that instrumental in developing one act, average age 15, from Newcastle and help propel them to international stardom, is unheard of. Even the Strokes had to go to England — and a lot of their fame rebounded here. The Vines did that as well.

So the most Australian characteristic about Silverchair is that you have a country where the population is small enough, and the media, especially Triple J, is hip enough, that they could have that kind of immediate effect and have that blow up overseas. By the same token, if Triple J had done all that stuff in exactly the same way and the record sucked, they wouldn't have gotten much past Tahiti. If the music hadn't been there, it wouldn't have mattered if they were Australian or not. But because of the channels that were available to them and the fact that they had the goods, I think that was a leg up they mightn't have got if they were from Bloomington, Indiana.

Were the band enjoying all the travelling and promotion and playing while you were with them?

It was one great, enormous good time. Sure there was a lot of work, but when you're 16 and in a big rock band — this is work? Would you rather be in school? I don't think so. It was interesting when you talked to them, too — their references were younger, while the dads would talk about Ritchie Blackmore and Deep Purple. To the guys, Tim Rogers was God.

Yet they often talked up the influence of their parents' record collections on their own music.

Kids do that in any case more than they care to admit. The idea is not to admit it. But they did cop to that. I remember asking Daniel something about influences and he said, 'Some dude named Donovan.' That put it all in perspective. But it just goes to show that he was paying attention. He may be coming at it from a different generation, a different decade, but he was listening to a lot of what was around him, be it Kurt Cobain, Tim Rogers or some dude named Donovan.

So who was the Silverchair class clown?

They were equals. Chris was probably a little quieter than the other guys; Ben and Daniel took the lead in these things. But Chris gave as good if not better in the exchanges with the outside world. And the outside world meant anyone outside those three, including the dads and Watson. Watson took all kinds of grief; they were always cracking wise and were at him. But that's what you do when you're young; you think you've got the world by the balls.

Did they care about anything at all?

You could tell they cared about what they did and that's what was really impressive. They were that young and that focused and that committed. When it was time to go out [on stage], there was no screwing around. On the bus there was a lot of screwing around but once they got onstage it wasn't a game. They really worked hard and clearly enjoyed the work. And that's why the shows were so rocking, whether they were playing outdoors or at this little St Andrew's Hall in Detroit, or later on when I saw them at Roseland in New York. I saw them at different venues and they measured up to the space no matter what it was or who was in it.

Tell me about the heater ...

[*Laughs*] I don't know where they got this bus. It was sub-freezing; it was December. At some point the heater on the bus packed it in. It was really, really cold. I could kind of deal with it, being used to it, but being from Australia I don't think they were quite prepared for how cold it was. We stopped at some anonymous place along the road and the driver, or it could have been one of the dads, came up with the idea of getting a space heater, which made sense. Apparently the only one they could find was a kerosene heater, which they put in the centre of the main lounge area of the bus. They lit this thing up and it was a little scary. Never mind fire; what about smoke inhalation?

We all laughed about it, but when I came back and told my wife, she said, 'Are you crazy?' It was cold, it was a long drive, and people were bundled up. Daniel was wearing about four coats. Afterwards we realised what a colossally stupid thing to do it was. But it was either that or be found frozen to death by the side of the road. We were like Neanderthals around a fire in the middle of the Ice Age.

Do you have fond memories of the tour?

I loved it. It was only a week, maybe a little less, but it was great. They were fun to be with, the shows were great and that's everything I like about being on the road. And the story hadn't been told to death; they hadn't really been interviewed that extensively and the parents hadn't done anything at all, which was something John Watson really worked at for me.

They didn't want to become part of the story and highlight the adolescence of the band. They wanted to present the guys as individuals with real brains and hearts of their own. It was clear the band hadn't been talked to death; I spoke with them each for an hour plus, which must have felt like an eternity for them. I was able to get things from them I hadn't read, even in Australian stories about the band.

So during winter 1995 and onwards into early '96 in the USA, was 'Tomorrow' unavoidable?

Not in a way that made you sick of it. Let's face it, '95 was a good year for stuff here: there was *Mellon Collie* [*and the Infinite Sadness*] from the Smashing Pumpkins, the Beastie Boys headlined Lollapalooza. I think it was the post-Cobain apex of alternative rock in this country. In fact, Silverchair fit in perfectly. They benefited from timing as well as craft and talent. Tool was coming up, the Pumpkins, Hole, Ministry, Nine Inch Nails — there was a lot blowing up. That was before Top 40 radio in this country restricted itself to hip-hop and dance. You'll get no rock on Top 40 radio now. It's been sub-divided to death. That's why it's so hard for Silverchair to get radio play now, because it's impossible to find a format that has a broad enough appeal. All you have to do is see MTV. It's all about targeting. It's very specific.

You hooked up with the band the next year in New York, right?

That was a real trip. They'd come in to do some post-production or some B-sides [for the 'Freak' single] and Watson called me and said, 'Why don't you come on down?' It was some studio down on 14th Street. I went down, it was early evening, we got to talk for a little bit, and Nick [Launay, the producer] was doing whatever people do in recording studios. Then it was time to do the B-sides and they had decided to do a version of 'New Race' — and Deniz Tek was there. I was thinking, 'Great, Deniz Tek twice in one year.' Radio Birdman had never played here, so to see him working here was great.

Everyone's having a good time. They do the basic track — the track, the vocal, Deniz's guitar solo — it doesn't take more than an hour. At the end, they're going to do the, 'Yeah, hup!' part of the background vocals. Daniel goes out; Ben goes out; Chris goes out; Deniz goes out. Then Nick turns to me and says, 'Get out there!' I went,

'You've got to be kidding.' He reminded me that it was my dream come true — Radio Birdman and Silverchair. So he gave me a set of headphones and we all stood around a mike going, 'Yeah, hup! Yeah, hup!' Fuck me, it was the best. I said, 'Now I have completely lived — I've sung with Deniz Tek and Silverchair on a Radio Birdman song! Thank you, God.' It was Aussie rock history in a bottle.

Did you get treated well in the mix of the song?

I was very conscious that since I was the ringer in the line, I better not screw up. Maybe it's just my imagination or my ego, but I think I can hear myself in the mix. I don't know. We were all around one mic; it wasn't like Queen or anything. When they issued the single they put my name in the credit, which was a really big thrill. It was my first time on a Number One record. That won't happen again.

What was your take on Freak Show, the so-called 'difficult second album'?

The thing is that they blew up with that first record, but I think *Freak Show* did better than a lot of people whose first records have blown up as big and immediately as theirs did. The novelty had worn off, so its success was based on the quality of the songs.

They were headlining bigger venues, too, the second time around. When people say the record's a failure, by what standard? I thought *Freak Show* was really good, I really enjoyed it. They were growing as players and I think Daniel was really growing as a songwriter. He's actually a really good ballad writer.

Do you think the band has gotten a reasonable rap over the course of their career?

A lot of people associate Silverchair with that mid '90s quasi grunge thing, and a lot of people forget he was 15 at the time. Not many people are writing songs then. They're playing in covers bands, probably playing Nirvana songs. So he's done his growing up as he's doing the thing. You're seeing the process, both the mistakes and the improvements. A lot of guys don't have to go through that. I think Daniel's underrated because everybody thinks they overrated him as a teenager.

3

The Freak Show

'Nick Launay slipped straight into our level. He was as stupid as we were.'

—Chris Joannou

The Easter Show might have been a mighty way to wrapup *Frogstomp*, but the band's first priority, by April 1996, was to get back to school. As Ben Gillies told Australian *Rolling Stone*, in the wake of *Frogstomp*'s runaway success, the trio needed to 'chill, and shit — go to school and hang out with our mates'. Swiftly, these three regular Newcastle dudes had become international rock stars, but their mates back home were all too ready to remind them where they came from. There were clear signs that the trio was uncomfortable in the glare of fame's spotlight, a part of their public lives to which they'd never adjust. Barely a day went past when the band didn't encounter a voice shouting, 'Silverchair suck! Silverchair are wankers!' from a passing car.

'It's really weird for our friends,' Gillies mused:

A couple of my really close friends at home, I've asked them a few times, is it weird for you, us just saying, 'We're going to New York for a week,' and they're like, 'Fuckin' oath it is!' Even for them, it's a spin-out that one day we'll be there talking to them, going to parties, and the next day we'll be on the other side of the world.

Johns insisted that, 'Our friends are cool, because we don't change at all, we don't think we're any better than anyone else. Our friends treat us the same. We're just the same people [who] go to our mate's house and hang out and play pool and fall asleep on the lounge.' The truth, however, was slightly different. The singer/guitarist suffered his first bout of depression after the madness of *Frogstomp*; it was a pattern that would repeat itself, more intensely, in mid 1997 and early 1998. Gillies and Joannou, meanwhile, also had their own dark patches. The songs Johns was about to write for their second album would express the discontent he was feeling towards the rock life.

When they came off the road after touring the life out of *Frogstomp*, Johns, Gillies and Joannou had two years of high school to complete, and it was a bit of a struggle to keep up academically. 'We do a lot of catch-up work when we get back,' Joannou commented, 'and we do have tutors.' Ever wary about 'rock star ego syndrome', Gillies noted that 'school is a priority to keep our feet on the ground, basically so we don't turn into rock stars.' 'I want to do music for the rest of my life,' Johns commented, 'and how well I go in Maths isn't going to help at all. Music comes before school for me because you can always go back and finish school.'

Despite the intrusions of Silverchair duties, the trio's ever watchful parents ensured that their education wasn't neglected. As Peter McNair, principal of Newcastle High School, recalls, 'the families' wishes were for school to be a separate life from their rock star [life]. Their peers were very cool about it, they didn't treat them any differently. School was a place of normality for these young men who were going through this amazing experience.' The band and their parents struck up a workable arrangement with McNair: the trio received special credits in music, after organising to have a music program added to the school curriculum (which the band funded). As Gillies said at the time, this made graduation way easier. 'It's really great,' he said, 'because one of the requirements of this course is to give them a recorded piece of music. So we can just give 'em the CD.'

In early May, producer Nick Launay headed up to Merewether to meet the band and listen to their new songs. But the three teens were keener to have him sit with them in Gillies's car as Gillies screamed around Newcastle at dangerous speeds, with Launay as the legally required adult 'supervisor' to a driver still on his L plates. During rehearsals, Launay found it a struggle to hold the band's interest for more than a few songs at a time. But by May 17, the band were formally rehearsing new songs for their second album, which they previewed at a Newcastle University show six days later.

Events off-stage made this a significant gig in Silverchair history. Watson — and Sony — were keen for the band to establish a cyber-identity, to capitalise on the unstoppable rise of the Internet. Sony's technical department had created a prototype website for the band, but postings were slow and the look of the site was no different from the sites of such other Sony acts as Celine Dion. Watson sensed that the band needed a more grassroots development. The morning after the Newcastle University show, he logged onto an unofficial Silverchair site based in New Jersey and was shocked to find not only the show's setlist and a song-by-song review of the gig, but quotes from Joannou's mother about the show. 'That was the moment,' Watson says, 'that I realised you could never be as reactive to this kind of technology wearing a corporate hat as you could being a fan.'

Watson learned that an Australian fan of the band, Duane Dowse, had filed the review. He talked Sony into providing some funding to help Dowse set up and maintain what became the award-winning chairpage.com ('silverchair.com' actually belongs to an American HMO). Watson then actively began to stream information to Dowse for posting on the site, with updates on concerts, new releases and band-related activities. In the subsequent eight years, chairpage.com has created as good a virtual community as any band could hope for. It certainly hasn't harmed Silverchair's reputation as a 'band of the people'. Because of its connectedness with a worldwide network of fans, the band has maintained a 'cyber-life' of its own, without relying on the traditional record company PR methods. It helped, too, that their followers were young and web-savvy; they embraced the new technology. And by providing special offers to members, chairpage.com encouraged loyalty.

To chairpage members, the band was cool; they weren't just part of the music industry machine. This underground network was the next logical step of the alternative rock world's doctrine of band/fan connectivity. Within a few years, a fully functional website became an essential part of every band's information machine.

Recording for Silverchair's second album was set to begin on May 30, after three days of pre-production, at Sydney's Festival Studios, where *Frogstomp* had been recorded. The official line at the time was that Nick Launay, who had very nearly struck gold with 'Tomorrow' in 1994, when Robert

Hambling had asked him to edit the song for radio, had been chosen over *Frogstomp* producer Kevin Shirley 'to complement the heavier, darker sound' the band was after. Truth was that Shirley had been offered the Silverchair album but opted to continue work with American stadium screamers Journey, whose album had run overtime. (He would later return to Silverchair, to mix *Neon Ballroom*'s 'Miss You Love' and the single version of 'Anthem for the Year 2000'.) At the top of the band's wishlist has been Seattle-based producer Steve Albini, who'd worked on Nirvana's final studio album, *In Utero*, and was renowned for capturing a raw, vital sound using little studio trickery. Johns frequently dropped Albini's name during interviews. Always wary of people's opinion, however, Johns figured that hiring Albini to produce *Freak Show* would make them easy targets. 'Everyone would say we did it because Nirvana did,' he told American *Rolling Stone* in February 1997. Manager Watson confirms this. It was as though Silverchair just couldn't shake off the ghosts of the grunge gurus.

Launay's relationship with the band was strong. He stayed at the Johns family home during album pre-production, and even sold Gillies a snare drum he owned that had been used by grunge heroes Soundgarden when recording *Superunknown*. Launay had lugged the drum with him on the train to Newcastle, fully aware that Gillies would love to own the thing. As a 'dry run' prior to the making of their second album, the band had already worked with Launay to re-record 'Blind', a track from their debut 'Tomorrow' EP, for the soundtrack to the Jim Carrey movie *The Cable Guy*. Band and producer had understood each other from the start. The *Freak Show* deal was set in stone when, during pre-production in Newcastle, Launay drove the band around their hometown while they 'egged' the shopping centre. When Launay pulled over and tossed a few eggs himself, the band knew he was the right man. 'He slipped straight into our level,' Joannou said. 'He was as stupid as we were.'

Launay's musical background was in stark contrast to Shirley, whose best-known work was with American arena-fillers such as Bon Jovi and Aerosmith. As a 19-year-old, Launay worked as a tape operator at London's Townhouse studio. A drunk John Lydon (then fronting Public Image Limited, but better known as Johnny Rotten of the Sex Pistols) locked producer Hugh Padgham, whom he disliked, out of the studio. This gave Launay a chance in the engineer's chair, and he went on to produce one of PIL's best-received albums, *The Flowers of Romance*. Launay also worked with Killing Joke, the Nick Cave-fronted Birthday Party and Gang of Four, all highly credible art-rock, post-punk bands. After working on Midnight Oil's smash hit *10, 9, 8, 7, 6, 5, 4, 3, 2, 1*, he had relocated to Australia.

10...1, a revolutionary record for a band reared on Oz rock's dirty riffs, sold almost 250,000 copies in Australia alone, and was one of Johns's favourite albums. It was also a favourite of John O'Donnell's, as were the records Launay had produced for Public Image Limited and Australian band the Church. Watson was also a fan: he'd already hired Launay to produce the debut album from Automatic, another Murmur signing. Ben Gillies voiced the band's approval of Watson's choice in a conversation with the *Seattle Post-Intelligencer*. 'We talked to him [Launay] a few times on the phone and he told us some of the cool ideas he had. We thought, 'That sounds pretty rad.' Johns also thought him 'rad': 'He's really open-minded. Anything we suggested, a lot of producers would have said, "Nah, you're 17, you don't know shit," but he'd listen to us.' Gillies backed this up when he was asked about making their second album: 'We spent a lot more time and were much more involved on this album. On the last record we were so young that we didn't know what was going on. Now that we're older, we knew what we wanted, and we knew some of the basics to getting to that.'

The band worked through their new songs in the Gillies garage, just as they'd done when they were nobodies. 'In the end,' Launay said, 'some songs were drastically rearranged, while others remained untouched.' During these rehearsals, Launay also acted as chauffeur, picking up the band after school and driving them to rehearsals. This time he made sure there were no eggs in the car. Of the songs shortlisted for the second album, several, including 'No Association', 'Freak' (the first single from *Freak Show*), 'Slave', 'Pop Song for Us Rejects', 'Learn to Hate' and 'Nobody Came' had all been aired live in shows promoting *Frogstomp*. There was also a group of never-before-heard songs slated for the album. These included 'Abuse Me' (later to become the first American single from the album), 'The Closing', 'Petrol and Chlorine' and 'Punk Song #1', which was renamed 'Lie to Me' during the *Freak Show* sessions.

'We wanted to make the songs more extreme and different,' Johns explained, 'so that means we made the fast songs harder and the slow songs softer. We also experimented with different styles and instruments.' It was hard to tell if it was simply teenage hubris or increased confidence in the band, but Johns seemed unfazed by the pressure of following up such a breakout hit as *Frogstomp*. 'If people don't think [*Freak Show*] is as good as the first one, or people think it's better, it doesn't really bother us. We don't feel any pressure. We don't really have a plan. We're just going to keep releasing music.'

At the time, Johns was namechecking such hardcore American bands as Helmet, Tool and Quicksand as new influences. The Seattle heroes — Nirvana, Soundgarden and Pearl Jam — were relegated to the wastebin of 1995. Johns described the new album as 'more influenced by New York hardcore scene kind of stuff, but it doesn't really sound like that. It's just influenced by it. It's just a bit harder — it's just rock.' Though *Freak Show* would prove the distance between Seattle and Newcastle hadn't increased that much, it did deliver a few new musical twists — strings, Eastern influences, pop melodies. It was a stepping stone to a brave new rock & roll world.

Recording of *Freak Show* began on May 30 and ended on July 16. (The band's reason for choosing Festival studios again: 'It's got better Nintendo games.') On June 6, Silverchair previewed some new tunes at the re-launch of Foxtel's cable music channel, Red, which later became Channel [v]. Among the crowd was crusty, behatted rock 'guru' Ian 'Molly' Meldrum, who flew in from Bangkok to check out the band. The faithful looked on in awe of their new idols, but the gig could have gone better — the venue's power shut down during Silverchair's set when the combined needs of PA, lights, catering equipment and more kicked in. Silverchair retired to their trailer, taking solace in a rider fit for three kings.

Launay was amazed by the band's energy in the studio:

Their enthusiasm is way more than any band I've ever worked with, [he told *Sonics* magazine], 'I said, 'Let's start at 11 o'clock.' I turned up at 10 o'clock and they've been there since nine, raring to go. It was like going in with a wild animal, trying to hold them back so we had

**enough time to put tape on the tape machine and push
the red button.**

The producer firmly believed they were a great live band, so
he attempted to record them as live as possible, which would
also keep them interested in what was going on. This wasn't
some static, repetitive studio exercise — Launay was startled
by how the band crashed around while recording, taking
'large, exciting jumps' while they laid down the tracks.

The producer introduced some studio trickery. He
squeezed Gillies's drum kit into a room 'about the size of your
average toilet', to achieve a bigger drum sound, and used
some backward recording techniques on 'Abuse Me', to
which Johns responded: 'Bloody hell, it sounds like I'm
singing in Arab.' But in the main, Launay's plan was to get
down on tape the raw energy of the band. In return, they
were impressed with the man and his work. 'Nick's done
some seriously weird shit,' Johns said, 'and if you saw him, he's
like a praying mantis with glasses. He's like a mad scientist.'
(One source of friction, however, was the band's concern that
Launay was working too slowly. Watson had to take on the
'bad guy' role and tell the producer to pick up the pace, without letting on that it was the band who were so concerned.)

On July 18, Gillies, Johns, O'Donnell and Watson flew to
New York to begin mixing *Freak Show* at Soundtrack studio
with Andy Wallace, the most highly regarded mixer of the
time, whose CV included work with Rage Against the
Machine, the Smashing Pumpkins and Silverchair favourites
Helmet and Sepultura. (The three loved Sepultura's *Roots*
album so much that they'd often break the on-road monot-
ony by chanting, 'Roots! Bloody Roots!' in the back of the
tour bus.) Wallace mixed all of *Freak Show* except 'Petrol &

Chlorine' and 'The Closing', which Launay worked on in an all-night stretch when Wallace was unavailable. This wasn't the only time Wallace's work on *Freak Show* was interrupted; the mixing stopped for a three-month stretch when he was occupied with Nirvana's posthumous live album, *From the Muddy Banks of the Wishkah*. 'Waiting three months for the mix to happen was really painful for everyone,' recalled Launay, who for the first time in his career wasn't mixing an album he'd produced. This time, the Silver-parents stayed at home while the record was being mixed. 'We didn't want any interruptions from anyone,' said Johns. 'There were really no visitors in the studio apart from our manager.'

Bassman Joannou figured that the band was growing up musically. As he told Brisbane's *Rave* magazine, prior to the record's release:

> They [the songs] are a bit more mature. We have taken a fair bit more time in the way the songs have been put together. We had more pre-production time, just running over the songs and making sure they sounded right. All we had to worry about was playing it right and getting the good sounds.

But mixing those good sounds was a stop-start process. Not only was Wallace occupied elsewhere but the band had to return to school — a key part of the juggling act that Watson, the band and their parents would struggle with throughout the *Freak Show* period.

Then Johns was accused of stalking by a Sydney prostitute, Paula Gai Knightly. She alleged Johns had begun following her in March, calling to her, 'I love you, Paula,' but by July had begun warning her: 'I'm a natural born killer. I'm gonna kill you tonight and I'm gonna enjoy it.' Knightly took out an Apprehended Violence Order (AVO) against Johns on July 24, and the formal application was set down for hearing. But before the matter could proceed, police withdrew it, as they learned that Silverchair weren't even in Australia at the time of the alleged stalking. Ms Knightly returned to her native New Zealand soon after, but not without contributing to Johns's increased wariness of those who wanted a piece of him. (Johns was on the receiving end of another AVO two years later, this time from a Newcastle woman with a long history of mental illness. Her application was also dismissed, but not before a Newcastle newspaper ran a photo of Johns with the headline: 'He's Got a Gun!')

The band had an Australian tour lined up from September 26 to October 7 — during school holidays, naturally, just like most of the touring done for *Frogstomp* — with American alt-rockers Everclear supporting. Silverchair had quickly graduated to headliners, even taking the lead over an American band who'd done serious business with their 1995 album, *Sparkle & Fade*, led by the grunge-pop hit 'Santa Monica'. As the tour drew to a close, Johns and band put in a set at Brisbane's annual Livid Festival that *Rolling Stone* magazine described as 'pure rock & roll'. Helped out by Everclear, Silverchair waged war on a cover of Black Sabbath's 'Paranoid', which closed their set. Then Johns and Joannou mooned the crowd, as all superstar teenagers should.

The tour's Sydney show had been a fundraiser for the Surfrider Foundation — both bands had contributed a song to *MOM* (*Music for Our Mother Ocean*), a fund- and awareness-raising album compiled by Surfrider and released that year. The band's association with the foundation stretched back to 1994, when they had played a benefit show for the grand fee

of one surfboard and wetsuit each. Later on, they would perform similar shows to raise funds for youth suicide
prevention, as well as giving money and collectibles to organ-
isations such as the Starlight Foundation.

Johns has aligned himself with many worthy causes, especially animal liberation groups — he's often stated that his best
relationship is with his dog. His guitar was frequently decked
with stickers pledging his allegiances. Though he was uncomfortable with being a teen role model, Johns was finding a way
of utilising his status. Whereas in the 1980s — the 'Me
Generation' — being a rock star was statement enough,
Generation Grunge had a different set of rules. Alt-rock heroes
such as Eddie Vedder (who had donated $50,000 to Surfrider
in 1995) and Rage Against the Machine's Zack de la Rocha
were proudly political, supporting mainly left-leaning agendas.
Silverchair were now finding their own causes to believe in.

It was around this time that Johns became a vegetarian —
later a vegan — a choice that his parents would also take up
in 1999. 'It's not any form of fascism or anything,' Johns told
MTV, about his choice to go meat-free:

> It started pretty much with animal-related issues. It was just
> a guilt thing. I'm the kind of person, as soon as I get some-
> thing in my head, I feel guilty about it, so I did it to get
> peace of mind. Once I was a vegetarian, I started to doubt
> whether I should be consuming any animal products at all,
> so I did the whole [vegan] thing.

Despite all their globetrotting in 1994 and 1995, Silverchair
had stuck with the established music marketplaces of Europe
and America, plus two quick shows in Tokyo and Osaka in
April 1996. So manager Watson was surprised to get a call

inviting the band to tour South America in November '96. It was a sweet deal, too: three well-paid dates over a week, in Buenos Aires, Rio de Janiero and São Paulo, the latter two as part of the Close-Up Planet Festival (Close-Up being a brand of toothpaste). Other bands on the bill included the reformed, we're-only-in-it-for-the-cash Sex Pistols, doped-up rappers Cypress Hill, Californian punks Bad Religion, and Marky Ramone with his new outfit, the Intruders.

Watson was surprised by the invitation because the band hadn't sold too many records south of the US border — roughly 5,000 copies of *Frogstomp*. Their bootleg sales in that part of the world were strong, however, and the worryingly titled *Sounds Like Teen Screaming* — a recording of a set from Triple J's *Live at the Wireless*— had been doing some reasonable underground business. The recently established MTV Brazil had also placed 'Tomorrow' and 'Pure Massacre' on high rotation, and each had held down the Number One video spot on the cable network for five weeks.

The band travelled light: their party was made up of the band, Watson, Susan Robertson (Murmur's promotion manager), Peter Ward, who looked after the band's front-of-house sound, and production manager Bailey Holloway. As for chaperones, this trip was the mothers' turn. The band arrived for the Buenos Aires Festival Alternativo on November 23, playing on the main stage between lipstick rockers Love and Rockets and expat Australian Nick Cave and his Bad Seeds. The sold-out event was held at the 25,000 capacity Ferroccarril Oeste. They shared a hotel with former US President George Bush Snr., and with the Reverend Moon and a gaggle of his followers. Silverchair were getting their heads around how strange their lives as reluctant celebrities were becoming. By the time the entourage reached Rio de

Janiero for the November 29 show at the Praca Da Apoteose, word had spread as to where the band was staying. A small but dedicated posse of Silverchair-lovers chased them down: one female fan even had to be shooed off by Watson when she became amorous with Johns by the hotel pool. South America loved Silverchair, clearly, especially their blond and blue-eyed frontman.

Australian *Rolling Stone*'s editor, Andrew Humphreys, covered the band's brief tour. The way he saw it, Gillies (whom he described as 'an exuberant, natural show-off') was the only band member really comfortable with the Silver fans:

> Gillies loves the attention and is in no hurry to go anywhere. Girls have begun to crowd the [hotel] pool's edge, and start quizzing Gillies as to his favourite bands. Before they go, he gives away a few strands of his hair, smiling broadly.

By this time, Johns and Joannou had long since returned to their hotel rooms. When Humphreys asked Joannou how the band reacts to the fans, he shot back: 'Gillies is the man. If he wasn't in a band, he'd be a pimp, controlling the action.'

Gillies's natural charm extended to the stage, as well. When Johns had problems with his guitar at one show, the drummer stepped up to the microphone to give his rendition of 'Twinkle Twinkle Little Star'. Now that was one song the band had never covered, not even back in The Loft: 'I started singing and then I realised the whole audience couldn't understand what I was saying. So I said something really rude ['fuck you'] and the whole audience started going, 'Fuck you! Fuck you!' I shouldn't have done that.' As Gillies sees it, at this point in his life, 'something just clicked' in his personality. He loved 'getting out there and talking to people and signing stuff. I was just having a good time; nothing more to it. [But] Daniel was never into it.' Joannou, meanwhile, shied away from off-stage flesh-pressing: 'I hadn't quite developed good people skills.'

Johns seconded Joannou's opinions, and also talked up Gillies's natural charm:

> He just loves talking to people and meeting people. I just hate meeting people. I'm not very social and I'm really shy when I don't know people. I hate it. It's just weird. Especially when you know that they're not there to be friends with you. They're just there because you're in a band.

Within a few days, Johns's caution had turned into something closer to paranoia, a hint of what was to come in the future. 'You always think they're watching to see what you're going to do wrong or something,' he told Humphreys.

However, this insecurity didn't stop the band from playing some of the most ferocious sets of their short lives. At Rio's Sambadrome, before a crowd of 18,000, they came on after American rockers Spacehog and tore into *Frogstomp*'s 'Madman', sending the crowd into overdrive. Humphreys captured the madness of the moment:

> The crowd goes fucking nuts. Girls in the front row are screaming hysterically as the mosh begins. Johns charges across the stage, feet shuffling, body shaking like an evangelical preacher possessed by the spirit of Jesus. Gillies's shirt is off, his long hair flying everywhere as he belts his drum kit and Joannou grinds into his bass. From the side of the stage, someone says, 'Fuck! They sound like Black Sabbath.' silverchair drive the point home, launching into a cover of 'Paranoid'. The gig, as they say, went off.

As the band moved between Rio and São Paulo, the number of (mainly female) fans lurking in hotels and airports increased. It was obvious: Silverchair were now stars in South America. However, they were still very green. When Joannou spotted Nick Cave stumbling back into his hotel at ten one morning, seriously 'tired and emotional' and supporting violinist Warren Ellis, in an even worse state, Joannou turned to his bandmates and said: 'He's just getting home? But it's 10 in the morning!'

Silverchair wouldn't make it back to South America until January 2001, when they appeared at Rock in Rio, the world's largest rock festival. But the 1996 tour left its mark — record sales in Brazil, especially, skyrocketed. *Frogstomp* went on to sell 30,000 copies, *Freak Show* 38,000 and *Neon Ballroom* a whopping 116,000. No formal count of bootlegs exists, but it's fair to say you could double, maybe even triple, the sales of official releases. Yet even though the tour was a raging success, the signs were there that the band — especially Johns — were becoming wary of the hangers-on and fair-weather fans they were meeting on the road. Writing about the Rolling Stones' 1978 American tour, *Rolling Stone*'s Chet Flippo had precisely captured the dynamic that surrounds touring bands:

> The public does not really exist for the performers. The audience is an abstract, picked up and packed into the trac-tor-trailer trucks along with the lights and amps, and unpacked into the next hall. The audience exists only as box-office receipts, only as dollars passing through the gates.

Such things bugged at least two members of Silverchair, as they have many other young bands in this strange, unfamiliar position.

Life went into overdrive after South America. Three days after the São Paulo show, the band played a secret gig for

American fan club members at the Troubadour in Los Angeles, billing themselves as the George Costanza Trio. There was another gig in Seattle, two days later, with a video shoot in Los Angeles for 'Freak' sandwiched in between, directed by Devo's Gerald Casale.

It was only a short trip, but the band struck trouble in Malibu, where Johns was arrested for driving a Mitsubishi Montero on Santa Monica beach (the same place where he had been hit by a bottle in late 1995). Acting on a pitch from Mitsubishi, Johns, Gillies and Joannou had joined Dave Navarro, then guitarist for the Chili Peppers (and formerly of Jane's Addiction), to test drive the 4WD, with Navarro to write up the results for *Bikini* magazine. It turned out there was more than a little Newcastle left in the trio. Bored with doing laps of the beach carpark, Gillies steered the 4WD onto the sand and, once in motion, spotted the Mitsubishi rep running alongside the car: 'We thought we were in trouble. Instead he reached in and slipped it into four wheel drive. We went up the beach a bit; we were driving through volleyball games, everything.' Joannou then took a turn at the wheel, and Johns started to drive the car back to the car park. It was then that they heard the police sirens. As Gillies tells it:

> This big black cop got out of the car — he was evil! He came up and screamed, 'Where's your licence, boy?' Daniel played dumb and told him that we drive on the beach all the time in Australia. [But] he took Daniel and threw him in the car. We were supposed to be going home the next day, but the cop was telling Daniel, 'You're going to juvenile hall, boy!'

After some fast-talking from the band's American publicist, Johns was released and the charges were dropped. His first task, though, was signing autographs for the police chief's daughter, a Silverchair fan. Back at the hotel, Johns's mother was unaware of her son's dilemma. (A poster made from a photo of the Malibu incident hangs in the Silverchair office in Sydney.)

Back in Sydney, a week before Christmas, the band shot another video, this time for 'Abuse Me'. When 'Freak' was added to Australian radio at midday on New Year's Eve, the band had ten days of R&R before starting their next Australian tour, this time in Hobart. And they had a new album to release, and the HSC to prepare for, as well. While Gillies claimed they were having 'the best time of our lives', it wasn't so clear that Johns and Joannou shared his enthusiasm. They'd spend the next 12 months bouncing between school and the rock & roll highway.

Freak Show was finally released in Australia on February 3 (and in North America February 4), seven months after recording had finished. Speaking with *Billboard* magazine, John O'Donnell explained the delay: 'The album was recorded in June, which essentially meant that we could have rushed to release it in 1996. [But] all around, the extra time has been used very well.' To which Epic Record's Jim Scully added: 'This is probably the strongest release for the [first] quarter [of 1997], and we wanted to make sure that we had enough time and energy to release it properly.' Of course it didn't hurt that *Frogstomp*'s sales were still going strong for most of 1996 — why release a new album when the old one is still selling well? That was elementary record company marketing.

Silverchair's second album documents a band in transition. As ever, they paid plenty of lip service to the moshpit marauders who loved nothing better than 'goin' off to the 'chair'. Songs such as the sludgy opener, 'Slave', and 'The Door' — a song with a riff so thunderstruck that Angus Young would have approved — were almost clones of the bulk of *Frogstomp*.

These were fast, loud rock songs to be played at maximum volume and high speed. Gillies and Joannou, especially, loved playing these songs live.

But there was more going on in *Freak Show* than 'Tomorrow' and 'Pure Massacre' revisited. 'Cemetery' was the album's centrepiece. The band had originally planned to hire Led Zeppelin's John Paul Jones to compose string arrangements, but he proved too expensive. Jane Scarpantoni was hired instead, and it was a savvy choice. Her sombre, yet elegant arrangements (recorded in New York, at the Jimi Hendrix-founded Electric Ladyland studios) pushes Johns to new vocal heights. And the interplay of his acoustic guitar with her cello and violins makes for the most adventurous music the band had made. So what if Johns's lyric ('I live in a cemetery / I need a change') is barely high school standard; 'Cemetery' showed the band how to make an impact using atmosphere rather than volume. And this was in spite of Johns's doubts about whether the tune fitted on the album, 'because it didn't really seem like a band kind of song'.

While writing demos for the album, Johns had given Watson a cassette that included 'Abuse Me' and 'Pop Song for Us Rejects'. Midway through the blank second side of the tape was a slow, sombre acoustic ballad, which Johns's parents had found and pointed out to Watson. Johns kept asking his manager to return the tape, because he didn't want him to hear 'Cemetery'. But Watson knew the song belonged on the album, so at the Newcastle University show (the show where chairpage.com was conceived), he cornered producer Launay and told him about it. He also told Launay that Daniel didn't know he'd heard it. The producer agreed to go along with the ruse. (Watson remembers his response: 'OK, so I don't know the song exists but I have to ask him to play it for me. Cool.')

Their ploy worked; Launay convinced Johns that by adding drums and strings 'Cemetery' would fit well on *Freak Show*, and the song was added.

Strings also left their mark on 'Pop Song for Us Rejects' — understated violins from Ian Cooper and ex-Go-Between Amanda Brown. For possibly the first time on a Silverchair song, the guitars were crisp and acoustic rather than distorted and electric, while the song's very hummable melody proved that the 'pop' in the title wasn't ironic. Indian instrumentation — tambura, tablas and sitar — elevated 'Petrol & Chlorine', another serviceable Johns melody. The song's a handy reminder of how much Led Zeppelin the trio absorbed in their youth: Jimmy Page and Robert Plant loved nothing better than to adorn their blues-based raunch with exotic Eastern sounds. Silverchair were listening and learning. 'It's Led Zeppelin only and exclusively,' Johns confirmed, when asked about the track's roots. 'We really like that they mixed different instruments with rock music and we want to do that same kind of thing.'

Johns had told the producer that the song 'needs drums like they have on those documentaries on SBS'. Pandit Ran Chander Suman, who played tambura and tabla on 'Petrol & Chlorine', was tracked down by producer Launay by calling the Indian consul and the Ethnic Affairs department in Canberra. Suman left an impression on the band, especially timekeeper Gillies, who talked him up during a late 1996 interview: 'That Indian guy that was playing these really weird drums; we asked him how long he'd been playing for and he said something like 60 years. And he said he still hadn't learned everything about it.' The truth about that day, however, is somewhat different. None of the band could endure the session, which ran well overtime. The Indian players worked to markedly different time structures, which slowed the recording down to a crawl. 'We were all really excited that day they came in,' recalled Gillies, 'but about an hour into it, you could see everyone going, "Fuck, how are we going to get through this?" It was fun for a while; we all had a go on the sitar and checked it out. But after a while it was so frustrating that we had to leave.'

Launay was left alone in the studio as the Indians droned on. 'He said it was one of the worst days he'd ever had in the studio,' said Gillies, although Launay now has more sanguine recollections. Speaking with *MTV News*, Johns revealed that Suman was 'one of the guys who used to play with Ravi Shankar, who did some of the Beatles' stuff. He has, like, a little group who he does stuff with and we've got some of that on the song and it sounds pretty weird.' This was true, although Suman didn't know of the sitar master's work with the Beatles.

So *Freak Show* wasn't all about Daniel Johns's million-dollar riffs or voice. Ben Gillies's deft brushstrokes of percussion were a highlight of 'No Association', a song in which Johns neatly inserted a line about 'contemplating suicide' from the 1979 underground classic 'Shivers', by the Nick Cave-fronted Boys Next Door. Johns had a lot to explain about *Freak Show*'s words. 'Freak', the album's debut single — which charted at Number One in Australia on January 20, 1997 — opened with a rhyming couplet, 'No more maybes / Your baby's got rabies', that he still has to downplay today. But the song would become a live favourite of the band, along with 'The Door', another *Freak Show* cut.

Whereas Johns had dismissed *Frogstomp*'s lyrics as throwaway observations from the couch, the same couldn't be said of *Freak Show*. Even though he was still having some trouble articulating his feelings, there was enough fear and loathing here to scare off Hunter S. Thompson. When Johns wasn't ranting about babies with rabies, he was growling (during 'Slave') that the 'only book that I own is called *How to Lose* / Pick a chapter I know them all, just choose'. And 'Freak' came on like a taunt to those critics wanting to cut these tall poppies down after the madness of Silvermania. As *Rolling Stone*'s Humphreys wrote in February 1997, 'silverchair have always been easy targets for the hipster crowd, a band that's somehow cool to hate, for no particular reason.' But it didn't help when Johns and Gillies told *Juice* magazine that 'Newcastle's the centre of a lot of fucking wankers.' The remark may have been taken out of context, but the backlash was immediate and it played on Johns's already fragile state of mind.

As John O'Donnell saw it, 'Daniel was definitely venting,' the album 'was definitely about him reacting to fame'.

During 1996 shows at Livid in Brisbane and at the State Sports Centre in Homebush, the crowd had tossed bottles and cans at the band, echoing the chaos of Santa Monica. They dodged the missiles and tried to keep playing. Johns relates:

> When it first happened, I was like, 'Fuck!' It's not that you're pissed off about getting hit with a bottle. It's more that you're pissed off because it fucks your show up. I don't get it, it's just weird. I guess it comes with playing in a band, that's what you expect. In the '70s, everyone just spat on each other. I guess in the '90s everyone throws bottles.

Although Johns stated he didn't 'really give a shit about it,' his anger seeped through the lyric of 'Freak'.

'If only I could be as cool as you,' Johns sneered, before declaring: 'Body and soul / I'm a freak'. There's even more self-flagellation in 'Petrol & Chlorine', where his world-weariness ('as my life just fades away / I wouldn't have a clue') is just plain worrying. Drugs and guns get a look in elsewhere, along with what could only be considered observations from Johns's herpes period. 'Your life's an open cold sore,' he yells during 'Pop Songs for Us Rejects', 'Got to get out the cream.' (It's a little known fact that microphones at festivals are herpes breeding grounds, so maybe the teenager had picked up his share of blisters over the previous couple of years.)

No matter how unintentionally comical much of this sounds, Johns's broody words were hardly what you'd expect from one of Australia's wealthiest teenagers. But Johns had sunk into what turned out to be the first of several depressions that followed the success of *Frogstomp*. When he was supposed to be writing new songs for *Freak Show*, he was holed up in his parents' house for a month, avoiding the world outside. Runaways would often turn up at their front door, asking for Daniel. Tabloid reporters and photographers frequently cruised past the family home, hoping for a sighting. It was just as difficult for Gillies; his family were reluctant to change their home phone number because of their business, so they'd constantly be fielding calls from fans and band-haters. But because of his more extroverted nature, Gillies seemed to handle the pressure better than Johns.

'I didn't want to go out and have someone go, "That's the guy from Silverchair," and fuck everyone else's fun up for the night,' Johns said afterwards, 'so I was just like, "Fuck this, I'm just gonna sit in my room."' It was a haven he would retreat to many times over the next few years. John O'Donnell noted how heavily it weighed on him. 'He wasn't the guy he used to be, hanging out with his friends. The tabloids started wanting pictures of him, people knew where he lived. We'd been telling the parents to get silent numbers, but they said no, it wasn't something people did.' John Watson remembers that time well:

> That was the month 'Israel's Son' was doing really well.
> Because I was really worried about Daniel, I had him stay at
> my house in Sydney for a while [on the suggestion of Johns's
> parents]. He was wrestling with the fact that he had become
> 'famous' and that life can be really strange sometimes.

What made it even more difficult for Johns was that he was
seeking refuge with one of the people who were dependent
on him for their livelihood. As a manager, Watson had the difficult task of balancing his and the band's livelihood, as well as
caring for their mental health. He wanted them to remain
big-selling international artists, while keeping them relatively
grounded as 'happy, healthy human beings'. 'From my reading
of rock & roll history,' he said, 'most bands end up frayed
because they're caught in this crazy world, the tumble drier
[of rock & roll] — and then they turn on each other.'

This juggling act would become even trickier for Watson
in the future. 'After *Frogstomp*, we were chased by the media
and all kinds of people,' Johns said in January 1997. 'That was
weird. We needed a while to get used to it. I realise now that
that attention goes with being in a band. [But] I don't feel like
a rock star or anything like that.'

Johns wrote most of *Freak Show*'s lyrics after the band
returned from their second American tour, which ended on
December 18, 1995. The non-stop nature of the trip and the
band's unstoppable success had been a lot to take in for the
band, especially Johns. 'I saw so much out there,' he noted, 'so
many weird things, that it really affected how I saw the world
and myself. Some [lyrics] were actually changed because they
were too personal. But they're a lot more real this time around.'
On *Freak Show*'s release, Johns took to introducing 'Cemetery'
as a song 'about a male prostitute', a not-so-subtle dig at all

those who've profited from the band since 1994. 'There's a lot of good people in the industry,' Johns insisted during an interview, 'and there's a lot of dicks. So you've just gotta live with the dicks and get on with the people that are all right.'

In early reviews for the album, critics picked up on the band's lyrical S.O.S. The message was clear: they were having trouble adjusting to life in the spotlight. 'It doesn't take much scrutiny,' wrote Michael Dwyer of 'Freak' in Australian *Rolling Stone*, 'to reveal a metaphor for the dirty business which has already swallowed silverchair up to their tender necks.' Writing in America's *Spin* magazine, Chuck Eddy echoed Dwyer's thoughts: 'If the whole world was gawking at my growing pains, I'd feel like a *Freak Show*, too.' Johns responded by sporting pierced eyebrows and make-up; Joannou and Gillies, alternately, shaved their heads.

The upside of *Freak Show*, however, is that there were very obvious signposts — the lush 'Cemetery', the experimental 'Petrol & Chlorine' — that Johns was taking musical control of the band and pushing them away from the sludginess of Seattle. The next album, 1999's *Neon Ballroom*, was an even bolder statement, and as far removed from grunge as these three Novocastrians could manage. 'It doesn't sound like Seattle,' insisted Gillies, when asked about *Freak Show*. 'Now that we've travelled around the world, our music tastes have been widened immensely. When people hear the new album, they won't say, "That's a Pearl Jam clone."' Joannou figured that the only reason they were compared to Nirvana was 'Daniel's hair'. Many rock writers agreed. Murray Engleheart emphasised the band's movement away from grunge and declared that the album 'should knock on the head once and for all any lingering doubts that the band is operating squarely in Pearl Jam's shadow'.

Speaking just after the album was mixed in New York, Johns pointed out the differences between *Frogstomp* and *Freak Show*. While admitting some songs were 'definitely heavier', he pointed to a more melodic direction, as well as highlighting the use of strings and sitar. 'It's got a bit more variety,' he said. 'It's more complex than the first album.'

In the same interview, Johns opened the door for bassist Joannou to co-write songs. Up until this time, the bulk of Silverchair songs had emerged out of rehearsal room jams: Johns would lock into a riff, Gillies would work out a rhythm pattern and Joannou would kick it all along with some heavy bottom end. Then Johns would lock himself away to work on the lyrics. 'It's not like Chris isn't allowed to join in writing the songs,' said Johns. 'He just hasn't really come up with anything yet. Maybe on the third album — who knows?' It was an odd comment, considering that all Silverchair music from 1999 onwards would be Johns's alone.

Johns was moving away from his two bandmates and friends. Although he would talk *Freak Show* up as an album where they worked together as a unit, the amount of time they'd shared touring over the past two years meant they spent less non-Silverchair time together. Before the band broke, they were mates who'd go to school together and then hang out at the Gillies home or go to the beach. They were tight, they were a unit. But now, when returning from a tour, they'd head in different directions. Gillies and Joannou would hook up with their respective Merewether crews and party hard, while Johns went home, holed up with his dog, Sweep, and wrote songs. It was at this time, too, that Gillies and Joannou would meet their first serious girlfriends: 'Before, every day, we used to go everywhere together,' Johns has said. 'But because we've been touring so much together, I just wanted to be by myself for a long time.' At the same time Daniel Johns was turning inwards, Silverchair was becoming *his* band, the outlet for *his* songs.

The critical response to *Freak Show* took a fairly predictable path. The Australian press praised it, the British panned it, and the American media sat somewhere between the two, confused as to whether the band were innovators or imitators. Australian *Rolling Stone*'s Michael Dwyer was typically insightful, noting that 'the casual sleeve peruser might conclude [from the song titles 'Slave', 'Freak', 'Abuse Me', 'Lie to Me'] that more bullshit than satisfaction had greeted silverchair in their fast-track transition from Newcastle garage to international smash.' He went on to praise the band for its 'more melodic, diverse and generally satisfying musical agenda.' The American parent of the magazine didn't have the same homegrown agenda, but still praised the album's diversity and the way 'bursts of guitar blend easily with strings, acoustic moments and quasi-Indian elements.' Writing in the Baltimore *Sun*, highly regarded US critic J.D. Considine figured 'the album would stand as an impressive achievement of musicians twice as old.' It's a fair comment, too. Even today, listeners who overlooked the band during its first wave are amazed by the maturity of music on display on their earlier albums.

Like most reviews, *The All Music Guide* admitted that the band 'were slaves to their influences' on *Frogstomp*, but acknowledged that with *Freak Show* 'their own style started to break through.' 'Every once in a while,' wrote *The Buffalo News*, 'rock needs a jolt of youthful energy. While silverchair has talent, it lacks originality.' *Spin* magazine, however, praised the album, noting its 'punkier speedups, fancier breaks and more dramatic climbing from quietude interlude to dude attitude.'

Most reviewers, however, couldn't resist such soft targets — if they were teenagers, went the standard line of thinking, surely they couldn't be originals. Typical was the review in England's *Metal Hammer* magazine:

> What exactly is it about this relatively unremarkable Australian trio that helped them shift so many copies of their debut album? They don't bite heads off pigeons [or] trash hotel rooms. *Freak Show* owes more than a drink to Nirvana ... but just remember we're talking about Nirvana without the apparent depth, experience or, indeed, the heroin habit.

But then, UK critics were never impressed by the band — a dilemma faced by almost every Australian act except for AC/DC and Nick Cave — and it showed in album sales, although Watson, justifiably, puts that down more to a lack of radio airplay. 'That was never going to happen at the time,' he figured:

> the whole country was into Britpop. Back then, none of the US rock sounds were working in Britain, so acts like Bush and Everclear couldn't get arrested there, either.

> Very few Aussie rock bands are taken seriously there. They seem to think we can either do soap stars and novelty acts or arty stuff like the Triffids and Nick Cave. Apart from INXS, nothing else in the middle has ever connected in the UK.

'That's always going to be the British tabloid rock take,' David Fricke told me. 'Oh, they're Australian, let's trot out the kangaroo jokes. The fact is that they missed out.'

Freak Show, just like *Frog Stomp*, did good business in Germany, France and Holland, but barely generated any commercial interest in the UK. But how to follow up the band's

2-million-plus *Frogstomp* success in the US? Manager John Watson was set to learn a lesson about dealing with the monolith that is the American music business, while the band was about to experience a little more controversy of its own. Johns had announced, just before its release, that the album's title was *Freak Show*. As he explained, he likened life in a rock & roll band to 'the old freak shows in the '40s, just travelling around, doing your show and going to the next town and doing it again. We saw there was a similarity and thought it would be a good theme for the album.' 'We reckon the music industry is like travelling freak shows,' Gillies threw in, 'You meet all these freaks along the way. You meet good people, but you do meet a lot of idiots. I'm not mentioning any names.'

What Johns and Gillies didn't anticipate was the controversy the album's artwork would stir up. First the 'Israel's Son' court case, and now this. Throughout the band's life it seemed as though every album would be tainted in some way, whether it was *Frogstomp*'s soundalike accusations or Johns's more recent reactive arthritis around the time of *Diorama*.

The nine images that decorated *Freak Show*'s sleeve — including a wolf man, a bearded lady and assorted circus sideshow weirdos — were found in the Circus World Museum, located in sleepy Baraboo, Wisconsin. With political correctness in full swing at the time, the band received some criticism of their artwork selection; many felt it was in questionable taste to highlight the physical deformities of these 'sideshow freaks'. The backlash was strong enough that their American label, Epic, had to issue a disclaimer insisting that the band 'are not in any way showing disrespect for the carnival performers of yesteryear. They simply think it's interesting that the human appetite for the bizarre seems to be timeless.'

It's more likely that the band just thought the images 'cool' or 'sick', but they had even bigger problems ahead. The American label had opted to lead with 'Abuse Me' as the album's first single, rather than their Australian Number One, 'Freak'. It was felt that a mellower song would sit more comfortably on radio. That turned out to be a bad move. Looking back, manager Watson still believes this decision to be the key reason *Freak Show* sold only 620,000 copies in the US, after *Frogstomp*'s 2,025,000.

What lay ahead for the band was one of the most restless years of their lives, as they tried to balance their last year of school with the demands of pushing their second album and trying to keep their respective heads together. Not only did they rack up more Frequent Flyer points than Rupert Murdoch, but they started to understand what was required to make Silverchair more than a one-album fling — hard work, and loads of it.

Bibliography

'Here Today, Here Tomorrow' *The Aquarian Weekly* 17/01/1996; 'Put Your Band in the Air' *Rave* (Brisbane) 18/09/1996; 'Quick silverchair Messenger' *Rolling Stone* Online 30/12/1996; 'silverchair: Down Under's Alternative Youth Wave' *The Buffalo News* 09/02/1997; Transcript: Interview with Daniel Johns, MTV *News* 30/03/99; 'silverchair' *Teen Magazine* 01/06/1996; 'Everything in order for silverchair' *Jam! Showbiz* Online 12/12/1996; Transript: Interview on MTV's *Modern Rock Live* 02/02/1997; Transcript: silverchair on MTV's *The Week in Rock* 22/11/1996; 'New silverchair Album "More Intense," Says Singer' *Allstar Music Magazine* 18/11/1996; Transcript: Interview on MTV *News* July 1996; 'silverchair Let Their Freak Flag Fly' American *Rolling Stone* 06/02/97; 'Teen Rockers silverchair Relish Their Golden Days' *Seattle Post-Intelligencer* 02/05/1997; 'Days in the Sun' Australian *Rolling Stone* February 1997; 'Anticipation Builds for silverchair Set' *Billboard* 11/01/1997; 'Band Gets a Higher Education: Interview with Ben Gillies' *Review* (Adelaide) 19/09/1996; 'silverchair in L.A.' *OOR Magazine* January 1997; 'silverchair body and soul' Australian *Rolling Stone* March 1997; *Spin* February 1997; *All Music Guide* (Allmusic.com); 'Freaks of Desire' *Metal Hammer* February 1997; *Baltimore Sun* February 1997; ''chair Man of the Bored' *TV Hits* 15/02/1997; 'How to Run a Freak Show' *Sound Magazine* Issue #4 1997

Abuse Me:

an interview with John Watson

John Watson has been Silverchair's manager since 1995, when he left his position in A&R at Sony to look after the band full-time. During his eight years at the helm, he's done everything from lugging gear to acting as surrogate parent and negotiating multi-million dollar deals. The way he sees things, 'the nature of management is that you want people to love the artist — and if people have to hate the manager in the process, so be it.'

Did you have a precedent for your plan when you signed Silverchair?

In terms of role models, we spent the first years of Silverchair's career trying to stop them becoming Ratcat. Ever since, we've been trying to stop them becoming INXS. I don't mean disrespect to either of those bands by that comment, I just mean that Ratcat exploded so big and so fast that everyone got sick of them within a year or two of *Tingles* [their 1990 EP, which contained the hit 'That Ain't Bad']. And INXS did an amazing job of breaking internationally but the price of those efforts was a backlash here at home. Having an Australian career was always important to Silverchair, so it was always important to them to keep the home fires burning — even if that meant doing less well in other countries. Given the fate of [2002's] *Diorama*, it's just as well.

Can you tell me about the band's signing with Murmur?

Had Sony not had Murmur, there's no way in the world we could have got involved with the band. Firstly, the nature of the deal we offered was one Sony would never have offered to an artist. Denis [Handlin's] brief was, 'Break all the rules.' A typical Sony deal would have been a worldwide deal for five or six albums with a pretty substantial advance attached to it and modest royalties.

The idea with Murmur was to give less on the front end but to provide more flexibility: shorter term deals, higher royalties, in some instances give some artists the ability to get releases overseas if Sony passed. Given the generation of bands coming through, it was incredibly important, the issue of creative control and a dedicated team of people who were on your wavelength.

How has your role as Silverchair manager evolved?

My role has changed a lot, but it's happened so slowly and gradually that it's only when you stand back that you can see it. The way I see it, it's best to think of your career as a truck going down a highway. Some artists want to party in the back of the truck and don't care what the managers do as long as they keep the hookers and blow coming. Some artists want to drive the truck and would prefer to have the manager out the front as a bull bar. Other artists want to drive the truck and want the manager sitting next to them, up front, as a navigator, going, 'You really should turn left up here.' The manager's voice is the one you hear calling — as you go over the cliff — 'I told you you should have turned left.' The last metaphor is the one I've always felt comfortable with. But at the end of the day it's up to the artist.

In the early days, the band had strong ideas about what they wouldn't do — things were either hell or they sucked. The more interest they took in things, the more responsibility they took. They always had good instincts for what sucked. That's great, but it's only a part of the picture. Knowing the right thing to do is the next part of the learning. The dynamic is that I'm always the guy going, 'What if we get David Helfgott? What if we get Van Dyke Parks?' Ultimately the artist should pick and choose and that's how it should be.

Frogstomp *cost just under $AUD40,000 to make and sold several million: how much larger was* Freak Show's *budget?*

The figure has never been made public and I'd rather not say. However, it would be safe to say that it cost a lot more than *Frogstomp* because we used Andy Wallace and a US mixing studio. And Nick [Launay] took a lot more time to record it. However, by the standards of bands who've sold a few million albums it was still comparatively cheap.

Was the choice of Nick Launay over Kevin Shirley, the producer of* Frogstomp, *made purely because Shirley went off to work with Journey?

Pretty much, although that sells Nick short. We were planning to use Kev but then he wanted to push Silverchair back because Journey was running over time. That was a concern because we originally wanted to have LP2 out by the end of '96. That ended up becoming impossible when Wallace's time shuffled around. In the meantime, the band needed to re-record 'Blind' for the *Cable Guy* soundtrack and we used this as a try-out with Nick. It went well, so the transition seemed natural and unusually painless.

Was Shirley keen to do the second record?

Yes. They've worked with him since — he remixed a couple of songs for *Neon Ballroom* and mixed the TV audio of *Rock in Rio* [where

Silverchair performed in 2001], as he happened to be down there already. Nick, meanwhile, was falling over himself to do *Freak Show*. He almost felt it was meant to be, having heard that early demo [of 'Tomorrow'] under such unusual circumstances.

Was Steve Albini on the shortlist?

Not really. I think Daniel loved the sound of his work and would have loved to make a record with him. But his association with Nirvana would have just invited more of those comparisons which everyone — particularly Daniel — wanted to avoid. When [Brit grunge wannabes] Bush used him, too, that really sealed it.

Was anyone else on the Freak Show shortlist?

Not that I recall. Andy Wallace was the dream candidate at the time because of his work with Helmet. That's why the guys were willing to wait for him when his schedule shuffled around. He'd come to the show in New York [December 10, 1995] and expressed interest in the band, so he was always in the mix for LP2, if you'll excuse the pun.

Wallace took a three-month break during the mixing of Freak Show: what happened?

There was a bunch of stuff, including the Nirvana live CD, although the main thing, weirdly enough, was a band who he actually produced from scratch. They were called Cola and had been signed in a big bidding war, so everyone was touting them as the next big thing. My recollection is that it was the only thing he'd tracked from scratch since [Jeff Buckley's] *Grace*, but I'm not sure about that. He spent most of the gap recording and mixing their album.

How radically did marketing plans have to be rewritten when that delay happened?

Abuse Me

Marketing plans were never written for a late '96 release as we knew by June-ish that we weren't going to make it by Christmas. If I may be allowed a sidebar here for a second, I still think that *Freak Show* was the best set-up I've ever seen for an album. We had all the marketing and promotional tools — new photos, bios, press kits, interview CDs, artwork files, EPKs [electronic press kits], a video, preview samplers, stickers — manufactured and delivered all around the world a full 10 weeks before the release. This probably doesn't seem like much but given how important set-up is to the fate of a release, it's extraordinary how often things run late. This means albums are often compromised.

What I'm saying is that *Freak Show* really benefited from the extra set-up time caused by Wallace's delays. This is part of the reason it did so much better than *Frogstomp* in Europe because we came out of the gate with a bang that made people pay more attention.

Was Nick Launay ever a possibility to mix the whole album?

No, although he was there for all of the mixes and added quite a lot. The combination of him and Andy [Wallace] was a great yin/yang thing because Nick always wants to keep polishing and loves to use lots of effects, while Andy likes to keep things fast and simple. Either of them would not have got the sounds you hear on that record.

There were a few name changes on songs from Freak Show, right?

Yes. 'Punk Song #1' became 'Lie to Me' and 'The Closing' started out as 'Cat and Mouse', while 'The Door' was originally called 'The Poxy Song'. As you might guess from that title, they originally didn't like that one. In the weeks before recording started, I was nagging them to try

113

and come up with a couple more tunes. They only had about 10 songs they liked at that stage and that didn't leave any breathing room if one of those tracks didn't turn out well in the studio. So they doubled the tempo of 'The Poxy Song' and decided they liked it after all.

What do you think prompted Epic to choose 'Abuse Me' over 'Freak' as the first Freak Show single in the US?

Oh boy. That was a big, big issue and is still at the root of the band's post-*Frogstomp* situation in the USA — along with releasing it into the wind of the pop revival, of course. The promo department at Epic felt that 'Freak' was too heavy musically and too young lyrically — 'No more maybes / Your baby's got rabies' — to get played across the board on all US alternative stations. If this happened, then the song would not have charted very well on the US airplay charts and they thought the limited exposure would hurt initial album sales. This would have meant that the album would quickly have been pegged as another 'sophomore slump' and the band would be assumed to be one-hit wonders.

What was your take?

Our view was that 'Freak' was a song that would mobilise the younger fans who liked *Frogstomp*. These people usually don't listen to radio during the day, anyway. As such, we felt that we'd be better off having half as much airplay on that tune because we believed it would connect better with the band's core audience — and sell enough records to avoid any perception of a 'sophomore slump'. We thought the more melodic 'Abuse Me' would appeal to a more mainstream audience who were unlikely to rush out and buy a 'chair album. As a result of all this, we — that is, the band, me and Murmur — were all strongly of the opinion that if it came first, the alternative music fans would think that the band had 'gone soft'.

At what stage did all this take place?

Well, it was only when the music reached the promo department that the issue raised its head. By then it was quite late in the piece, around November '96. It really threw a spanner in the works. We fought them [Epic] for several weeks and there were many memorable conversations. Eventually it turned into a complete stand-off, with both sides honestly believing they were completely right.

We were therefore in a no-win situation. If we forced the promo department to work 'Freak', then they would have egg all over their faces if they made it work. This hardly provided an incentive to get them to get it played on the radio. On the other hand, if we reluctantly agreed to let them work 'Abuse Me' first, then they would look like idiots if that song didn't work. So they had a powerful incentive to get that song lots of airplay.

How involved were the band in this?

I distinctly remember discussing this with the band. We had a conference call — I was overseas — during which the final decision had to be made. Daniel said, 'Well, it's just a question of doing what sucks the least, isn't it?', which summed it up perfectly, I think.

So, what next?

What then happened was those promo people — many of whom were tremendous supporters of the band and honestly thought they were doing the right thing — got massive airplay for 'Abuse Me'. In other words, they were right that the song was well suited to what radio was playing at the time. However, we were right, too — the song didn't mobilise the band's fanbase in the numbers you would normally expect from that kind of exposure.

This meant that the album started to lose heat and each week it slid down the charts, creating momentum — but it was all going backwards.

By the time Epic got to 'Freak', radio programmers had the perfect excuse: 'We played the last song a lot but it didn't really connect with listeners — so why should we play this one which is less accessible?'

And the end result?

I should point out that the 'Freak' CD single sold three times as many copies as 'Abuse Me' in the US, even though 'Abuse Me' was their first song — and only song, apart from *Neon Ballroom*'s 'Miss You Love' — to ever get significant daytime airplay on mainstream stations. So that showed we were right — 'Abuse Me' had broader appeal but 'Freak' was more appealing to the band's audience.

One other important point is that Epic's last-minute change of heart on the singles order really compromised the video for 'Abuse Me'. We had everything planned perfectly for *Freak Show* and the 'Freak' video was no exception. That clip was all very well set up and still looks great. However, the 'Abuse Me' video was thrown together far too quickly and the result is probably the worst video the band ever made.

How did the band come to choose the images for Freak Show's cover?

I read a story about the Lobster Boy in a magazine while the band was on tour. It was an amazing tale. There's also a cult paperback about him. He was one of the last superstars of that world, but he became an abusive alcoholic who was implicated in several murders. Then he was murdered by his own family who couldn't take any more of his abuse.

I showed the story to the band and they thought it was amazing, too. The thing we liked about it was how things are actually a lot different from how they appear on the surface. I guess that fitted well with many of the lyrics on the album, which were about the perversions associated with attention and about how things can seem great on the surface, but there's a lot of trouble underneath.

That idea was carried into the album art. The cover image of his boyish face seemed really angelic, then when you opened up the album and took out the disc you discovered his disability. You might then have felt compassion for his condition — unless and until you found out what kind of person he became. So your outlook twists a few times over the course of looking at one image.

The whole 'freak' theme was triggered by the song, initially, but kind of took on a life of its own as we kicked it around more and more. Just one of those metaphors that works at lots of levels.

4

So Where'd That Year Go?

*'There they sit, three antsy teen rockers in skate-rat duds,
trapped in a fate about as fun as spending a Saturday
night with the parents.'*

Launch.com Online, February 1997

If the band had lived the two previous years in top gear, 1997
was twelve months spent in overdrive. Their first date for the
year was in Hobart on January 10, and their final show was
on December 20 at the Perth Entertainment Centre. In
between they played a hundred gigs, toured the US and
Europe three times, and completed four Australian jaunts, as
well as shows in Canada and the Philippines. The Philippines
show was a first — and a last — for the band, as out-of-control fans kicked in doors, inflicted $10,000 worth of damage
on an orchestra-pit hydraulic system, and drifted into the
unpatrolled backstage area to meet their idols. It was a long
way from Madison Square Garden.

The year had some particular thrills. They opened the
ARIAs with a blistering version of *Freak Show*'s 'The Door'.
They toured with such A-list peers as Bush, the Offspring and
Collective Soul, and had a song featured on the *Spawn* sound-
track, the film of the hugely popular Todd McFarlane

action-adventure book series. Epic promoted *Freak Show* in the US with a toll-free number that played grabs from various songs. And, finally, they graduated from high school — an event they celebrated with a tour that they still regard as a career high, the 'Summer Freak Show'.

But there were also endless days of promo for radio, print and TV. Some of these were exciting: they did a midnight in-store signing at Blockbuster Records in Atlanta, performed at Virgin Records in New York's Times Square, attended the MTV awards, and appeared on the hugely influential *Late Show* with David Letterman. (Gillies told one reporter, 'All our friends love Letterman and all of them have been, like, "Fuck, you're going to meet Letterman!" It's going to be pretty cool.') Yet these were exceptions; the usual media grind of quickie interviews and smiling on cue for photographers was a serious drag for these hyper teenagers.

Silverchair had a lot to prove with their new record. By 1997, the bands that had heralded the arrival of grunge — Pearl Jam, Nirvana, Soundgarden, the Smashing Pumpkins — had either split or started exploring new musical sensations. Instead, it was punkish acts such as Californians the Offspring that were shifting serious numbers of units in the album charts, as the wall came down between the mainstream and alternative worlds. It was also the year that 'rocktronica' (aka electronica) — a flashy fusion of rock attitude and dance beats — was declared the future of music, thanks mainly to groundbreaking albums by the Prodigy (*The Fat of the Land*) and the Chemical Brothers (*Dig Your Own Hole*). Silverchair were out to show that they could still satisfy the fans, still cut it live and that they weren't 'one-zit wonders', as one wisecracking writer put it.

First up, Silverchair had an album to launch. They did it in style in the Circus Oz tent in Sydney's Moore Park, on

January 20. The venue made perfect sense: the album was called *Freak Show*, after all, and the three had regularly been comparing life on the road to a travelling circus. More than a thousand people, including high-profile media from *Spin* magazine, MTV and elsewhere, either squeezed onto the wooden benches around the tent's edge or into the moshpit, to check out the band's 55-minute long, eleven-song set. The stage was decorated with cutouts of the muscle men and circus oddities from the album's cover that had caused such a fuss in America. In the crowd looking on was Snazz, the tattooed man from the 'Freak' single cover, who'd also appeared in the 'Abuse Me' video.

When the pre-show murmur died down, a shirtless MC appeared on stage and introduced the opening act, a fire-eating sword swallower. Once he'd done some freaking of his own, the lights went down and the band appeared on stage, as if out of nowhere, Johns wearing a T-shirt that proclaimed 'Nobody knows I'm a lesbian', which was subsequently auctioned for charity for over $1000. The new album's first single, 'Freak', turned up early in the set, along with a mix of five more *Freak Show* tunes (the Indian-ised 'Petrol and Chlorine', however, was deemed too tricky to recreate live) as well as *Frogstomp* standards 'Pure Massacre' and 'Tomorrow'. Then Gillies and Joannou disappeared in a puff of smoke, leaving a solo Johns to strum his way through the sombre 'Cemetery'. Despite a heavy-handed, parallel-import-themed speech from Sony head Denis Handlin to close the night, the launch was a success. The band proved to a tough local audience that they had the presence — and the tunes — to be a worthy headliner. Tall poppy syndrome be damned.

While launching the album was the band's immediate priority, Watson and the band's parents had an equally challenging task. They were trying their best not only to keep the band in good mental shape but to ensure they didn't miss too much school. Typically, teen stars would drop out of the formal education system, prefering to use an on-the-road tutor, thereby capitalising on the chance to squeeze every last drop out of what could be a short-lived career. But this wasn't the case for Silverchair. While the band did rely on a tutor at times, those close to them knew that attending school as often as possible would keep them sane and grounded. And the trio's schoolmates were always there to keep their egos in check, something they didn't get when dealing with the music business. They were about to enter their final year of high school, and had committed themselves to finishing it, even though they'd now dedicated themselves to careers in music. This was standard working-class thinking: always have a back-up in case the bottom drops out of your dream.

Watson found himself turning down more requests for interviews and photo shoots than ever before; he figures he rejected up to 90 per cent of requests during the *Freak Show* phase. He also made sure that while touring overseas the band never performed more than five shows a week (most bands averaged at least six), at one point turning down a six-figure-fee show at Wembley Stadium so the band could swing an extra two days at home. On another occasion, they spent $40,000 on airfares to get them back to Newcastle for a welcome six-day break between gigs.

As they'd proved with their Surfrider shows and various other acts of charity, Silverchair didn't consider the rock life to be just about the cash. Before accepting any offer, the band's parents had to sign off on the deal first. Thanks to the runaway success of *Frogstomp*, the band were financially comfortable and had more control of their career choices. While these self-imposed restrictions may have contributed to fewer sales for *Freak Show* in North America, the challenge now was to hang onto the joy they felt when playing and recording music. Which, in the end, was what they really desired.

While the gloss was starting to wear off their very atypical teenage lives, there was the occasional golden moment. At the band's February 24 show at the Palace in Los Angeles, Ozzy Osbourne turned up with his daughter Aimee, whom Johns would date for a short time. The band coped well with playing before one of their (and their parents') idols, dedicating their crashing cover of Black Sabbath's 'Paranoid' to the man known for sometimes biting heads off bats. Sammy Hagar, occasional Van Halen vocalist, was another Silverchair convert, fronting at a show and asking to have his photo taken with the band. Even porn star Ron Jeremy showed up backstage. After dates in Europe during March, with their tutor Jim Welch in tow, the band breezed through Australia for four dates, releasing 'Abuse Me' on March 24 as the second single from *Freak Show*. It went gold soon after.

It was after their March 30 set at Melbourne's Offshore festival, alongside Blink-182 and Tool, that drummer Gillies took the drastic step of getting rid of his hair, which he'd often vowed to grow down 'to the crack in my arse'. He'd complained to Johns that his mane was restricting his playing, so Johns completely shaved Gillies's head. 'I'm a gimp,' Gillies laughed afterwards, to which his father, David, added: '[He's] bald as a baby's bum — just like Yul Brynner.' Gillies premiered his clean scalp a week later at the Surf Skate Slam Festival on Sydney's Maroubra Beach. The band then disappeared for another two months of touring, this time swinging through Vancouver, Mormon capital Salt Lake City, Milwaukee, New York, Houston, Dallas, Los Angeles and San

Francisco, before more European festival dates. *Freak Show* had gone gold (500,000 copies) in the US by May, but its sales still didn't match the frenzy that had surrounded 'Tomorrow' and *Frogstomp*.

If Frequent Flyer points were a reliable predictor of record sales, *Freak Show* was set to outstrip even *Frogstomp*. But as the Toronto *Sun* shrewdly observed when reviewing the album, *Freak Show* was 'a stronger and less popular album' than its predecessor. Johns realised this, too, but stuck to the party line that 'as long as you keep writing good songs that people like, and that you like, I think that you can just keep going for as long as you want.' Always looking towards the long-term, Watson even admitted he'd trade reduced record sales for more critical kudos. 'It wouldn't bother me if *Freak Show* sold half as many copies [as *Frogstomp*],' he said, 'but got treated with a little more respect.' (Watson's request was granted — *Freak Show* shifted 1,414,000 units, just under half *Frogstomp*'s 2,898,000.)

Despite the work they were putting in to promote *Freak Show*, and reviews that were, in the main, more positive than for their debut, the album wasn't a breakout success. Although it debuted on the US *Billboard* album chart at Number 12, it slipped away quickly. Of course it would reach the top spot on debut in Australia (which it did on February 10), while in Canada it debuted at Number 2, in Germany at 28, France at 20, the UK at 38 and New Zealand at 8. But these were good, not great figures. Yet although the band's established markets reacted with some caution to *Freak Show*, there was a sharp rise in sales outside North America. Such new(ish) Silverchair fanbases as France, Holland, Germany and South America started buying their records in good numbers. The band were going global.

But their excellent rock & roll adventure was starting to become, well, not so excellent. While non-stop international travel was a dream come true for these Novocastrians when 'Tomorrow' went big, they were now several international tours down the line. The idea of racing around the corridors of five-star hotels in the middle of the night, knocking on strangers' doors and running like hell, as they'd boasted of in the past, had lost its appeal. As Johns had made quite clear with *Freak Show*'s title and many of the songs' lyrics, the band were having some trouble adjusting to the leeches and star collectors that frequent the music industry, and the personal cost — his first major depression — was a clear sign that he mightn't have the right stuff for this life.

As one writer observed, 'Daniel, almost 18 now, looks shy and vulnerable, his eyebrow pierced and wearing silver-glitter eye shadow, his fingernails painted with half peeled off nail polish.' Another writer, on the road with them in LA, noticed how swiftly Gillies and Joannou tired of high jinks — while Johns didn't even bother getting involved:

> Their devilish grins fall away, replaced with bored expressions similar to the one worn by Daniel Johns, who is staring out a window. There they sit, three antsy teen rockers in skate-rat duds, trapped in a fate about as fun as spending a Saturday night with the parents.

The band were also losing patience with one of contemporary rock & roll's necessary evils: fencing inane questions from VJs and DJs, designed to generate the snappiest 'grab' — usually just a few seconds long — for a short-attention-span marketplace, all in the name of flogging the product. When promoting *Frogstomp*, Gillies, Johns and Joannou cheerfully played bullshitters, talking up mythical pasts and twisting answers to the same questions into any number of different responses. But now that they believed more strongly in their work, they found little opportunity to speak with even a little intelligence. Their conversation with *Modern Rock Live* typified the dumbing-down approach.

> MRL: I actually read in an interview, I don't know if it was you, Daniel, or Chris, or Ben, I don't know who mentioned that the last record you did, after listening to it ... you guys weren't particularly happy with it.
>
> Daniel: Um, no, we're happy with it, it's just that we're more happy with the new album. The first album had three or four songs on it which we didn't particularly like but that we had to put on to make up an album's worth of songs. But we're as happy as you can be with the first album.
>
> MRL: Well, I can tell you, I've listened to the new CD and it's amazing. I mean you guys have definitely ... for a band that had a quick turnaround between two albums you guys seem like you were very focused in the studio. I mean is that how you went into this record, going, 'OK, this is our second album, we have to be really focused?'
>
> Chris: Um, it was kind of ... we had a bit of time off in between and we thought, 'Let's work a bit harder on this one.' It took three weeks instead of nine days and we sorted out a lot of sounds and just made everything better.

Just as vacuous were the caller questions. 'Does one person write the songs, or do you collaborate?' asks one. 'I was wondering', asks another, 'what are your views on musicians and their drug addictions and stuff? 'Cause you guys are real famous now and are you, like, into that stuff?' A third rings in to ask the band if they ever feel nervous on stage.

In a discussion with *TV Hits*, Gillies was asked: 'Would you agree that your audience is still pretty young? Is that what you're into — screaming teenagers?' You can almost feel Gillies cringe, before he politely replies: 'I think we've got the weirdest crowds in the whole world. Sometimes teenage girls, older girls, young guys and older guys and sometimes you have 40-year-olds.' Gillies's permanent grin must have been stretched just that little bit tighter when the next question posed to him was: 'So it doesn't bother you that your audiences on the *Frogstomp* tour mainly consisted of teenage girls?' Then came the topper: 'Are you in search of a typical or original sound?' Through gritted teeth, Gillies replies, 'This album is close [but] I think the third album will be the real Silverchair sound.' Another interviewer asked Johns: 'When you're on tour, do you get a lot of older women coming onto you?' Johns snapped back: 'We wish.' It was a frustrating time for a band that was doing their best to prove they were a serious rock & roll force, not some disposable music industry creation.

During the course of early promotions for *Freak Show*, the question, 'How does it feel to be Seattle clones?' was asked repeatedly, like some kind of mantra. Initially, the question was fended off, but the more it was repeated, the feistier the band's responses became. Speaking with the Edmonton *Express*, Joannou laughed it off, stating: 'That's kind of worn off now, because the whole Seattle thing has kind of quietened down a bit. It's not as full-on as it used to be.' But Gillies snapped at a similar question from *Request* magazine's Jon Weiderhorn, describing people who compared them to Nirvana as 'full of shit' and elaborating:

> We don't listen to Nirvana. Personally, I don't really even
> like Nirvana. The thing is, people don't realise that Nirvana
> was influenced by old '70s bands like Led Zeppelin and
> Deep Purple and Black Sabbath.

Johns also found himself playing down soundalike accusations when he spoke with the *Orange County Register*. 'You can always hear a band's influences on the first album,' he said. 'It's that way with everyone. We're over it.'

Johns was seriously understating Silverchair's case. When *Frogstomp* went mad, everyone recognised their musical roots, but still wanted a part of them. They were fresh-faced, they were new, they were from regional Australia for God's sake, there was a story here. Now with *Freak Show*, they were constantly defending themselves against the same Seattle soundalike accusations, even to the point of having to give music writers lessons in the history of rock. The band was getting to understand how fickle the rock & roll world could be. 'If people can't take us seriously,' Johns told the *Denver Post*, 'they're never going to.' He amplified the response when speaking with the Toronto *Sun*. 'It's good to be able to say "fuck you" to everyone who said we weren't capable of producing a second album.'

Australia, nonetheless, still loved the band, irrespective of what their critics said. Back home in June for one-off shows in Brisbane and Darwin, they set new sales records when the tickets for their Brisbane Festival Hall show sold out within a day, a feat they'd repeat six years later as part of their 'Across the Night' tour. (Both tours were helped no end by chairpage.com leaking the tour dates just prior to their on-sale date.) It was the first time in the venue's history that an Australian band had sold out their 4000 seat venue so quickly. Their concert at Darwin's MGM Grand Casino also set new ticket sales records.

Yet in spite of the thumbs-ups that *Freak Show* had been receiving, and the occasional high such as the album launch, the tough mixture of touring, studying and being teen role models was causing the band some real trouble. Especially Johns, who'd given up meat the year before. 'Johns is slim to the point of thin,' wrote the *Sydney Morning Herald*'s Bernard Zuel in April, 'his jeans and shirt hanging loosely from him.' Not long after, Microsoft's *Totally Live News* noted that Johns looked 'dangerously emaciated'. Frustrated by the impositions his stardom was placing on his family, and feeling as though his life was out of his control, Johns was slipping into the first of several serious depressions, one that was manifesting itself in his sunken features and rake-thin physique. It was almost as if he were trying to physically disappear.

Even the laddish Gillies admitted he was having some dark days of his own, trying to cope with the mix of rock and study. 'Sometimes, you just kind of get so sick of it you don't want to do it any more,' he said. 'It's like, "This isn't worth it." Then in the end, if I didn't do all the bull, I wouldn't be able to travel around the world. It kind of makes it worth it in the end.' Johns wasn't so taken with the glamour of globetrotting. 'I just enjoy being at home,' he said at one point, mid-tour. 'I just sit at home with my dog and watch telly. I don't know if sitting home every day is normal, but that's what I do.'

In Sydney on June 2, the band spent a day in the now very familiar Festival studio, this time with producer Wayne Connolly, cutting the song 'Spawn' for the soundtrack of the same name. (A reworked version of the song would reappear on *Neon Ballroom* as 'Spawn Again'.) The 'Spawn' track was to be remixed by UK whiz kid Vitro, for a soundtrack of unusual collaborations: nu-metal band Korn with the Dust Brothers;

speed-metal band Slayer teaming up with Atari Teenage Riot; Filter joining forces with the Crystal Method; and so on. The *Spawn* album epitomised a moment when hard rock acts were hoping to grab a little of rocktronica's cool. 'If anyone heard the song without the techno remix they wouldn't think it was us,' commented Gillies. 'One section of it has a riff like Sepultura. It's real heavy.' It was the second time one of Silverchair's full-throttle rockers had been electronically tinkered with. (Paul Mac's remix of 'Freak' was a bonus track on the 'Abuse Me' single.) At the same session, Silverchair also thrashed out a cover of the Clash's 'London's Burning', which was destined for a Clash tribute disc featuring Bush, Rancid, the Mighty Mighty Bosstones and Moby. The band were starting to develop a taste for crossing over into unfamiliar musical territory. It was an area Johns would explore even further, a few years on, when he collaborated with Mac for the *I Can't Believe It's Not Rock* EP.

After more European festival shows, the band made it back to Sydney for a surprise gig at Luna Park on July 26. The audience was made up of 200 Triple J prizewinners, while the show was a benefit for the Reach Out appeal, which raised cash and awareness for youth suicide prevention. The live video for *Freak Show*'s final single, 'The Door' was taken from this one-off show. The band's set was revealing. Such firestarters as 'Slave' and the obligatory 'Tomorrow' set the moshpit alight, but Johns's wayward behaviour was leaving its mark, too. He dabbled with an instrumental version of the national anthem, 'Advance Australia Fair', between songs, and introduced 'Abuse Me' as 'a song about masturbation'. Johns's attitude mattered little to their fans, however, as 'Cemetery', the third single from *Freak Show*, raced into the Australian charts at Number 5 on July 7.

After two weeks of school, the next stop for the band was Europe. But as they rolled through Sweden, Holland, Germany and Austria through August and September, as well as playing a handful of Canadian and American dates, what they really needed was a break. Badly. That finally came in October, after the band had performed 'The Door' at the ARIAs. By the time the three were announced winners of the Channel [v] award for Best Australian band — which they've won every year since — Johns was long gone. Claiming an asthma attack, he was halfway back to Newcastle, with his father at the wheel.

Apart from the Australian release of 'The Door' on October 6 — *Freak Show*'s fourth Top 10 single at home — much of October and early November was absorbed by the HSC exams, which they completed on November 14. It was a burden the three were desperately keen to have out of the way, partly in the hope journalists would finally drop it as a point of discussion. The three realised their career paths were already laid out before them, but figured they'd gone this far with school, so they might as well graduate. And at least school gave them a much-needed break from the spotlight.

Johns, as he frequently and freely revealed, was fast becoming the band loner. 'After spending so much time on the road over the last couple of years, and being surrounded by so many people all the time, it's good to be able to get away for even a few hours with just your dog,' he told *Hit Parader* magazine. 'You get time to think a little and get a hold on everything that's happened. You can always trust your dog.'

The band said goodbye to school with their first major Australian tour, the 'Summer Freak Show'. Strangely, while they'd covered much of the planet promoting their first two albums, they'd rarely toured Australia beyond the capital cities and larger regional centres — it was almost as if they were working in reverse. Now they were set to play twenty shows over five weeks, commencing on November 21 and swinging through the capital cities and such less-visited towns as Mackay, Ballarat and Dubbo, where they played in a spider-laden aircraft hangar on the RAAF base. Magic Dirt — whose lead singer, Adalita Srsen, would become Johns's occasional girlfriend — opened these all-ages shows. It was the last time Australian audiences would see the band for a year.

The 'Summer Freak Show' was the Australian rock event of 1997. Now chaperone-free — all the band had turned 18 — and without their on-road tutor (who had been given the choice position as head of band security), the trio started to cut loose. While their peers were in the midst of Schoolie's Week, the traditional drunken post-exams blast, the band were busy with their own version of this teen rite of passage. Sure they had to work, but there was plenty of downtime and the shows were a (well paid) riot. This was the end of the *Freak Show* road, which had begun back in Hobart in January. The band remember it as a career high, probably the most enjoyable tour of their lives. 'Yeah, that was a peak,' said Joannou. 'We'd finished school, we were without our parents, we were playing all different-sized venues; it was so much fun.' Gillies's recollections are a little foggier: 'It was drinking galore, freedom, lots of fun. We let our hair down and had a good time.' Mind you, drinking only took place after the shows. The band had — and still has — a firm 'no alcohol before shows' policy.

At the Melbourne Festival Hall show in mid December, Johns was torn between darkly comic monologues about his lifetime loser status ('I was only a seconder at scouts — I mean, imagine that, I was even coming second in scouts, for

Christ's sake') and playing the full rock dude. He flicked plec-
trums into the crowd and stopped at one point to try on a bra
thrown from the moshpit. 'How do you put these things on?'
he pondered out loud. 'Don't know much about them.'

Writing for on-line site *Addicted to Noise*, Andrew Tanner
saw the changes in the late 1997 version of Daniel Johns:

> Johns, who only a year ago was the most diffident of front-
> men, now prowls the stage with growing confidence, his
> long blond hair fashioned into a mane of spiky dreadlocks.
> He looks sort of like a younger, leaner Johnny Lydon.

As he became even more withdrawn off-stage, this teen loner
was undergoing a transformation — once he plugged in, he
became physically assertive and could whip a moshpit into a
frenzy. It was in direct contrast to the *Frogstomp* model. Johns
wasn't just a more imposing presence on stage — he was getting mouthier. During the Melbourne show he fell into a rant
about critics who figure his dark emotions couldn't ring true:
'The people who say stuff like that are just dumb old fucks
who can't remember what it's like to be young,' he snarled.
'Just because you're a teenager doesn't mean you don't have
those emotions. Those people are just jaded, silly old cocks.'

Gillies and Joannou looked on as Johns, *sans* guitar, threw
himself into the Paul Mac remix of 'Freak', which closed most
shows. (Mac even joined the band on-stage at their Sydney
University show on December 8.) Then Gillies — now
sporting a mohawk — stepped out from behind his kit and
whaled on some tom-toms and a gong bass drum as 'Freak'
built to its climax. Crowds would erupt as the band freed
themselves from their regular Silver-roles, losing themselves in
the song's heavy rhythms. 'We were trying to do something

different,' says Gillies, 'We were playing along to a tape but we didn't care — and the audience didn't seem to, either.' 'We wanted to do something really different in our set,' Johns explained, 'that no one would expect. We've been toying with the idea of doing the "Freak" remix for a while now. It seems to be going down really well.'

The *Freak Show* campaign ended in Perth on December 20 — Silverchair's hectic year was over. But instead of winding down, Daniel Johns was about to disappear into some of the darkest days of his life.

Bibliography

'silverchair: Monsters Under the Bed' *Launch.com* Online February 1997; 'The Boys Are Back in Town' *Cleveland Scene* January 1997; Transcript: Interview on MTV's *Modern Rock Live* 02/02/1997; ''chair Man of the Bored' *TV Hits* 15/02/1997; 'Minor Threat' *Guitar World* March 1997; 'silverchair in L.A.' *OOR Magazine* January 1997; 'Solid Silver: Aussie rockers silverchair shun their rock star image' *Edmonton Express* 02/02/97; 'Raging Against the Machine' *Request* March 1997; 'Australia's silverchair Rockin' Along' *The Orange County Register* February 1997; 'silverchair Not Kidding Around With Fame' *Denver Post* 15/04/1997; 'Sounds Like Teen Spirit' *Toronto Sun* 13/04/1997; 'Men at Work ... Boys at Play' *Sydney Morning Herald* 04/04/1997; 'Growing Up With silverchair' Microsoft *Totally Live News* May 1997; 'Still in High School, the Members of silverchair Are Sitting Pretty' *Rocky Mountain News* 15/04/1997; 'silverchair: Mixed Up' *Time Out* (Brisbane) 18/06/1997; 'silverchair: Born Show-Offs' *Hit Parader* August 1997; 'silverchair's Rite of Passage' *Addicted to Noise* Online 23/12/1997; 'Q&A: Ben Gillies' Australian *Rolling Stone* December 1997

5

Ballroom Blitz

'I couldn't leave my house without thinking something terrible was going to happen, whether it was getting beaten up or being hounded by photographers. I was really freaked.'

—Daniel Johns

Coming off the long and winding road that was the *Freak Show* promo trail, Daniel Johns was exhausted. Mentally and physically drained, he was in dire need of some serious downtime. Joannou and Gillies were also feeling some pain, but they recovered through travel. Joannou and his girlfriend headed off to Thailand, Gillies and his girl travelled to North Queensland and Byron Bay. When they returned, both kicked back in 'Newie' with their mates, 'surfing and hanging out' and doing a whole lot of nothing.

'It was such a luxury, just hanging around at home,' Joannou said, of the first half of 1998. 'Beforehand, you'd be carted off all the time; it was nice to sit around at home.' But it wasn't always easy for him to adjust; he admits that some nights he had to stop himself when he reached for his bedside phone and started placing a wake-up call. 'For seven days a week you had an itinerary. It felt funny, at first, being alone, because you'd been in this group of 10, 12 people for so long, travelling around all the time.'

Unlike his bandmates, as Johns readily admitted, he was no 'social butterfly'; he much preferred holing up in his parents' Merewether house with his dog and his guitar. 'I was pretty lonely,' he remembered, when asked about life after *Freak Show*. 'We'd just left school and all our friends were going to university. Ben and Chris were going out with their girl-friends, doing their thing, and I was living in a house by myself, just writing.'

By early 1998, the pressure was on Johns to generate some new tunes for the band's third album. The stop-start nature of touring prevented him from writing on the road, and the demands of playing live, travelling and doing press were intrusive and cramped his creativity. In the past, many of the band's songs had emerged from jams; now Johns wanted to write alone. He was taking over as the band's main songwriter, and his only chance to write was when the band returned to Australia.

At the same time, Johns's musical mood was changing. While still deeply enamoured of the red-meat rock on which he'd been raised, the positive response to the more pensive, orchestrated songs of *Freak Show* ('Cemetery', 'Abuse Me') had opened his ears to a whole new world of sound. Gillies's tastes were changing, too; he was opening up to dance music, a form which had meant nothing to him up to then. Johns wanted to create music that wasn't dependent on volume and his full-throated roar to express what he was feeling. He was also underwhelmed by the type of music American radio had opted to play instead of *Freak Show*, such bland, corporate rock acts as Matchbox 20 and Third Eye Blind. The way he saw it, Silverchair needed a serious musical makeover.

But Daniel Johns had more immediate problems. The past four years had taken their toll. First there was the massive hit of 'Tomorrow' and the band's rapid ascendancy in America and elsewhere. Then there was the pressure of hitting back after such a huge first-up hit, as well as the Apprehended Violence Order, the 'Israel's Son' controversy, graduating from school, becoming a public figure and teen role model and the obligatory backlash — it was a lot to digest. It was easy to forget that he was all of 18 when *Freak Show* ground to a halt in December 1997.

Johns felt he had lost control over his life — instead, it was in the hands of people in the music business. He'd even thought about splitting up the band at the end of the *Freak Show* tour; it was a low point he would revisit a few years on, after the global tour to promote *Neon Ballroom*. 'We were either going to stop or keep going,' Johns told *Kerrang!* magazine, simply. 'I decided that music's always been my dream since I was a little kid, and to throw it away would have been something that I'd regret when I was 30 years old. I'd look back and go, "Fuck!"' (There is more to this, of course: It turns out that Johns had issued the band an ultimatum about their direction. But more of that later.)

By now, Johns's parents had convinced him to start seeing a psychotherapist to help him cope with the type of pressure most 18-year-olds aren't exposed to. Johns later said that he saw the therapist to 'learn to associate with people', although he stopped the initial treatment after two months. By that time his participation in consultations consisted of him walking into a room, sitting down and saying, 'Just give me the tablets and I'm going.' He didn't take well to the idea of being picked apart by someone who didn't know him. One piece of the therapist's advice he did take was to move out of his family home — he rented a two-bedroom home near Merewether beach. The house's interior decorating style was best described as spartan: a couch, a television, a bed, a stereo and not much more. Johns only stepped outside to walk his dog, Sweep, see his therapist, or hit the video store (where he quickly racked up a $1600 bill, renting 'anything to pass the time and help me get through another day'). His always-supportive parents looked after his groceries and any other day-to-day needs, while keeping a watchful eye on their oldest son. As Johns later revealed, he was sinking deeper and deeper into a funk of alienation and depression. And then he stopped eating.

As Johns tells it:

> As our popularity grew, so did people's expectations. When you're a guy in a band, everyone thinks you should be happily swimming in girls. But it's just not that way unless you're a really confident person to start with. Every time the crowd got bigger, I felt more empty when I walked off-stage. Towards the end of 1997, I gradually began to feel more and more alienated from people.

After moving into his house by the beach things took a turn for the worse:

> The psychological problems that surfaced on tour intensified and my view of reality became distorted. I began to feel really anxious and paranoid. I couldn't leave my house without thinking something terrible was going to happen, whether it was getting beaten up or being hounded by photographers. I was really freaked by phones. When mine rang, I'd have to leave the room to get away from it.

Johns figured that the only part of his life he could take charge of was his food intake. It was his way of controlling 'the chaos I was feeling inside'. He had hit on this 'solution' to his psychological problems as early as 1997, but now he started to push himself, trying to discover how little he could eat and still get by. He saw it as a personal test. Quickly, he was down to eating two or three pieces of fruit a day.

'The only way I can describe it,' he said afterwards:

is to say that it felt comforting to be in control of something, like I hadn't totally lost it. The problem is, you think you're gaining control over something, but in reality you're losing control over the functioning of your body.

Within a few months it got to the point where I was eating just so I wouldn't collapse. If I felt like I was going to black out, I'd eat a piece of fruit or a cup of soup. At the time, my parents and my brother and sister were the only people I trusted and could see without feeling anxious. Of course they were all worried sick about me, but I couldn't really see how bad it was.

In the midst of this self-deprivation, Johns found himself unable to shake a cold, which was hardly a surprise, given his diet. He visited his family doctor, who gave it to him straight: if he didn't start eating he was going to die. What he'd done was seriously damaging his immune system. Being a vegan — and suffering paranoid delusions that his food had been poisoned — didn't help Johns's decline.

'When I was about 17, I had this great phobia about different foods I couldn't eat because I thought they'd cut my throat,' explains Johns. 'It seems silly when you look back on it, but at the time it was scary to eat cereal because I thought it was sharp and it would cut my stomach.' Johns's doctor went on to explain that he was already displaying the physical signs of those with advanced eating disorders: receding gums, exposed teeth, protruding bones and sunken cheeks. That was a turning point.

By this stage, Johns's weight had slipped under eight stone. His doctor prescribed Aropax, an anti-depressant that would mollify his anxious state of mind. Johns moved back in with his parents to start his physical and mental recovery. (The move might have been coming anyway. Johns's neighbours had started complaining about his barking dog and his tendency to play loud music late into the night.)

What Johns didn't realise was that the anti-depressants he'd been prescribed were just as effective at blocking out the rest of the world as locking himself away in a rented house or giving up food. While Gillies and his father swam laps in the local pool every morning, and Joannou kicked back at his parents' home, Johns was sinking into what he would later call an 'anti-depressant haze', a wobbly state of mind that it would take him three years to shake off. As much as his bandmates wanted to support him — Gillies even helped him move into his house by the beach — Johns had shut off the world. His bandmates felt frustrated by his inertia. 'I saw him a few times,' says Gillies:

I was friends with the guy, but when all he wants to do is sit around all the time and do nothing, after a while you go, 'Fuck, this is boring, let's go and do something.' But if you did go out, someone would say something [to Johns]. It was frustrating seeing a friend go through it. We'd achieved so much and we could have done anything we wanted — and then that happened to him. You care about the guy, but there's nothing you can do. All you could say was, well, I hope he works it out.

Manager Watson was also relegated to outsider status. 'He made it pretty clear that he didn't want people to contact him. He wanted to be on his own.' Nonetheless, Watson was getting updates from Johns's family and felt very concerned: 'We had a lot of pretty intense conversations.' Several years later Johns explained that his condition was 'too personal' to share with family and friends. And although he insisted he wasn't suicidal at the time, 'When I was really bad with the eating disorder, I thought that I might die and I think everyone that knew me thought I might die if I kept going.' He would never sink lower.

While Johns may have been slipping away from his family, his bandmates, and the world in general, he had started to write the songs that would form *Neon Ballroom*. Initially, however, he wasn't writing songs, per se (there was too much pressure to write songs), but poems, reams of poems, over a hundred in total, scribbled on scraps of paper. He had no music to accompany his words, which was in complete contrast to the band's songwriting methods in the past, which had typically begun with jamming in the Gillies garage, followed by Johns writing lyrics to fit the music. But now Johns was the main songwriter — and if this approach worked for him, so be it. Writing these poems provided an emotional outlet for Johns. The process allowed him to slowly come to grips with his insecurities and his depression. What better way to understand your problems, especially for an introverted loner such as Johns, than to write them down? His next step during the early part of 1998 was to take all the poems he'd written, cut them up, and make a collage of the words that made the most sense to him.

'With the previous two albums,' Johns explained:

the music was written first and then I just went home and wrote lyrics. I didn't ever want to get too poetic with lyrics in the past, because lyrically I've been very influenced by old-school punk bands like Minor Threat and Black Flag. [But] with this album I wanted to really focus on what I was feeling at the time. I really wanted people to focus on the lyrics and what I'm trying to say in the songs and then focus on the music, rather than the other way around.

The poems were never intended to be lyrics for Silverchair songs. 'It was just basically a form of expression. [But] I liked the words so much that I changed it to a more lyrical format and put music around it.'

As *Rolling Stone* magazine later noted, Johns's lyrics — derived from these poems — were 'full of sickness, needs, obsessions, uncertainties and pain'. Rather than rely on the atrocities he saw on the six o'clock news, as he did for the songs on *Frogstomp*, rant how 'baby's got rabies' or decry the machinations of the music industry, as he did during *Freak Show*, Johns now had some deeply personal, real-life pain to write about. Not surprisingly, this would make for some of the most powerful songs of his brief songwriting career. Growing in confidence, Johns felt he was finding his own songwriter's voice with these songs:

On the second [album], I got into this mind frame where if it's too melodic, that's too wimpy. I didn't want to be perceived as too feminine because people always thought I was gay. I was self-conscious about that with the second album. With this album [*Neon Ballroom*] I just said, 'Fuck it, I'm just going to do what I want to do.'

As the songs slowly came together for the album, Johns was putting all this personal baggage into the most poignant lyrics he'd ever written. Interestingly, neither Gillies nor Joannou would ask Johns about the meaning of his new, anguished songs when the band reconvened in mid '98. To them, that was Johns's job, to write the words — analysing them was for the critics and fans. 'I don't think we've ever picked through his lyrical content,' Gillies told me. 'It's been more, "Cool, let's play."'

'Ana's Song (Open Fire)', the second single from the album and one of the most stirring (and richly melodic) songs Johns would ever write, emerged from his six months of isolation. The song wasn't just a metaphor for anorexia, although Johns quite blatantly roars the words: 'Ana wrecks your life/Like an anorexia life', as the song builds to its climax. 'It was the first time I exposed my eating disorder to anyone,' Johns said.

> The lyrics of 'Ana's Song', particularly 'In my head, the flesh seems thicker,' are about my desire to see how far I could take it. I'm sure the reason some people get eating disorders has to do with a distorted body image, but often it has nothing to do with looking a certain way. It's about gaining control over a part of your life.

> It's about an obsession, whether it's an eating disorder or whether it's a distorted image of one's self.

Pointedly, Johns then revealed a home truth about his adolescence that few people knew. It would explain a lot of the thinly veiled anger in many of his songs, both old and new: 'I've always had a fascination with the darker side of life. I'm a bit fixated on it.' He would repeat this in 2001, telling me, 'I've always had an obsession with death. Love and death, I'm always thinking about those two extremes.' One reason, he suggested in 1998, was that 'I had a hard time in high school.'

This was news to most people, because the party line was that the band fared well enough at school, even if Gillies and Joannou sided more with the sporting jocks than the lean, blond, more creatively inclined Johns. Newcastle High principal Peter McNair strongly believes that the band members were treated well at school by their peers; any problems Johns experienced happened outside of school hours. 'When we started playing at 13, I was called a fag and beaten up.' Johns explained. 'Even though Ben and Chris were in the band with me, for some reason they weren't subject to the same ridicule. Probably because I was the lead singer and they played relatively masculine instruments.' Joannou and Gillies understood this. 'I suppose with him being the frontman, it was unavoidable,' said the drummer. In another interview from the period, this time with *Juice* magazine, Johns described how this hassling intensified. 'I was getting beaten up, constantly being called faggot, people throwing shit into our pool and hassling my family. That was really hard. There was a point during *Freak Show* that Silverchair was about to end because I didn't want to inflict anything else upon my family.'

Johns had been through a lot of teen trauma. But now he was developing the songwriting confidence to let out anxieties and aggression. Unlike most teens, he actually had a very public outlet for his pain. Accordingly, the songs for *Neon Ballroom* had started to flow as the band convened for the first time in two months, on February 22, to record a song with Nick Launay for the *Godzilla* soundtrack. The song, 'Untitled', was an old tune. It had first been recorded for the *Freak Show* album, but didn't make the cut. It had then been considerably reworked for *Godzilla*. The session was the first time Johns,

Gillies and Joannou had been in the same room since December 20 of the previous year, but Johns wasn't ready to debut any new material to his bandmates.

Just as they'd given producer Launay a 'dry run' with 'Blind' prior to recording *Freak Show*, the band were now test-driving themselves: could they record another album? Were they comfortable together in the studio? Reassuringly, making music still felt right and the session went well. Still, the next four months were consumed with Johns's slow recovery and the gradual development of songs for *Neon Ballroom*. Launay was locked in to begin pre-production in early June, so Johns had a lot of fine-tuning to do, which he did in isolation, transforming his scraps of poetry into full-blown rock & roll anthems.

Four months since they'd last plugged in together, Silverchair finally got back together in June, in a Newcastle rehearsal room. They chose this space over Ben Gillies's parents' garage (even though The Loft was now seriously soundproofed) so they could better amplify Johns's vocals. Producer Launay, who was again staying at the Johns family home, convened this first meeting. With the exception of the one-off 'Untitled' session, Johns hadn't spoken with his bandmates for six months. There was a lot of bad feeling at the time, especially between Gillies and Johns. The drummer felt rejected by his close friend, who'd shut him out during his breakdown, while Johns, despite the confidence he was showing as a songwriter, was worried that Gillies would hate the style of the new, deeply personal music that he was writing. He wasn't sure that this music was right for Silverchair.

Johns's reservations about premiering these new tunes to his bandmates made some kind of sense. While they were written with rock's basic guitar/bass/drums/voice format in mind, the emotions in the songs were much deeper than, 'come on, abuse me more, I like it'. And some of the songs, especially 'Emotion Sickness' and 'Steam Will Rise', were far more restrained than the riff-heavy rock of *Frogstomp* and *Freak Show*. Johns could hear strings in many of the songs — they were way more cinematic than anything he'd tried writing before. An uncertain Johns even had vague notions to hang onto these tunes for a solo album. 'I was really nervous,' he said, after he'd finally played the songs to Joannou and Gillies. 'I didn't know whether or not to keep them and do a solo album or whether to show them. I thought they'd go, "What the fuck is that?"'

To Johns's way of thinking, Gillies was the true rock dog of the band; he figured he'd reject these songs as 'too wimpish'. 'I thought Ben would be like, "No, man, metal! We want metal!"' But as Johns played the songs to the band on an acoustic guitar, with Launay looking on, Gillies started suggesting rhythmic ideas and Joannou quickly jumped on the bass. It was a flashback for the band — after all their globetrotting of the past three years, they were almost back to where they first started, when life seemed a hell of a lot simpler. All it would have taken was for Gillies's mother to tell them to turn it down and the scene would have been complete.

Later, Johns explained to *Rock Sound* magazine that some of the more restrained passages in his new songs did throw his bandmates, just a little, but added:

They could see that these ideas were going round in my head and that there was no other option. Ben and Chris are enormously alike — they have the same interests and the same view of the world, whereas I'm different. But I respect them, you know? They're my friends. Our temperaments are at odds with each other but that's OK. We complement each other, which is the essence of silverchair.

Gillies had brought one song, entitled 'Trash', to the pre-production sessions for the new album. It was a throwaway he described as 'heavy, fast, punky'. But it didn't make the final cut for the album, though it did appear later as a B-side. Joannou had also tried to write music, but as he admitted, 'it really sucked.' With the exception of 'Spawn Again', co-written by Johns and Gillies, a track resurrected from the soundtrack for *The Cable Guy* (where it was simply called 'Spawn'), the songs on *Neon Ballroom* were all Daniel Johns compositions. From now on, Johns would be the band's songwriter, which didn't sit well with Gillies's mother. She was hoping some of her son's tunes would make the final cut, as they had on the first two albums, thereby generating songwriting royalties. But that's not how it panned out.

After the near-breakdown he'd experienced at the end of the *Freak Show* tour, Johns was straight with Gillies and Joannou. He told them that the only way he could continue as part of Silverchair was to write all the band's music. He had conceptual ideas for their future recordings, and these couldn't come out of the type of jams that had produced the bulk of their first two albums. Joannou and Gillies didn't think about it for too long — they were too enamoured of playing in Silverchair to shoot down Johns's plan. It turned out to be the smartest move the band could make, as their music matured greatly, even if the perception of Silverchair from then onwards would be as 'The Daniel Johns Band'. Despite the freedom this deal gave him, Johns still had some emotional baggage to deal with. He still felt like a prisoner of Silverchair, albeit one who had been granted creative day release.

Unlike famously fractured trios, such as the Police and the Jam — bands divided by the 'creative differences' cliché — Silverchair had come up with a design for survival. Johns was the creative force, frontman and loner, Gillies and Joannou were both the band's musical engine room and good mates. They all had their place in the band, on-stage and off.

'Emotion Sickness', which was to become *Neon Ballroom*'s mood-swinging, richly evocative opening track — and Johns's favourite cut on the album — was a vivid snapshot of his fragile state of mind. He explained it as being 'about any kind of mental disorder or problem', but the finished version of the song is proof positive that he connected deeply and emphatically with the song. David Helfgott's mad-professor piano heightened the song's white-knuckle intensity.

'It's about depression or anxiety or anything like that,' Johns said. 'It's about trying to escape it without resorting to an anti-depressant or some kind of pill.'

'Paint Pastel Princess' was another lyric from Johns's darkest days. It was a metaphor for Aropax, the anti-depressant that his doctor had prescribed. 'The song's about how taking that type of medication prevents you from feeling highs or lows — every day is the same,' he explained, likening Aropax to Prozac, which 'keeps you on the same level, but at the same time they numb you. Unfortunately, I need them, but it doesn't mean I have to like them.'

'Anthem for the Year 2000', a riff-crunching rock beast — which later became *Neon Ballroom*'s lead-off single — was another song to emerge from this frenzied songwriting period between the 'Untitled' session and the recording of *Neon Ballroom*. But whereas 'Ana's Song' and 'Paint Pastel Princess' were deeply felt lyrics about the trauma Johns was going through, 'Anthem' came from somewhere else entirely.

A dream, in fact. It was also one of Johns's fastest turnarounds. 'I had a dream we were playing at this huge stadium,' he told *Guitar* magazine:

> and we had no instruments because everything had broken. Thousands of people had their hands in the air, clapping.
>
> And I started singing, 'We are the youth, we'll take your fascism away,' over the handclaps, in order to compensate for the lack of instruments. So I woke up and straight away wrote [the song]. I did it from start to finish in, like, five minutes. It was the quickest song I'd ever written, and the first verse starts with drums and vocals — just like the dream, only with the handclaps.

'I wanted to write a stadium rock song,' Johns told America's K-Rock radio station. 'I want it to really rock.' He was correct on both counts. (In a curious footnote, the band approached AC/DC rhythm guitarist Malcolm Young to add guitar to the track; he politely declined.)

Although Johns had been downplaying the political nature of his words — despite such titles as 'Israel's Son' and 'Pure Massacre' — 'Anthem for the Year 2000' was overtly political, if a little glib. The song's social conscience was something he couldn't deny. He even drew links between its theme and the outbreak of One Nation and Hansonism that was creeping into Australian politics and society at the time:

> I think the government treats us like shit, they think the youth is a bunch of people who are wasting their lives on drugs and loud music. The song draws a parallel between politicians and how they view youth and how they put certain restrictions on them. It draws a parallel between that

Wait until tomorrow: (l to r) Daniel Johns, Ben Gillies and Chris Joannou 1995.
Courtesy of John Watson

Pure massacre: Mayhem in the moshpit at the Sydney Big Day Out, 1995.
Photo by David Anderson

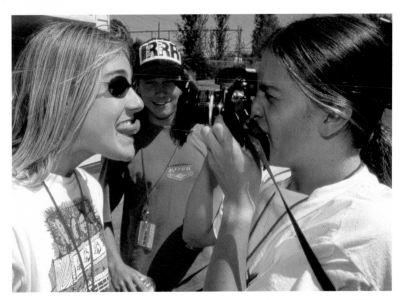

In focus: Gillies (right) snaps Johns backstage at the Sydney Big Day Out, 1995, while Joannou looks on. *Photo by David Anderson*

Llamas in pyjamas: Backstage at the Newcastle Workers Club, at the Llama Ball, August 1995. *Courtesy of John Watson*

Thunderbirds are go: Backstage, Rio, late November 1996. *Courtesy of John Watson*

Abuse me: Johns in drag on the last date of the Summer Freak Show tour, Perth, December 1997. *Courtesy of John Watson*

All that glitters: With manager John Watson (second from left), backstage at Homebake, Sydney, December 1999. *Photo by Tony Mott, courtesy of John Watson*

Reading to rock: At the massive Reading Festival, Leeds, August 1999. *Courtesy of John Watson*

Man of the people: Gillies prior to a show at the Brisbane Tivoli, March 1999. *Courtesy of John Watson*

Thunderstruck: Joannou lets rip at the Falls Festival, 2000. *Photo by © Martin Philbey*

Hair today: Johns at the Melbourne Big Day Out, January 2003.
Photo by © Martin Philbey

World upon his shoulders: An almost crippled Daniel Johns at the video shoot for
Diorama's 'Without You', April 2002. *Courtesy of John Watson*

Back in brown: Johns at rehearsals for the ARIAs,
October 2002. *Photo by David Anderson*

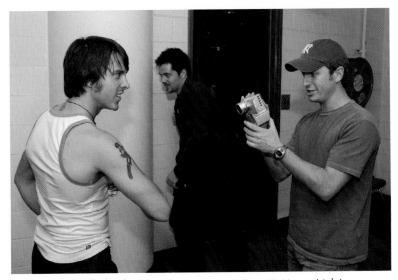

Soulman: Gillies flashes his James Brown tattoo to Rove McManus (right), backstage at the 2002 ARIAs. *Photo by David Anderson*

After all these years: Johns, pre-performance at the 2002 ARIAs. *Photo by David Anderson*

Winners, grinners: Joannou (right) holds one of the five ARIAs Silverchair claimed in 2002. *Photo by David Anderson*

Luv your life: Johns preaches to the converted, Wollongong Entertainment Centre, March 2003. *Photo by David Anderson*

and the record industry and taking away from young stars and using young people — and taking their innocence.

On closer inspection, maybe 'Anthem' wasn't just a political rant — it was closer to Johns's current state of mind than even he knew at the time.

Just like 'Anthem', 'Satin Sheets' — another song from Johns's hermit phase — wasn't as deeply personal as the bulk of *Neon Ballroom*; it was more observational. He described it as a comment on class, taken from a time when 'die yuppie die' was a counter-culture catchphrase: it was about 'the corporate world looking down on people'. 'If I walk into a restaurant or something,' said Johns, 'there's this whole yuppie mentality of people who think I shouldn't be there because I don't brush my hair. But I've probably got more money than them.' Clearly Johns hadn't quite shaken off the anti-everything stance to which the band blindly swore allegiance back in 1994.

'Miss You Love' and 'Black Tangled Heart' were other poems-cum-songs written during band downtime. But they reflected a different Johns trauma: his inability to form a lasting relationship:

> I've had girlfriends, but I've never had a relationship that's lasted longer than a month. I think I've got some kind of phobia [a word Johns would repeat endlessly when talking up *Neon Ballroom*]. I'm scared of getting too attached to someone. Just when someone gets close to my heart, that's when I cut them off.

As Johns freely and frequently admitted, the bulk of *Neon Ballroom* was personal, not political. He didn't picture himself as some kind of youth spokesman, even if he'd been burdened with that tag, very much against his will. 'I find it a lot more creatively satisfying to express myself the way that I feel inside my head or inside my heart,' he said, 'rather than focus on things that are more political. Because I don't know about political issues — I just know what I feel strongly about.'

By June 23, the trio were finally back in Sydney's Festival Studios, where both *Frogstomp* and *Freak Show* had been recorded. But for the first time in their lives, Silverchair entered the studio with a set of songs that felt honest and real and not in any way related to grunge. Despite the emotional baggage they were carrying, they'd never been so prepared to make an album. 'The first two albums were traditional hard rock music,' Johns said when the band began the *Neon Ballroom* sessions. 'This album's a lot more ambitious. You have all your bands and they're either pop or rock or whatever and they always stick to that. [But] we didn't want to be labelled as a certain kind of style. We wanted to change and try different things.'

One constant, however, was their choice of producer Nick Launay. Before agreeing to go with Launay, Johns had called him at home and talked for an hour, running him through the new songs and what instruments and production techniques he felt would bring them to life. Launay was in full agreement. 'Nick's really good because he's really willing to listen and doesn't try to dominate the sessions,' said Johns. 'A lot of days, me and him just sat around fiddling with effects units and effects pedals and different miking positions and stuff.' It was clear that Johns was learning to love the studio. This would prove handy, because the singer/guitarist was about to share the studio with a string section, a choir, various non-Silverchairists — and he was also about to go head-to-head with *Shine*-man, pianist David Helfgott.

Though they might have resided in completely different musical universes, Helfgott and Johns had more in common than they knew. Born in 1943, Helfgott had been a teen star, winning the state finals of the ABC Instrumental and Vocal competition six times. (Coincidentally, Johns and Silverchair had also come to prominence through the ABC, in their case via massive airplay on Triple J.) Just like Johns, Helfgott suffered terribly from the impact of being a teen prodigy. After a complete emotional breakdown, he disappeared from view in 1980. He staged a comeback a decade later, culminating in an astounding recording of Rachmaninov's Third Piano Concerto and sell-out shows around the world. His wild ride of a life story had been documented in Scott Hick's 1996 film, *Shine*, which featured Geoffrey Rush in an Academy Award-winning performance as Helfgott. Johns's life story paralleled Helfgott's in intriguing ways. (For his part, when asked about their connection, Helfgott joked that he and Johns shared a lawyer.)

The day before Helfgott's arrival at Festival had been adventurous enough: the New South Wales Public School Singers choir had been brought in to add their voices to 'Anthem for the Year 2000'. Conducted by George Tobay, the young voices gave the song an eerily similar mood to Pink Floyd's 'Another Brick in the Wall'. The next day, August 19, was Helfgott's turn in the studio; he was scheduled to add piano to the epic 'Emotion Sickness', which would become *Neon Ballroom*'s opening track.

During pre-production, when he presented the song to the band, Johns figured it needed a 'manic kind of piano part', designed to 'exaggerate its sadness'. On Watson's suggestion — after his proposal to use indie-pop piano player Ben Folds was shut down by Johns — the band decided Helfgott was the right man for the job. The band agreed after a meeting at Watson's house during which Helfgott, at one stage, excused himself so he could slip upstairs and brush his teeth — with Watson's toothbrush. Throughout the meeting, he kept putting his arm around Gillies and muttering, 'Very different, very different.' The drummer didn't know what to make of the wildly emotional Helfgott. Then the band met with Larry Muhoberac, who was writing the piano part for Helfgott. While Johns lay on the floor shouting out the notes he was imagining Helfgott would play, Muhoberac — a renowned player who was once Elvis Presley's pianist — made sense of the songwriter's untrained stream of consciousness. Strangely, it worked.

Now in the studio, and once he'd familiarised himself with the seesawing music of 'Emotion Sickness', Helfgott behaved true to character. He hugged and kissed anyone who came near him, while mumbling all the time. Unable to keep still — and needing the same kind of affection that he generously gave to anyone nearby — there was only one way Helfgott could settle down sufficiently to record the part: Muhoberac shared his stool, hugging him with one arm and pointing to the musical score with the other, while Launay talked the pianist through the recording process via his earphones. Helfgott clearly connected with Johns, too. At one stage he reached across and quite innocently grasped the singer's crotch. 'There was one time he grabbed my dick. He didn't know that he was doing it,' Johns said. 'He just has to be intimate.'

Johns — as documented on Robert Hambling's *Emotional Pictures* documentary, which was shot as the album progressed — clearly fell under the spell of the unstoppable Helfgott. 'David was great,' Johns said after the session:

> It was the first time he'd ever played on a song that wasn't really classical, so it was an interesting experience for all of us, I think.

> David played his piano part like a classical composition. Then he started improvising around what he felt, which was exactly what I was looking for. Only a pianist as inspired as he is could have managed what he did.

Producer Launay was another Helfgott convert, describing the session as 'probably the most amazing day of our lives.' And true to character, Helfgott had the final word: 'The prodigies are alright, it's the parents who need advice,' he mumbled. 'I have plenty of emotion sickness myself.'

The band's only regret was that they weren't able to capture on tape the words Helfgott muttered as he began to play: 'Here we go into musicland.' It would have been the perfect opening line for an album where the band proved there was more to Silverchair's music than screaming riffs and hammer of the gods rhythms.

As the *Neon Ballroom* sessions continued into the first week of September, more guests added their parts. As the album's liner notes will attest, Paul Mac 'attacked' the piano on 'Anthem', 'Spawn Again' and 'Satin Sheets'. (Mac hit the keys so hard that during recordings for their next album, *Diorama*, a piano tuner was needed after every session he worked on.) Midnight Oil's Jim Moginie, who was to become a Silverchair studio regular and ended up on a shortlist to produce their next album, added what the band fondly dubbed 'keyboards Mogenius' to 'Anthem', 'Ana's Song', 'Miss You Love', 'Dearest Helpless', 'Do You Feel the Same', 'Paint Pastel Princess' and 'Point of View'. Sydney musical journeyman Chris Abrahams played piano on 'Black Tangled Heart'. Jane Scarpantoni, whose string arrangement on *Freak Show*'s 'Cemetery' was the centrepoint of that album, added various arrangements to *Neon Ballroom*, along with eight other violinists and cellists. And Johns's longtime companion, his dog Sweep, howled during the album's closer, 'Steam Will Rise'. It was every bit the team effort.

Johns was particularly engrossed when working with Scarpantoni. Whereas 'Cemetery' had been written as a ballad and only had strings added as an afterthought, Johns was now writing with strings in mind — especially strings as arranged by Scarpantoni. 'She was classically trained,' he figured, 'but had a rock mind. She understands my language; I describe things more as scenery or pictures, and she latched on and got the right kind of mood.' Not that Johns completely understood her language. A priceless moment on Hambling's *Emotion Pictures* is when she mentions the classical term 'legato' (which is translated in layman's term as 'smoothly') to Johns. He mugs for the camera, replying, 'Yeah, right, more "legato".' But you sensed that Johns was storing the information away, as his musical vocabulary increased day by day. The studio was no longer somewhere to bash out songs and then rattle around the corridors on trolleys, as he, Gillies and Joannou had done in the past. There were no girlie mag centrefolds decorating the vocal booth. Now it was a place where Johns could give some life to the musical pictures in his head. This was serious business.

Despite being 'smoothed out' by the anti-depressants he'd been prescribed, Johns was at his best in the studio. He was finding out that the thrill he'd lost in performing had been substituted by this new kick. It was now more of a home to him than the stage or even The Loft in Gillies's garage. A significant shift had occurred in Silverchair's world — the band renowned for 'going off' live were becoming studio craftsmen.

'When I first started,' Johns reasoned, 'it was more about playing live and everything was about energy. Everything was about being really loud and playing live. [But] the thing that

keeps me doing it is just creating music and exploring different elements of musical and lyrical angles.' Despite their
musical progress, and the diffusing of some tension in the
rehearsal room during pre-production, the *Neon Ballroom* sessions were still the most taxing of the band's recording life.

Johns was recovering from his eating disorder, and Gillies
and Joannou could sense the tension that permeated every
session. 'It was like this elastic band of tension was pulled tight
around us,' said Gillies. 'It was everything — Daniel wasn't
well, we were having to do another record, thinking whether
this is what we really wanted to do. We were also thinking that
if our lead singer's not well and doesn't really want to do it,
well, then, shit, I don't want to do it.'

'Ana's Song' was the last track recorded for the album. It
took some hard talking by Johns to convince everyone else
that the song belonged on the album. Johns hadn't revealed
the song to Watson until late in the sessions, when they were
doing string overdubs at Sydney's Paradise Studios. Watson
recognised that it was the ideal second single, but after a few
listens to the song, knew that its anorexia theme was a major
controversy waiting to happen. Watson called John O'Donnell
and told him to drop everything and get down to the studio.
The Murmur boss agreed that it was a great song and also
agreed there was no way it could go on the album.

They phoned Johns and told him just that. 'We told him
he had no idea of the scrutiny this would subject him to,' says
Watson. 'He was just coming out of a dark place — he didn't
want to be thrust back into it. Particularly not as the single
that's meant to sum up the whole album. Which, of course, it
does.' But the song's lyrics were simply too personal, too close
to what Johns had (just) survived while he was writing the
album, for it to be excluded. He told Watson and O'Donnell

that he wanted to make an emotionally true record. 'Because it was so honest as a song,' Johns said, 'I didn't want to censor myself at all.' It was a wise move. 'Ana's Song' was in.

After almost two months of recording — a far cry from the rushed sessions for both *Frogstomp* and *Freak Show* — Johns and Launay discovered one final hitch with *Neon Ballroom*. Having spent a week in Mangrove Studios laying down vocals and various other music (mainly provided by Midnight Oil's Moginie), they detected a strange, muffled quality to Johns's vocals, which in playback sounded as if a sheet had been laid across the speakers. It was never determined what the exact cause was, but his vocals had to be re-recorded. (By the time of their next album, the studio had been rebuilt.)

A genuinely pissed-off Johns took a fortnight's break to regain his physical and emotional strength. In those two weeks 'there was a lot of smashing things because of the frustration' but Johns felt gratified when his vocals were finally done. 'All the struggles were worth it. We've made an album that combines lots of different sounds and instruments that you don't usually hear together,' Johns commented at the end of the recording sessions. Then he, Watson and Launay got ready to decamp to Los Angeles for three weeks of mixing, where Launay would mix every track bar 'Miss You Love' and the single version of 'Anthem for the Year 2000', which were presided over by Kevin Shirley.

'We wanted to carve our own little piece of turf, blending futuristic noises with more classic influences,' Johns said as he left for LA. Then he added, in a telling kiss-off to grunge, 'We're fed up with all the usual comparisons that people keep making about our music. I wanted to make guitar pretty much a non-issue. I wanted us to make an album that was different from everything else that's out right now.'

Neon Ballroom hit the Australian stores on March 8, 1999. As statements of musical independence go, it was a success. Though not shy of Johns's trademark force-10 riffs, it breaks the band out of the grunge ghetto that had characterised *Frogstomp* and *Freak Show*. The opener, 'Emotion Sickness', sets the tone for the entire album. Instead of a monster riff to open the disc, there's a neo-classical orchestration, introducing a tense, terse psychodrama enhanced by Helfgott's piano interlude and a surging musical arrangement. Johns's voice drifts for much of the song, floating, until he suddenly bursts into life, screaming 'Get up! Get up! Everything is clearly dying,' as if they were his final words on Earth.

The song's selection as the album's opening track was a smart move on the part of Johns (and manager Watson), even though Launay and several of those at Epic weren't so sure. If *Neon Ballroom* had opened with 'Anthem for the Year 2000' (already a Number 3 hit in Australia by the time of the album's release), it would have been seen as an entirely different album, as many reviews are dictated by an album's opening cut, which typically establishes the mood of what's to follow. Johns realised that, but boldly went with his instinct — and the contrariness of the move must have appealed to him, too:

> We were warned not to do it, because it would alienate and confuse people, and turn them off the album. But I found that really intriguing. As soon as someone said that to me, I said, 'Yeah, I'm definitely going to do it.' It shows the ambition behind the record and sums up what I was trying to do.

'Ana's Song (Open Fire)', the album's third track, drove home the point that this was a new Silverchair. With Jim Moginie's keyboards adding woozy texture, Johns worked his way through his troubled year as if he were on the analyst's couch. Gillies's powerhouse drumming and Joannou's solid bottom-end left their mark, but it was Johns's searing honesty that elevated this track, as it did the bulk of *Neon Ballroom*.

Johns's personal anguish was underscored on several tracks by Scarpantoni's classical leanings, which meshed perfectly into the lush 'Paint Pastel Princess', the turgid 'Black Tangled Heart', and 'Miss You Love', a gentle, waltz-like ballad with a dark underbelly. 'I wanted to write a song that people could dedicate to their lover on the radio or dance to,' Johns confessed, when asked about 'Miss You Love'. But this was a love song with a twist —'It's actually about not having love and not being able to find love, and being lonely.' If there was one track on *Neon Ballroom* that summed up Johns's tortured soul, this was it: an anti-love song, combining a gorgeous melody and a perversely glum lyric.

However, the band still had a moshpit — their established fanbase — to satisfy. Tracks such as the pure punk fury of 'Spawn Again' and 'Dearest Helpless' were throwbacks to the simpler times of their first two albums. Although neither track were standouts on *Neon Ballroom* — 'Spawn Again' was actually pretty dreadful — they both packed a kick like a mule, bound to send bodies flying live. Still, you couldn't help but think Johns was paying lip service to the fans who had snapped up *Freak Show* and *Frogstomp*. These songs were for them, not for him.

But how much musical experimentation could Johns get away with before his audience started looking elsewhere? It was a conundrum that marked much of *Neon Ballroom*. If anything, *Ballroom* adequately managed to fulfil Johns's need to scratch his creative itch without overly shocking the band faithful. For every lush, near cinematic moodpiece there was a raw, bleeding rocker. As each-way bets go, the album was a winner. But with the benefit of hindsight, perhaps Johns was selling himself just a little short, even if the album does contain the best songs he'd written to this point: 'Miss You Love', 'Emotion Sickness' and 'Ana's Song (Open Fire)'. *Neon Ballroom* may have been an album of both killer and filler, but it was a necessary stepping stone for the epic, ambitious sprawl of 2002's *Diorama*.

Astute local critic Barry Divola, writing in *Who* magazine, got it right. When reviewing *Diorama*, he described *Neon Ballroom* as 'an experiment that didn't quite have the cojones to back up the vision'. Yet even without knowing what was to follow, most critics acknowledged *Neon Ballroom*'s broader vision. *Massive* magazine took a *vive la différence* approach: '*Neon Ballroom* is different, silverchair is experimenting and the results are awesome.'

Craig Mathieson, a close follower of the band, gave it a four-star review for Australian *Rolling Stone*: 'It's an ambitious, varied record, one brimming with intelligent ideas — some not always realised — but worthy nonetheless.' He then added that '*Neon Ballroom* is a sustained, adult work … the musical sophistication takes silverchair beyond being a [typical] three-piece.'

Most overseas press also praised the band's ambition, if not always the mixed bag of an album it had produced. American *Rolling Stone* awarded the record a three-star review, but measured their praise. 'The problem is that the kids can't decide what they want to do when they grow up,' wrote a mildly condescending Neva Chonin. The review softened up, though, finally admitting that, '*Neon Ballroom* is what you'd expect from a young band going through its awkward stage.' (In their 'feedback' section, most Silverfans disagreed. One disgruntled fan fired back: 'This album was the best thing to come out of one of the worst times ever for rock.') Similarly, Ken Advent in the *Cleveland Free Times* wrote that 'silverchair is making a concerted effort to stretch the band's musical boundaries ... when silverchair is on top of their game, there are flashes of a visionary band like Pink Floyd filtered through the heavy guitars.'

Johns's development as a songwriter was often singled out. *Electric Music Online* praised the album's 'sonic oomph' but added that 'the biggest credit has to go to Daniel Johns. His songwriting skills have improved out of sight — no longer is he simply copying his peers and influences, [he's] writing songs with their own structure and sound.' New Zealand's hard-rock mag *Rip It Up*, which gave the album a mixed review, admitted that 'all the time you know Daniel John's songwriting skill has progressed beyond playing three chords and shouting very loudly.'

As the reviews started filtering in, Silverchair's attention turned to their upcoming tour. In order to recreate the lush, orchestrated sound of much of their new album, they spent two weeks at home, in late November 1998, auditioning keyboardists. The band had put out feelers within the industry and had tried out half a dozen players before settling on Sam Holloway, late of moody Melburnians Cordrazine, whose debut (and farewell) album, *Welcome to Wherever You Are*, had made the Australian Top 10 before the band imploded. Holloway was not only classically trained, he also looked good on stage and had a laddish nature that sat well off-stage with Joannou and Gillies, who admitted that Holloway's 'good blokiness' was as big a factor as his keyboard skills.

After the band dispersed for the Christmas and New Year break, they began rehearsing with Holloway in Newcastle on

January 4. His first public appearance with the band was on January 21, but the show was so low-key, only the faithful chairpage addicts knew about it. Billing themselves as the Australian Silverchair Show, the now four-piece shocked locals at Newcastle's Cambridge Hotel as they tried out new songs and early standards. 'We just thought it would be a fun, low-pressure way to kick off a tour,' said Gillies. 'We've got a lot of new songs, so we wanted to try them out in front of a real crowd.' It was their first public appearance for over 12 months and the last time for a couple of years that they'd get to play such an intimate, low-stress show. From now on in, every show would be about selling the product.

The next day, the revitalised band was in Sydney, shooting an anarchic clip for the album's first single, 'Anthem for the Year 2000', with American Gavin Bowden. He'd shot clips for MTV darlings the Red Hot Chili Peppers, Live and Rage Against the Machine, which definitely gave his CV the right kind of buzz. After all, Silverchair's career needed a kickstart after the moderate performance of their second album in the US. A massive crowd scene forms the heart of the video. In keeping with their new 'keep it different' policy, the band had sent out invitations via their fan club and chairpage, again, inviting anyone interested in being involved. On the second day of shooting, 1200 faithful turned up in Sydney's Martin Place, transforming it into a seething mass of Silverchair fans. Johns had expected 300. 'Anthem' blared repeatedly through an outdoor PA during the shooting, as the army of extras staged their scripted riot and were sprayed with industrial-strength hoses.

Another feature of the clip was a cameo from Australian actor Maggie Kirkpatrick, best known as 'The Freak' from Australia's long-running '70s TV drama *Prisoner*. In the clip,

Kirkpatrick plays a robot, a Pauline Hanson-like figure that serves as a visual metaphor for the song's 'authority sucks' message, what Johns described as 'youth rebelling against people who are supposedly more important'. It turns out that Kirkpatrick shared more with the band than even she knew: not only was she a Novocastrian, but her niece and nephew were schoolmates of the band. 'My first reaction was, "Why me?",' she told the *Sunday Herald-Sun*. 'I later found out that the boys were from Newcastle, and being an old Newcastle girl myself, I was more than prepared to help them out. I encourage anyone from my own town.'

Not that Silverchair had much time to swap hometown stories with the TV star. By the time the water cannons had been shut down and Martin Place dried and cleared, the band were on a plane to Melbourne, en route to a headlining spot at the Peaches & Cream Festival. Ahead of them lay a very heavy year's worth of travelling, playing and messing with their audience's heads.

Bibliography

'silverchair frontman Daniel Johns talks openly about his painfulbattle with depression, anxiety and a life-threatening eating disorder' *Teen People* November 1999; 'Growing Up the Hard Way' *Kerrang!* 13/03/1999; 'Growing Pains' *Guitar* April 1999; 'silverchair — True Confessions' *Juice* April 1999; MTV News Feature March 1999; Transcript: Interview on 92.3 K-Rock New York April 1999; 'Emotion Sickness' Australian *Rolling Stone* May 1999; 'Ballroom Blitz' Australian *Rolling Stone* Yearbook 1999; 'Daniel Speaks' *Big Hit* April 1999; 'silverchair — Three lads in the fishbowl' *Chart* April 1999; 'silverchair — Strictly Ballroom' *Rock Sound* April 1999; 'silverchair — Graduated from school and heading for the Neon Ballroom' *Circus* July 1999; 'silverchair: Lighting Up the Neon Ballroom' *Metal Edge* June 1999; 'The Ballistic Rebirth of silverchair' *Watch* April 1999; 'Future Rock' *Guitar One* May 1999; 'Aussie trio unveil 'futuristic' style' *Kerrang!* 09/01/1999; 'silverchair stomp preconceptions with *Neon Ballroom*' *Jam! Music* Online 12/03/1999; 'Anthems for the Year 2002' *Who Weekly* 15/04/2002; *Massive* March 1999; Australian *Rolling Stone* April; American *Rolling Stone* March 1999; *The Cleveland Free Times* March 1999; *Electric Music* Online March 1999; *Rip It Up* (New Zealand) March 1999; 'Aussie rockers pose as tribute band for surprise hometown show featuring new music' *Addicted to Noise* 22/01/1999; *Sunday Herald-Sun* 21/02/1999

The Peacemaker:

an interview with Nick Launay

British-born, Sydney-based Nick Launay produced *Freak Show* and *Neon Ballroom*. In the process, he coped with inner-band tensions, argumentative Indians and a sweet, strange genius named David Helfgott.

How did you first become involved with the Innocent Criminals?

Robert [Hambling] rang me about 'Tomorrow'; this is before either of the two Johns heard it. He said, 'You've got to hear this tape; it's amazing, I want your opinion.' He was working for SBS. They were inundated with tapes and CDs [for the *nomad* competition] but hadn't determined who was going to listen to them. He volunteered, and got it down to two or three — at the top was the Innocent Criminals. He played it to me and I was blown away by a couple of the songs.

What was the reaction of the other judges?

The SBS people didn't like the Innocent Criminals because it was too aggressive, too whingy.

What happened next?

Robert called Daniel's phone number and got his Mum, who said he was at school. Robert assumed that Daniel was her boyfriend or her husband. Once he realised the age he went back to the SBS people and said, 'This is insane; these people have got to win.'

How did you react to 'Tomorrow'?

To me it was the most tuneful song, the most memorable song on the tape. I spoke with Robert and suggested quite a radical rearrangement. He called me back the next day and asked if I could chop it up. I wasn't working at the time, so I edited it on my two-track. I did a cassette of it, gave it to Robert, he took it back to them. By then I was really into it and played it to three record companies — and Robert played it to I don't know how many. No one bought it. They [the SBS staff] then asked Robert if he could ask me to go into the studio with them. I said, 'Absolutely, yes,' but I was leaving the next week to go to America. Then I got horribly ill; I couldn't get out of bed, I had to leave for America late, still ill. So I got on the phone to Phil McKellar, who did a great job. He was the Triple J guy, and the free Triple J studio time was part of the prize. I told him what I was going to do — add a guitar solo, that kind of thing.

When did you next hear 'Tomorrow'?

When I came back from America, on Qantas, I heard this song which I thought I really knew. It sounded like something I'd done or been involved with but I could not work it out. Then I looked at the magazine and it said 'silverchair'. I thought, who the hell is silverchair? When I got back home I finally worked it out and found out it had been number one for seven weeks.

Did you want to produce their first album?

I wanted to work with them when I started editing the [demo] version — and told everyone that. By the time I got back they were already in the studio. I wasn't offered the job because I was out of the country. I honestly thought, having taken the demo of 'Tomorrow' around to record companies and having it rejected, that I could have taken it around after I got back and got them a deal. But it happened much quicker than that, which *never* happens.

What did you think of Frogstomp?

I think it was perfect. It was done quickly, it was done with Kevin Shirley, who's very 'get them in, bash it out', which is very different to what I do. I would probably have worked on getting better takes, getting into sounds. I wouldn't have necessarily made it less raw, but I would have worked longer on it. Maybe two weeks [laughs]. The band's attention span then was very short. When I worked with them a year later, when they were 16, it was still very short.

So what happened then?

When it came to doing *Freak Show*, I'd met up with them a few times, but it didn't click with them at all that I was the guy who did the edit on 'Tomorrow'. I think halfway through doing *Freak Show* the conversation came up and the penny dropped. They had no idea. Anyway, I was about to go to America again and John Watson called me and asked would I like to do the next Silverchair record — and he said to bear in mind that Andy Wallace was going to mix it. I said, 'Well, that's not a bad thing.' I was about to go to America and meet a band and see if I wanted to work with them. That definitely wasn't as exciting as working with Silverchair, so I came back.

What went on during pre-production?

I went up to meet them and it was the funniest thing. I arrived there by train. I brought with me, from America, a big snare drum that I'd bought that used to belong to Soundgarden and I thought it might sound good on their record. I'd talked to Ben a few times and told him that if he really liked it he could buy it, which he did. So I arrived with this really heavy thing — it's made out of sewer pipe, solid steel and it's eight or nine inches deep. I'm outside Ben's house and I saw these kids on skateboards. It's stupid, I know, but it's only when I got up close to them and they're going, 'You Nick?' that I realised they were really so young. It was really bizarre to me — they were such a great band and they were so young. Nothing was serious.

You were their chauffeur, right?

Well, then Ben came up to me and said, 'You got a car? You wanna go for a drive?' And I said, 'Yes, but I came by train.' And he said, 'No, I've got a car.' And I was thinking, why was he asking me this? Then I realised they were so young they had to go with an adult. So we went into the garage and he's got this big, powerful car. And they jump in, all excited, when out jumps Ben's mum. She said, 'Hang on a minute, where are you going?' Then she pointed at me and said, 'Young man, can I have a word with you inside, please?' And she said, 'They're young, they're impressionable and they're hoons. You're the adult, you've got to be responsible.'

I got back in the car, feeling like I've been told off. I told the band and they just went, 'Yeah, yeah, yeah,' and as soon as we were around the corner Ben just floored it. It was just insane; they're all laughing their heads off. Then we went up this hill and there were all these girls coming back from school. The guys slowed down — and then the girls suddenly realised it was Silverchair. Off we took, with girls running behind. Then we drove around Newcastle and they showed me the sights. It was hard for me, because I didn't want to come over like the adult but at the same time I had to be careful because an accident could have happened at any time. I had to tread a very fine line.

What's this about you going 'egging' with the band?

We went in and rehearsed and played a few songs. That lasted about half an hour, given their attention span. I said, 'Can I hear another one?' They said, 'Nah, that's the lot.' I said, 'Well, that was three songs, not enough for an album.' So I think I squeezed six songs out of them. Then we went for another drive. They said to me, 'Have you ever been egging?' I had no idea what that was. So they stopped at the gas station and got some eggs, and they were driving around egging things, which I thought was just insane. But the excitement level … I was a bit of a kid, too, and still am. I guess they thought I was OK, because I got the job.

How did you connect with Johns?

I relate to him very well — we're both arty, skinny types. We're not blokey types. Newcastle is a pretty blokey type place, which isn't Daniel.

Tell me about how the Indians came to play on 'Petrol and Chlorine'?

Daniel said to me that he didn't think there should be drums on the song. It was quite a shock. Ben was like, 'What?' I asked whether he meant it should just be guitar, vocal and bass, and he said, 'No, but I don't reckon it should be drums.' I asked what he wanted for percussion — shakers, that type of thing, and he said, 'No, no, no hippie shit. I reckon it should sound like one of those docos on SBS.' The next day I bought in some CDs of Indian music and African music and Latin American music and played them to him. When I played the Indian

CD he went, 'Yeah, that's it.' It was a tabla he was hearing. Then I thought that I should play him some Beatles stuff — I played him 'Within You Without You' and he heard what we thought was a sitar. He thought that was cool.

I ended up calling the Indian Consulate who had a list of musicians. One of them was a guy called Pandit Suman. I went out to Bankstown; he had a studio where he taught traditional dance. We got talking and I played him what we'd recorded of the song. He picked up a tabla and started playing and it was absolutely perfect, spot on. I complimented him and he told me that he used to be in a band in India. He showed me a picture that had three or four musicians in it. He pointed to one and said, 'This man is called Ravi Shankar.' I thought, how about that? I'm in Sydney, Australia and the first guy that I find has played with the guy who played with the Beatles. But he hadn't heard the Beatles song Shankar played on. I played it to him and he identified the instrument, which I thought was a sitar. It's a one-stringed instrument [the tampura] that follows the vocal. I said that's what we wanted and he said he'd organise everything.

Tell me about the day in the studio.

The day came and we realised we needed someone to go there and pick them up. I called John O'Donnell and the only car Sony had was a limo. So we sent a stretch limo to pick them up. Two hours later all these Indians, in full dress, arrive in this big stretch limo. It was hilarious.

So they came in, but they'd never used headphones before and we found out that their timing is different — they don't count in fours at all as we do. They work out the meter and then go from there. I didn't know this at the time. Daniel was dying, he was going nuts — this guy can't count! It was a combination of hysterically funny things; they even started arguing in [an] Indian [language] at one point. In hindsight, if I'd got Silverchair to play live with them, it would have been much quicker. But the basic recording was already done. It worked out, but it took a few hours.

A lot had changed within the band by the time of Neon Ballroom.

There was a lot going on. The first album, they had all the songs, they went in and played it and bashed it out in seven days or whatever. The second album, one half was rock songs and half was experimental, where they had no idea what was going to happen. I think they found that fun, they were more curious about how things worked. *Neon Ballroom* was a completely different thing. That whole thing about being so famous and not being able to go outside had really hurt Daniel, plus he'd started on his not eating thing. He didn't hang out with Chris and Ben at all. He stayed in his room, didn't go out. Everyone was worried about his mental state.

How did you convince Daniel to play his new songs?

No one knew what songs he had and he was convinced the songs he had weren't right for Silverchair and that was it. He had a lot of pressure on him from the record company to make another Silverchair record, which he didn't want to do. He'd been listening to a lot of different kinds of music. He didn't relate to Ben and Chris — and he's not a communicator, he wasn't about to get on the phone. He didn't know how to deal with this.

I went up there, lived in his parents' house for maybe a week, got him to play me the songs. Then I went to Ben and Chris. Chris was no problem, he had a very good view of it, he accepted that if Daniel didn't want to make an album, that was it. But he wanted his friend back. Ben was different. He's a tough kid, he said he didn't know what was going on, why wasn't Daniel talking to him, he thought they should make another album, blah, blah, blah.

What do you think was really going on?

The more I got into it, it became very personal, and Ben was really, really upset that his friend hadn't called him. I told him that I thought that he was Daniel's best friend in the world. I told him, he doesn't believe you'll like any of his songs and he doesn't want to play them because he's scared you'll reject them. He told me he wouldn't do it, he likes what he does and he didn't want to do a rock record, anyway.

Ben was listening to dance music; they were all growing up. Chris was great; he was like the glue between them. He told me where Ben's head was at. So what I proposed was a day of rehearsals. They'd go in, Daniel would play them the songs and then they could tell him what they thought. It was really emotional; on-the-point-of-crying kind of stuff. Basically, we went in, Daniel sat on a chair, with no eye contact with either of them, and went, 'I've got this song.' He played it and of course it was a beautiful song.

Then Ben would go, 'I reckon that's heaps good — what if you put a beat to it?' Ben, of course, is one of the best drummers in the world, so he started playing this beat to this song that Daniel felt shouldn't be a Silverchair song — and it worked. Before you know it, they're all laughing and talking. I remember turning to Chris and saying, 'Will you look at these two? They should give each other a hug.' I don't think they did, but it was a major turning point. Over the next week we found out he had a whole album's worth of songs, half of them rock songs, half of them not, and everyone loved it.

Do you think Ben felt rejected because none of his songs made Neon Ballroom?

I think he did and does from an artistic expression point of view, but from an ego point of view he doesn't. I think the tension about that kind of issue came from their individual managers — that is, their Mums. And I don't mean that in a nasty way; it was just a concern thing. They look after their own son's interests; all Mums do. I think that was something Daniel was aware of and that's why he was very resistant to showing these songs; he didn't want to upset Ben. It was a caring thing — it wasn't a case of, 'My songs are better.' This tension has happened with every single band I've worked with.

On Neon Ballroom *you had a memorable experience with David Helfgott: what was the genesis of that?*

It started when we met Larry [Muhoberac, who composed the arrangement for 'Emotion Sickness'], me, Daniel and Watson. He was perfect, because he understood rock music and classical music. Larry would say to Daniel, 'Well, what do you think should happen?' And I remember Daniel being in this huge almost fluorescent green beanie — he looked like an alien — saying, 'Oh, I dunno, you know, kind of, Bling! Bling! Bling!' And Larry asked him [how] these blings should go. And Daniel would tell him in the funniest way — he'd dance around the room, doing it with these great gestures. And Larry could actually do it. Daniel turned around and went, 'That's it.' And they went through the whole song.

The stuff he was coming out with was brilliant — and I don't think Daniel realised. He'd never done anything like this before. I really do think that these two songs ['Petrol & Chlorine' and 'Emotion Sickness'] are the beginning of what he would go on to do. This was definitely a turning point. He realised that as long as he could articulate the music he was hearing to talented people, he'd be OK.

Was it difficult to record Helfgott's part for 'Emotion Sickness'?

Difficult? Yes. The biggest problem was that, again, like the Indian musicians, when he plays, everyone follows him. But with Silverchair he was listening through headphones and playing along, which is something he hadn't done. So we had to do it line by line. With his kind of piano playing, it's extremely fast — he plays so many notes in one run. We had to work out how we'd get this crazy guy to do it.

He doesn't stop talking — he has no inner voice, everything he thinks, he says. When he met Ben, he was going, 'Ah, Ben, Ben, the timekeeper, very strong, he's the man with the beats.' Then he met me and said, 'The decision maker! The decision maker! Where would we be without the decision maker?' He hugs you while he talks to you. He's very tactile. A beautiful person. He kept saying how angel-like Daniel was — 'You've been sent to sing to us like an angel.' That's exactly what it's like to work with Daniel.

How did you keep him in check?

He couldn't sit still at the piano unless someone was hugging him; he also needed Larry to be near him to tell him what came next. The end result was this crazy thing of me playing one part of the tape, him and Larry sitting on a bench at the piano with Larry hugging him with one arm and pointing with the other, saying, 'OK, David, now we're going to play this part,' and talking him through it.

As Larry explained this to him in a very schoolteacher way — because you have to — David would be saying, 'Very exciting! Like this bit!' When he was being counted in he said he was going to be like a racing car, waiting for the start. Just as I'd count to four, David would shout, 'And here we go!' Then he'd slam this poor piano, and as soon as he'd finish the last note he'd shout again, 'There she goes! It's a good one!' Could you imagine doing that for three hours?

It took a long time to do the song, and we had to be very patient, but we did it. Then we had to take the tape and put it through ProTools to get rid of all the talking. It was a wild experience for all; I left the studio that day with my mind blown. I was very lucky to have been in that room. He's unique — an amazing musician and an amazing person.

What are your memories of the Neon Ballroom *sessions?*

Very comfortable. Compared with other bands, it went extremely smoothly. When you're making artistic stuff — be it painting, making music, whatever — and you've got more than one person, friction is what makes it great. The closest band I can think of [by comparison] is Talking Heads. In my mind there's no doubt that those musicians are the best musicians David Byrne could work with. But he was so close to it he couldn't see it. It's the same with Daniel; Ben and Chris are the best musicians he could work with. Whether he sees that, I don't know. It's a tricky thing.

6

Can I Get a Hallelujah?

'Eating disorder rocks teen star'

—*Courier-Mail*

'Oh shit, we're all going to die really, really dramatically.'

A nervous Daniel Johns was sitting in Sydney airport, alongside Gillies and Joannou. Those were the first words he uttered when the band convened to begin the Australian leg of their 1999 world tour, promoting *Neon Ballroom*. It was March 2, and the trio were en route to Brisbane — and then much of the Western world — as the story of Johns's near breakdown started to become public knowledge. After some pre-release album promotion with one-off shows in London, New York and New Orleans, this was the start of the real grind.

After arriving at Brisbane's Dockside Apartments, prior to their March 3 show at the Tivoli Cabaret, Gillies, Joannou and new boy Holloway hit the pool, as a rainstorm burst through the 98 per cent Queensland humidity. Johns was holed up in the hotel with a journalist, talking about himself, a situation that would be repeated throughout this year of touring.

Rolling Stone music editor Elissa Blake was travelling with the band, writing a cover story for the magazine's May 1999 issue. But what she thought would be a regular band-on-tour piece quickly changed into something radically different and far more serious. Johns needed to spill. He felt it was important — almost a community service, in fact — to let Blake know exactly what he'd been through during 1998, prior to the recording of *Neon Ballroom*.

Almost nonchalantly he turned to Blake:

A lot of people have been very worried about me.

Do you want to talk about it?

Yeah, I do.

What was going on while you were writing this album?

I was dealing with a lot of psychological things. I cut myself off from everyone that I knew for about six months.

Was it depression?

It was associated with depression. I started getting really bad anxiety trouble. I ended up getting medication because every time I left the house I'd be really badly shaking and sweaty.

Johns then proceeded to detail his season in hell: the isolation, the panic attacks, his eating disorder, his fear that in the midst of his breakdown he might actually die. He even showed his medications to Blake — nine sheets of coloured pills, including two different varieties of sleeping pills. 'I'm just trying them out,' he said.

In a seperate interview, Johns had spoken to a newspaper staffer two days earlier, and the morning after the first Australian show of the tour the local media had picked up on the story. 'Eating Disorder Rocks Teen Star', was the *Courier-Mail* headline that manager Watson read over his bacon and eggs. He was livid. Once again his band was front-page news for all the wrong reasons. 'It's disgusting,' Watson spat. 'I'm sure there are more important things in the world to put on page one.'

But Johns had chosen to share his problem with his audience. Possibly, among his millions of fans, was someone who could benefit from knowing that even Daniel Johns suffered typical (albeit extreme) teenage problems. Once Watson had calmed down, he began to accept what his youthful charge was trying to do by being so frank with journalists. 'I have a great deal of concern for Daniel as a human being,' he told Blake, explaining that 'he wanted to help other people and now we just have to do our best to help him.'

When Blake's story was published, Australian *Rolling Stone* was flooded with responses. Many were written by teenage girls with similar eating disorders who felt comforted by Johns's revelations. They wrote that they were relieved; they didn't feel alone anymore. Some even sent poems to Johns via the magazine. The volume of letters was overwhelming, and Blake forwarded many to John Watson, who then relayed them to Johns. Blake commented that it was the strongest response to a story that the magazine had ever had.

More was happening within Silverchair than the frontman's very public personal problems. Things had begun changing on-stage, as well. It was as if by turning inwards off-stage, Johns enabled himself to suddenly explode when he plugged in and played the band's new material. Six weeks earlier, at Cobram's Peaches & Cream festival, on the first official date of the tour, he turned up in a spangly, glittery top found in a Newtown op shop, which would become standard stage-wear during the *Neon Ballroom* tour. The old cargo pants and band T-shirts were dumped in the bottom of his closet. In the same way that his deeply felt songs were now the focus of the band, Johns had become the centre of attention on stage, slashing at his guitar and windmilling his arms like a young, blond, even-scrawnier Pete Townshend. The band chaperones were gone, school was out, and Daniel Johns had morphed into a seriously watchable, albeit unpredictable, rock star. In part, he was giving his fans exactly what they craved: a wild-haired, electrifying frontman. But Johns also knew there was a big difference between 'person' and 'persona'.

This inner conflict was astutely noted by *Rolling Stone*'s Craig Mathieson, who spotted the differences between 'Daniel of silverchair' and Daniel Johns. 'It's a complicated relationship,' he wrote. 'Daniel from silverchair puts Daniel Johns in the public eye, where he feels uneasy. But Daniel from silverchair also sells the albums, which satisfies Daniel Johns' self belief in his songwriting and quietly fierce ambition.'

Not long after taking the stage in Cobram — a show watched by Sarah McLeod from the Superjesus, who was soon to become Joannou's live-in partner — Johns launched into a barely-decipherable tirade, one of dozens documented during the tour. 'Right,' he yelled:

> put your hand up if you had a stage in your life where you felt alienated from the rest of the world. OK, yoga is for you. It stretches the mind and everything is about spiritu-ality. Spirituality or drugs. You're gonna take your pick, right? Or Jesus, but Jesus at times can be very stressful.

Because you don't know whether to read the Old or New Testament. Two different stories; it fucks me up.

You could hear a collective sigh of relief from the crowd when he ended his rant by screaming: 'Are you ready to rock & roll?', as the band crashed into 'Pure Massacre' behind him.

What this audience — and most other crowds during the almost one hundred dates Silverchair played during 1999 — didn't know was how hard it was for Johns to get on stage at all. While he might have been busting some of the most outrageous moves of his life while playing — roaring at the crowds, playing, as one review described, 'as if the power chords had taken over his body' — Johns was in the midst of a serious prescription-drug dependency. He needed pills to help him play, pills to help him come down from the show, pills to help him sleep. Every day was a variation on this medicated theme. Joannou, Gillies and Holloway were becoming tight; on tour they were often found together at the back of the bus bellowing such classic rock tunes as 'Sweet Home Alabama' at the top of their lungs. But Johns would be a million miles away, staring out of the window as the road flashed past him. Looking back, Gillies and Joannou agree that there were many moments on the *Neon Ballroom* tour, as there were during its recording, where 'you could just feel this tension in the air.'

Johns's manic on-stage persona didn't help. His live raves took any number of perverse variations. In London, he responded to an audience taunt by referring to himself as 'a lesbian wanker'. In New York, before a crowd that included *Neon Ballroom* collaborator Jane Scarpantoni and *Rolling Stone*'s David Fricke, Johns fell into a rap about becoming Posh Spice, 'because I'm a bitch and I'm gonna be married to a famous soccer player'. At an important LA show, watched by startled Epic A&R staff, he gave an impromptu Bible reading. In Chicago he declared the Windy City 'my favourite city in the whole world. Favourite people, favourite neon lights, favourite balconies, favourite people on balconies.' In Melbourne he tried to explain to the sold-out crowd that eating a beaver saves trees, because 'Beavers eat trees, right? So the more beavers there are, the less trees, right? So, save the trees by eating the beavers — then there'll be less of them to eat the trees.' Sometimes it was as though he was disgusted by his audience, who he figured just wanted to hear 'Tomorrow' — which Johns now played solo, in a truncated, acoustic version — and bang their heads. At other times it was as if Johns was playing some kind of macabre joke on himself and on the concept of 'rock star'. (Looking back now, he laughs long and hard about some of the peculiar statements he made on stage.)

Johns had also begun to talk to himself, frequently, between songs. Almost like a tennis player he was urging himself on ('I can do it'), or screaming obscenities. 'I hate you, I fucking hate you,' he yelled at himself in Minneapolis, before telling the crowd, 'OK, listen. We spent several fucking hours signing hundreds of CD covers and it was all for you. They're fifteen bucks — over there.' While the rest of the band played on, Johns was coming on like a bizarre cross between rock & roll madman and stand-up comic.

The fans were starting to notice how lost the frontman seemed. A German fan, writing on chairpage about Silverchair's Dusseldorf show on April 4, noted that 'there was almost no contact between the band members', comparing the show, negatively, with the first time she had seen the band, in 1996, when 'they were three funny young guys who just had fun playing music.'

Two nights after the Dusseldorf show, back in the UK, Johns actually stopped the band's set midway through 'Pure Massacre' when a stage-diver was kicked by a security guard. 'Hey, what the fuck do you think you're doing, man?' Johns drawled, as the band crashed to a halt. 'You don't go kicking people like that.' Johns then led the band back into 'Massacre' as if nothing had happened. There was a similar incident in Vienna in mid April, when a stage invader was dragged away by security in the midst of 'Anthem for the Year 2000'. 'Fuck the security!' Johns screamed. Then he repeated his antagonistic refrain, before returning to the song. Now it seemed as though both audiences and security were getting under Johns's skin. And the tour still had eight months left to run.

The notices for the tour were as mixed as Johns's attempts at humouring himself and his audience. Reviewing their March 4 Sydney show, the *Sydney Morning Herald* noted that 'what was meant to be a triumphant kick-off for the world tour was largely a forgettable evening.' Astutely, reviewer Jon Casimir wrote:

> Johns increasingly appears to be fronting another band. While his colleagues cling to casual (almost invisible) stage behaviour and costume, Johns is now resplendent in spangly shirt and shiny eye shadow ... he has also acquired the full catalogue of Rock God poses. There is a distance between the band members ... Johns seems self-conscious, as if age and experience have leached some of the raw joy from the job of performing.

Writing about their Melbourne Forum show in *Inpress* magazine, Greg Cormack observed not only that 'Johns was definitely running this show,' but that 'not a smile, not a high five or even a word seemed to be exchanged between the three throughout the set.'

Daniel Johns was experiencing the odd sensation of emerging from his shell onstage and yet feeling something close to contempt towards his audience. The anti-depressants weren't helping his confused state.

The band were in Chicago on March 15 when *Neon Ballroom* debuted at Number One on the Australian album chart, repeating the runaway success of *Frogstomp* and *Freak Show*. It went on to sell 204,000 copies at home. The album was also released that day in North America, making its debut on the US charts a week later, at Number 50. In Canada its first chart placing was 5, while the album's European chart debuts were the best of their career: 29 in the UK, 13 in Germany, and 23 in France. *Neon Ballroom* marked a strange turnaround for the band's commercial wellbeing.

In America, *Neon Ballroom* achieved roughly the same sales as *Freak Show* — 633,000 to *Freak Show*'s 620,000 — not a notch on *Frogstomp*'s two-million-plus sales, but a none-too-shabby effort when you realise that the charts that year were dominated by apple-pie pop from Britney Spears, Christina Aguilera and the way-too-cute Backstreet Boys. Rock radio, meanwhile, was dominated by the po-faced Creed. But sales of the band's third album increased elsewhere. It sold 101,000 copies in Germany, compared to *Freak Show*'s 68,000; 116,000 in Brazil, compared to its predecessor's 38,000; and 25,000 copies in Sweden, which was 8000 more than the previous two albums combined. On May 10, when 'Ana's Song (Open Fire)' debuted at Number 14 on the Australian singles chart, it became the band's eleventh consecutive Australian Top 40 single. Silverchair had become the most successful Australian chart performer of the 1990s.

And still Silverchair kept touring — and Johns continued to behave in comical, sometimes bizarre ways. At times it seemed as though he had moved beyond his audience, who still bayed for such older songs as 'Tomorrow' and 'Pure Massacre'. On other occasions he was quite clearly playing up his role as frontman: Why not give the crowd some razzle-dazzle to go with the rock? In Tampa, Florida, on May 2, Johns took up the persona of rock & roll evangelist again. 'Can I get a hallelujah?' he asked the crowd at the worryingly titled Rockstock festival. 'Let's hear it for Jesus!' he yelled. 'Let's hear it for Satan! Let's hear it for sex, drugs and fucking rock & roll!'

His bandmates were often uncomfortable with his strange turns. Joannou felt that Johns was challenging himself by digging a metaphorical hole on stage and then seeing how he could pull himself out. But it wasn't something the bassman enjoyed watching, especially when Johns turned abusive: 'Sometimes you thought, this is good, he's becoming his own person. Other times you thought, oh boy, where is he heading tonight? There was definitely a case of, "Just three more months, just three more months."'

Gillies, meanwhile, maintained his 'man of the people' role, signing autographs and chatting with fans at shows long after Johns had left the building. He figured it was a fair trade-off for not having Johns's responsibility as band mouthpiece. And he didn't mind the attention, either.

Another sign of Johns's increasingly unpredictable behaviour was the way that he vented his frustration towards his audience. If he wasn't grumbling about their lack of response, he was lecturing them on the subject of animal rights. In St Louis, after trying on his combination of 'Do you believe in Jesus?' and/or 'Do you believe in Satan?', he turned on the crowd at Pointfest (another cringingly titled summer festival).

'You guys are too quiet!' he yelled. 'I've tried but you aren't saying anything. We're going to play now so you shut the fuck up and we will play. Just sit there like you are and rock out like you fucking should!' Then during 'Freak', he gave the crowd the finger, and changed the lyrics to 'Body and soul/Suck my dick'.

Johns's onstage behaviour just kept getting stranger and angrier. In Boston on May 30 he posed the question: 'Do any of you believe in shooting ducks?' Clearly, not many in the crowd knew they were being addressed by an Animal Rights advocate (the band set up an Animal Liberation stand in the foyer at their Australian shows, and Johns even got himself an Animal Liberation tattoo), because when they replied in the affirmative, Johns shot back: 'Anyone who answered "yes" is a fuckwit.'

In Atlanta three nights later, a protest group calling itself Be Level-Headed picketed the Hard Rock Fest '99, where the band was playing, citing 'Suicidal Dream' and 'Israel's Son' as 'particularly offensive'. The band dropped both songs from their set, in response to a request from the event organisers. Mid-set, Johns stopped the show to point his finger at the church-related group that accused them of promoting violence: 'That's what we do with our music, we promote violence, according to the church. The church is always right. So we promote violence, sorry. Can I get a halle-fucking-lujah?' Johns then jammed 'Advance Australia Fair', a tune completely lost on the crowd.

Occasionally, Johns would slip up and hint at the source of his irritation. 'Thanks, that's our only hit,' he said after playing a desultory take on 'Tomorrow' in Denver. 'That's when we were an Australian teenage grunge sensation. Now we're just a rock band, according to the press.'

Despite Johns's wayward behaviour and the sometimes-indifferent responses to the shows, the band were still an A-list attraction. In Vancouver on July 14, Johns got into a shouting match with a surly punter while Hole's Courtney Love and Samantha Moloney looked on. In San Francisco, he remained uncommunicative throughout the band's set while Limp Bizkit's Fred Durst stood at the side of stage, mouthing most of Johns's lyrics.

It was still unclear whether Johns loved or hated his audience. When he wasn't getting into verbal sparring matches, he was inviting them up on stage to join in. He tried this out in Dallas in early June during 'Anthem for the Year 2000'; by tour's end in Australia it became a regular feature of a night with Silverchair. Once Johns had assembled a choir onstage, he would encourage them to chant 'We are the youth' at the top of their lungs. The lucky ones stood on a specially prepared choir stand, while wearing T-shirts printed by the band. It was anything-goes chaos.

But despite the many faces of Daniel Johns — Rock God, crowd-baiter, blasphemer, hit-and-miss comic, evangelist, choir master — he was still alienated from both bandmates and crowd. While Gillies, and sometimes Joannou and Holloway, were signing autographs and posing for snaps with fans after their shows, Johns would either be holed up on the bus or safely back in the hotel.

In Australia during July, Johns encouraged another on-stage invasion during 'Anthem'. 'Listen to me now, I am the boss,' Johns told the audience and security staff. 'Don't listen to anyone else!' But when one female fan tried to get too close to Johns, he freaked. 'Let go of me now,' he said. 'I've dealt with psychos enough this week.' A few days earlier, on July 26, Johns had been cleared of an allegation of harassment filed by one Jodie Ann Marie Barnes, another Silverchair obsessive.

There was another lap of Europe, supporting old buddies the Red Hot Chili Peppers, and a final fling in America, before they were ready for an album-closing circuit of Australia, in late November and early December. The some-times bizarre, physically and emotionally draining 'Neon Ballroom' tour ground to a halt in Sydney's Domain on December 11, when the band headlined the annual Homebake festival, a locals-only bash that had developed in the mid 1990s as a sort of 'all Aussies Big Day Out'. With Triple J having gone nationwide, and TV shows such as *Recovery* spreading the word about homegrown music, it was a good time for local bands — many of whom were inspired by Silverchair's success.

Silverchair had already announced that the Sydney Homebake show would be their last for at least a year. They were exhausted after the past five years, and needed a break from music, the road and each other. In an interview just prior to the show, Johns dreamed out loud of 'seeing friends and not being tied to a schedule. Stuff that doesn't involve promoting the band or being Mr Silverchair.' Backstage, the rumour spreading like a Chinese whisper was that this was it, the band was breaking up. Side stage, Natalie Imbruglia looked on, alongside her sister Laura. The pop star (and former *Neighbours* actress) had hooked up with Johns two months earlier at the ARIAs, where their relationship — which began when they'd met in London a year earlier — had blossomed as they locked into a deep, serious conversa-tion in the Gazebo Hotel, the location of the after-party for her record label, BMG. In fact, they were still talking the next morning, when they were spotted at a King's Cross bar.

Taking the stage after such bands as Powderfinger, Jebediah, Eskimo Joe and Deadstar, the sight of Johns in his amazing technicolour rocksuit — a purple, spangled, mirrored, custom-made rocksuit, no less — sent the Homebake crowd wild. Despite the success that many of the bands on the bill had experienced, none boasted a star like Johns. The band understood the significance of the event, too, so they'd invested more money in lights and visual effects. While playing festivals in Europe, earlier in the year, they had seen how big bands incorporate spectacular light shows into their performances. Silverchair wanted some of that, especially knowing that they'd be off the scene for some time to follow. 'We spent a lot of time on the lights because we wanted it to be remembered,' Gillies said afterwards.

Liberated by the fact that this was the end of the tour — and thrilled to be back in front of an Australian crowd — the band shed the year's baggage like an old skin. They poured themselves into 'Israel's Son', with Gillies — introduced to the crowd by Johns as '154 kilograms of glory!' — taking the lead, pounding his drum kit like it had done him wrong. Johns called for some 'hallelujahs', before the band unleashed the seesawing 'Emotion Sickness', with keyboardist Holloway doing a fair take on Helfgott's frenetic piano part.

By the time the band reached 'Miss You Love', the Domain had been transformed (as reported in *Rolling Stone*) into 'stadium rock proper, from the single spotlight on Johns for the first verse to the background drench of red in the chorus and the rapturous crowd singalong.' Not long after, Johns — as he'd done frequently during the *Neon Ballroom* shows — riffed on Lou Bega's 'Mambo Number Five' and Christina Aguilera's 'Genie in a Bottle', before tearing into 'Freak' and 'Anthem for the Year 2000'. He, Gillies and

Joannou then ran off stage, with the thunderous roar of 20,000 fans ringing in their ears.

'We're not supposed to do an encore,' Johns told the masses a few minutes later, 'but we'll do it because we love you.' They brought down the curtain on the night, the tour and the album with a roaring 'Spawn Again'.

'That show had a special chemistry,' Gillies said afterwards:

It was really the icing on the cake for the past six years. It was a new millennium, it was the end of *Neon Ballroom*, and it had been a really long haul and we all made it. It was like a celebration.

Joannou captured the band's mood and mixed emotions perfectly: 'As soon as we did the Homebake show and said "Thank you, goodnight," we went, "Hang on." It was weird. It was over too quickly.' Despite spending much of the tour wishing he were elsewhere, suddenly he didn't want it to end.

As the band drove back to Newcastle, they were readying themselves for a whole lot of nothing. While they settled back into their domestic routines, unsure if the band would tour or record again, Daniel Johns got busy writing a rock & roll opus.

Bibliography

'Eating Disorder Rocks Teen Star' *Courier-Mail* 04/03/1999; 'Emotion Sickness' Australian *Rolling Stone* May 1999; 'Ballroom Blitz' Australian *Rolling Stone* Yearbook 1999; 'Lethargic silverchair Fail to Fire' *Sydney Morning Herald* 8/03/1999; 'Feedback Section' *Inpress* 10/03/1999; '*Rolling Stone's* Gigs of the Decade' Australian *Rolling Stone* September 2000; 'Making of Diorama: The Resurrection of Daniel Johns' Australian *Rolling Stone* June 2002; 'The Uneasy Chair' Australian *Rolling Stone* September 2002; 'Silverchair's Greater View' Australian *Rolling Stone* April 2003

Miss You Love:

an interview with Elissa Blake

In 1999, Elissa Blake wrote the controversial and perceptive *Rolling Stone* cover story that revealed, in intimate detail, Daniel Johns's eating disorder. She was also the first journalist to cast eyes on his amazing swag of prescription drugs.

How long have you spent with Silverchair, and in what kind of situations?

My first contact with them was through a handful of phone interviews when I was a news reporter at the *Age* in Melbourne. It was around the time *Frogstomp* started to take off in America, and the band seemed genuinely shocked by their success. I think we were all shocked. It wasn't that they lacked talent or didn't deserve it, but success like that happens like a tidal wave. It's sudden and huge and somehow starts to be larger than the band itself.

Talking to Daniel and Ben in those days was like talking to your kid brother. They sniggered at the questions and answered with an 'I dunno' or 'it's all so weird' — that kind of thing. But I remember they were always so polite and grateful for their opportunities. They were never snotty.

Some of those stories went on the front page of the *Age*. They had the 'gee whiz' factor. The senior editors thought they were a novelty story because they were so young and Australia hadn't had a big chart success in the US since INXS.

What came next?

After that, I met them briefly at the ARIA awards, but didn't have closer contact until 1999, when I was writing the *Neon Ballroom* feature for *Rolling Stone*. By then, Daniel had started to look and behave like a troubled rock star. There was a lot of speculation within the Sydney music industry that something serious was happening with him. He looked dangerously thin and he seemed to be pulling away from the other band members. Chris and Ben seemed to be regular knockabout blokes who laughed a lot, had long-term girlfriends and surfed most days. Daniel had started wearing eye make-up, had gone vegan, seemed to be withdrawing emotionally, and was rumoured to be in an on-again-off-again relationship with Adalita from Magic Dirt. Adalita had talked about her own drug use, and now the media were starting to wonder if Daniel was using some kind of hard drug. Most suspected heroin.

The other huge rumour doing the rounds was that Daniel was gay and was either trying to hide it or was about to come out — either way, the rumour was that he was struggling with his sexuality. God knows where that rumour came from. All I know is the morning I went to the airport to fly to Brisbane with the band, I had in my mind that I had to ask Daniel about his sexuality and/or his heroin use, and I had no idea how I was going to do that.

What was your initial reaction when Daniel Johns started revealing the details of his eating disorder?

I was really shocked. I had never suspected he had an eating disorder. When you see a painfully thin rock star you tend to think drugs, not anorexia. It was incredible, and I was trying to hide my surprise so that he didn't get self-conscious and stop talking.

The topic came up when I asked him to talk me through each of the songs on *Neon Ballroom*. He told me the first track, 'Emotion Sickness', was about trying to maintain a normal state of mind to avoid the need for mood-altering medications. He was talking about depression within the first five minutes. I was surprised, but it seemed like he'd made a decision to talk openly; it was almost confessional. I abandoned my list of questions and just listened. Whenever he paused for a while, I just asked him to keep going. He didn't volunteer any personal information, but when I asked how he was feeling, he answered freely. I could have asked more, but I could see he had limits and wasn't about to spill all the details of his life — and nor should he have. He talked in a stop-start kinda way, making direct eye contact every now and then. He was gauging my reactions pretty closely, which is unusual in an interview. I'm sure he'd decided that week that he was going to talk openly to journalists about his depression and anorexia.

So you think it was premeditated?

He seemed resolved to speaking about it, and had obviously thought through it. I don't think it accidentally started spilling out in that interview. Some have said that maybe this was a calculated move, to spill all and sell more albums. But I don't think he had a choice. So much of the album was about his personal experiences, how could he not talk about it in interviews? I guess he could have made up stories to hide what the lyrics were about, but that would have been unsustainable. If he really wanted to keep it private, he'd have written a different album altogether. He said he wanted to express his feelings in his music and he wanted to help other teenagers who might be going through the same thing. It sounds idealistic, but I believe his motives were genuine.

This sounds ridiculous, but we were sitting in a hotel coffee shop doing the interview when this enormous late afternoon storm started blowing in across Brisbane. Daniel would say something really important about his thoughts on suicide and then a clap of thunder would break over our heads. It was creating a really weird atmosphere and we both knew it. At the end we were able to laugh about it. The mood couldn't have been more dramatic — it was almost silly.

Can you describe your reaction when he whipped out his stash of prescription drugs during the interview?

That was the most surprising moment. About an hour after our interview was over and we were just getting ready to get in the car to go to the soundcheck, Daniel suddenly pulls all his tablets out of his bag to show me. I hadn't asked for that; it was totally out of the blue. I wondered if he was trying to shock me — he had a smile on his face. But I think he himself was amazed by the number of tablets he was taking. It was like, 'Hey check it out!' I didn't know what to say. I mean, really, what are you supposed to say in these circumstances? He'd put them away in a flash, so it wasn't really discussed. I'd asked what they were all for and he claimed not to know. I don't think he wanted to discuss it any further.

He told you his eating disorder wasn't 'a reaction to fame or the pressure', but didn't actually reveal a root cause. Any theories?

I don't like to speculate. From my limited understanding, anorexia is often an attempt to control something when everything seems out of control. Daniel says he was simply trying to push how far he could go with it, like some weird not-eating experiment. I suspect that's a flippant answer and not the whole truth. I've heard anorexics say that at least they can control their bodies and have some order over what they do and don't eat. It's an area where no one can tell you what to do. But it can also be a lack of care for yourself, that you don't care about yourself enough to eat properly. Almost a rebellion against yourself. Sometimes someone feeling that way can be living so much in their heads and emotions that they neglect their bodies or don't care about them, as if eating is an annoying chore. It's hugely complex and different for everyone. Only Daniel knows what was really going on.

Is it typical of the man, from your perspective, for him to be so frank?

Daniel had always been pretty open in interviews. He'd never refused to answer a question or given a deliberately unhelpful answer. He seems to take interviews fairly seriously, as part of his job. I reckon he's the kind of guy who prefers to tell the truth and doesn't think he should have to hide things. Having said that, he rarely starts telling personal stories voluntarily. Like most musicians, he prefers to keep his private life private. But in this instance, it really seemed like he had something to say and he had to get it out. His music has become increasingly personal so we may hear him continue to talk openly about his life or he may choose to let the music do the talking in future.

Listening to Neon Ballroom before your interview, did you get a sense that he'd been through something very heavy? Did you view the album differently after the interview?

It was strange, because the lyrics seemed dark but his singing voice was so beautiful. I was really struck by the risks he was taking with his voice, really singing those high notes rather than the screaming style he used on the earlier songs. So it sounded like he was working some stuff out and things were shifting. The album had a lot of drama in it. After the interview, I was able to hear how delicate a lot of those lyrics were underneath the heaviness of the sound. I think a lot of people were touched by that.

Could you sense a distinct difference at the time between the personality of Daniel and those of Ben and Chris?

Yeah. I think at that time Daniel was trying to get back in touch with his sense of humour. Chris and Ben are such jokers and Daniel had been part of that, mugging at the camera and saying stupid stuff. But around that time, he seemed so much quieter, but as if really wanting to get that humour back. He's not the kind of guy who is deliberately dark or wallows in his darker emotions; he seems to prefer a happier state — you can hear that on *Diorama*.

Daniel is more introverted than Ben and Chris, and I guess you could say he has that artistic temperament where he can disappear into his own headspace. But that doesn't mean he's weird or reclusive or especially different. All three of them are pretty sensitive, funny guys.

Do you think that Johns would have this kind of fragile mental state, regardless of what he did for a living?

Again, it's impossible to say. He's definitely a man unafraid to express his emotions and he's highly creative. I think those qualities, and all the highs and lows that go with them, would be part of his life no matter what he was doing. Maybe if he'd had less pressure at such a young age he may have felt more in control of his life. But depression affects people in all occupations and at all different stages of life, so it's hard to say. He may have felt worse if he didn't have a creative outlet. He talks about music being a life force, so he's lucky he's found that.

Were you surprised when he fell ill, again, not long after making Diorama?

Yes, I was surprised. It seems incredibly unlucky. I wonder if he puts so much into his creative work that his body tends to pack it in if he doesn't get enough rest. That's pretty common. It just seems so extreme in Daniel's case. But I guess if he was just a regular person we wouldn't hear about his health; he's very much under the microscope.

From a magazine editor's perspective, what's your take on the Silverchair phenomenon?

I think they had great songs at the right time when they first started out. They have consistently struck a chord, lyrically and musically, with other young music fans. Add to that a teen idol quality in Daniel — girls love him. That can't be ignored but it doesn't belittle the quality of the band's records. Also, Daniel's openness has brought about an incredible loyalty from Silverchair fans. He's a survivor, and fans love that about him. I think they also appreciate his growing writing ability and the risks the band take on each new album. This isn't an arrogant band just trying to make money or have as much fun as possible. There's something musically exciting about them.

7

Love, Peace & *Diorama*

'I see all the musical qualities in Daniel I heard and saw in Brian Wilson. I know there's a lot of dark meat on that bird but lurking in there is the voice of the human spirit.'

—Van Dyke Parks, 2001

In 1994, Daniel Johns pointed to the row of houses on a hill overlooking Merewether, the snoozy seaside town where he, Gillies and Joannou grew up. With just a hint of disdain, he stated, 'the rich people live up there.' Nowadays, however, he lives right alongside them.

During 2000, the band spent their time off enjoying the spoils of several years' worth of hard slog. Joannou had bought a good-sized property on the NSW Central Coast, the former site of a bed and breakfast, encompassing a main dwelling, a guest house and a studio, for a little over a million dollars. Gillies, who lived in a rented apartment in Merewether, had bought several small properties in and around Newcastle. Johns, meanwhile, had found a home in the stretch of Merewether known as 'millionaire's row' — his home is now worth somewhere near $2 million.

But rock star chic it is not. It's almost as if Johns's anti-rock-star mindset has crept into his interior decorating. The spacious interior is decorated in a minimalist style: here a lampshade, there a Brett Whiteley print. There's a shining piano in his lounge room, on which he composed most of the band's fourth album, *Diorama*, during another long stretch spent alone with his dog. Next to the piano is a home entertainment centre, the kind so big you'd expect to see it in a multi-screen sports bar. Some of Johns's own art — a hobby he's pursued for years and a handy outlet when he's not writing music — is framed and scattered around the lounge room. The sun shimmers off a swimming pool, which looks pretty much unused. A telescope stands in an otherwise empty room. There's a home studio downstairs. The only real rock-star trapping is a framed copy of Black Sabbath's *Paranoid* album, a gift from former girlfriend Aimee Osbourne, who gave it to him for his 18th birthday.

The view of the Pacific Ocean from Johns's deck is stunning, virtually uninterrupted. A queue of tankers can be spotted on the horizon, awaiting their call to enter the industrial harbour of Newcastle. On some nights, their horns are the only noise that cuts through the silence. Five minutes down the road, Johns's parents live in what was once a typically modest Merewether house, but now, post makeover, is a stylish two-storey suburban home.

Daniel Johns has no problem with Merewether's drowsiness. In fact, he's so comfortable with the solitude that he rarely left the suburb during 2000 and 2001, as he began piecing together the songs for *Diorama*, the band's fourth album. On a typical day, he'd have only Sweep for company. His parents would phone, he'd say he was OK, he was working, don't worry. These days would fall into a familiar pattern: he'd drop Sweep at his parent's home; they'd walk his dog on the beach. Johns would go home, sit at his piano and continue working on his songs. But there was little of the darkness of early 1998, when he almost died. He was just lost in his songwriting — an obsession that led him, months later, to virtually live in the studio while they were recorded. Some nights during the writing it was just too much; there was music everywhere and Johns would wear earplugs to bed, because he 'could hear melodies in the cicadas outside'. Other nights he would put in an all-night stretch, wrestling with the kind of complex arrangements that would surprise some and shock many when *Diorama* was eventually released in April 2002.

One such session took place the night the sprawling 'Tuna in the Brine' was completed: 'I remember feeling so drained and so tired because I'd been thinking about all the parts for weeks,' Johns says. 'When I finished it, it must be the feeling people get when they do intense meditation. My body felt really long, my spine felt really elongated; it was like I was on top of the world, looking down on everything. It was better than any drug.' Even though the rain was belting down, Johns (with his ever-present dog) went and stood outside, soaking himself in an effort to come down from this natural high. Then he headed back inside and stood in the shower 'and pretended I was still in the rain'. He finally crashed at about 6.30 in the morning.

Johns insists that this obsessive, hermitic behaviour is normal for him, almost expected. Although he didn't speak the actual words, he was clearly thinking back to the time prior to the making of *Neon Ballroom*. He had been in a worse way before, and his family were starting to accept this reclusiveness as part of his nature. 'They've seen me much worse,' he insisted. One of Johns's new songs, 'The Greatest View', recognised that his family were watching out for him, without being intrusive. He knew he was a lucky man.

Silverchair only came up for air twice between their head-lining spot at the 1999 Homebake Festival and the release of 'The Greatest View', *Diorama*'s first single, in February 2002. They appeared at Victoria's Falls Festival on New Year's Eve 2000 and then at Rock in Rio three weeks later. It was off-stage that most Silverchair activity happened during 2000, when they split, very publicly, from their label Sony.

The split was a difficult one. While re-negotiating their Sony contract, having now delivered the agreed three albums, Watson insisted the band be signed directly to Sony America for releases in the world outside of Australia. This would elim-inate the label's requirement to pay a 'matrix royalty' back to Sony Australia. It would also give the label the incentive to work the band's records harder, particularly in North America, because profits would stay in-house. Watson felt Silverchair needed 'someone in Sony behind a desk in New York whose fortunes would rise and fall with that of the band'. But it was too big an ask; if the label agreed, they would have had to set up the same kind of deal for stars Ricky Martin (who was signed to Sony Latin America) and Celine Dion (signed to Sony Canada).

When Sony passed, Watson stitched up a lucrative deal with Atlantic in America, as well as setting up his own bou-tique label, Eleven, in October 2000. Eleven would release Silverchair's music locally, with manufacturing, distribution and publicity handled by EMI. The Atlantic deal — particu-larly in light of what would happen with *Diorama*, commercially, outside of Australia — was especially sweet. It was 'frontloaded', which essentially meant that the band would receive a hefty advance regardless of the record's for-tunes, whereas in Australia their deal was 'backended', which meant a higher royalty rate on sales. 'We've done better with this record than any other,' Watson admits – quite a revelation, given that *Diorama* became their poorest-selling record, globally, by several hundred thousand copies.

The band's departure from Sony also ended — temporarily — their relationship with John O'Donnell, who, along with Watson, had launched the whole crazy trip in 1994, when they signed the band to Murmur. He was, understandably, gutted by their departure. 'It was heartbreaking,' he said. 'It was like walking away from mates. But I totally understood why they left; I would have done the same thing.' O'Donnell would leave Sony a little over a year after Silverchair, and in a happy coincidence, he now heads EMI.

Sony retaliated to the break-up by releasing a two-CD greatest hits set in November 2000, which the band refused to help promote. (In 2002 Sony quietly released the *Silverchair: The Best of Volume 1* set, a repackaged single-CD version of the greatest hits set.) 'I have no qualms with the songs,' Joannou told *Rolling Stone*, when *The Best of: Volume 1* appeared, 'but it's nothing that Silverchair would have liked to do in their career. It's something you do when you're retired.'

The first Eleven Records release was an unexpected treat. Johns had developed a strong bond with Paul Mac, who'd played piano on *Neon Ballroom* and had remixed the song 'Freak'. They strengthened their rapport during 2000 when they collaborated on the experimental five-track *I Can't Believe It's Not Rock* EP, a record so deliberately underplayed that on release in December 2000 it was sold only via the Internet, with some of the proceeds going to charity.

Johns and Mac premiered some of their songs with a performance on the ABC TV drama *Love Is a Four Letter Word*, an episode that was filmed not long after the EP's release and aired in April 2001. Mac played keyboards and Johns —

decked out in porn-star shades and one of the most garish cardigans ever seen on the small screen — sang and played guitar, grinning madly. It didn't seem to matter that the performance wasn't live; they were both having a blast. The program's producer, Rosemary Blight, couldn't praise their performance enough. 'Daniel Johns was fantastic,' she gushed. 'He arrived with the brilliant Paul Mac, played great music, sent the crowd wild.' Johns rounded off a big day out by smiling for photos, signing autographs and playing soccer with the series' star, Peter Fenton, former frontman for indie rock band Crow. No one in the Sydney studio knew what an emotional struggle it had been for Johns to get to this point.

After the *Neon Ballroom* tour, Johns was determined to wean himself off the anti-depressants that had kept him going throughout '98 and '99. It was tough therapy. Johns also returned to the therapist's couch, an experience he found 'uncomfortable', but more rewarding than in the past. 'All of a sudden,' he said, as his anti-depressant dependency waned, 'I started appreciating the ups, which I hadn't felt for such a long time.' It was around this period of recovery that Johns and Mac started to piece together *I Can't Believe It's Not Rock*. 'This was never a record we set out to make,' Johns said on the EP's release. 'It happened by accident, but now that it's done, I really like it.'

(While all this was happening, Joannou was spending time with his girlfriend, Sarah McLeod, and Gillies took a job at Sound World records in Hunter Street, Newcastle, stocking shelves and ringing up sales. Not used to the 9-to-5 grind, today he says, 'I don't know how I lasted six months.')

The Mac/Johns partnership was an unlikely liaison. Before going gold with his 2001 solo album *3000 Feet High* — also released by Eleven — Sydneysider Mac was best known for his role with drug-guzzling dance duo Itch-E and Scratch-E. He left his mark on the local industry when, while collecting a Best Dance Artist ARIA in 1995, he publicly thanked Australia's Ecstasy dealers. He's that kind of guy: funny, open and as affectionate as a headful of the 'love drug'. These are not the kind of traits you'd ascribe to Johns, who's troubled, insular and cautious around everyone except those few people he believes don't want a part of him. He doesn't trust too many people, but he connected powerfully with Mac.

'I love the guy,' Johns told me, without hesitation, while he was recording *Diorama*:

> **Music is our middle ground but we have a really good friendship. There's something about when we play music together. It's great.**

> **He's really important to me. When I was writing *Diorama* a lot of people were really reserved about giving me an opinion but he stood up and said, 'Do it. It's a good thing.'**

Their connection, however, ran deeper than just the music. When Johns was in his anti-depressant stupor after the *Neon Ballroom* world tour, he'd spend days with just Sweep for company, rarely leaving the house. His on-again, off-again relationship with Natalie Imbruglia was in an off-again phase. Even when he and Mac started work on *I Can't Believe It's Not Rock*, Johns still had days when he had to be prised from the couch.

The first part of the collaboration happened at Mac's home studio in the Blue Mountains, when Johns would travel down from Merewether to jam and hang out. There was one day, in particular, when Johns just couldn't face the trip to

Mac's home. Mac knew the solution. He jumped in his car, drove the two hours from his Blue Mountains home to Johns's spread in Newcastle, and played chauffeur for the day. Their bond was formed.

Johns's psychological recovery moved up another gear when he agreed to play both the Falls Festival and Rock in Rio. Both appearances were significant. Scotching the rumours that their Homebake finale was the end of the band, they agreed to ringing in 2001 at the Falls Festival, an annual alt-rockfest held at Lorne, a coastal town a couple of hours drive west of Melbourne. The festival stretched over two days, with the midnight New Year's Eve slot reserved for the headliner. As was their way, Joannou and Gillies arrived earlier on the day, drifting through the crowd and checking out other bands on the bill, including Machine Gun Fellatio and the Vandals. Johns, however, arrived with just enough time to change and prepare himself for the set. Wearing a knee-length, fully sequinned coat, every bit as extraordinary as the one he sported during the final shows of the *Neon Ballroom* tour, Johns led the band through a favourites-heavy set, including a slightly reworked 'Ana's Song' and 'Freak'. They also debuted two new songs planned for their fourth album, 'One Way Mule' and 'Hollywood'. 'It was great, we had a ball,' Joannou reported from backstage after the well-received set. By that time, Johns was well and truly out of there.

The band's next public appearance, three weeks later, would be the biggest of their career. Silverchair hadn't toured South America since the craziness of 1996, but were invited back for a key spot on the Rock in Rio Festival, the largest rock & roll gathering in the world, described by many as a cross between the Big Day Out, Woodstock and Britain's mammoth Glastonbury Festival. And then multiplied by 10.

In fact, it had been the invitation to Rock in Rio that had motivated the band to play the Falls Festival. When the pitch was made to Johns by Watson, it was done speculatively. Johns had been the key instigator in the band's decision to take at least a year off. He was tired of touring, tired of playing live, and needed to get his head back together. But now, 12 months on from the millennium-closing Homebake gig, he felt enthused enough to play the higher profile shows. Working with Mac had helped him rediscover the joy of making music. He was now up for returning to his Silver-life.

Understanding the enormity of an invitation to Rock in Rio, Gillies's was shocked at Johns's enthusiasm: 'I thought, Holy fuck! We'd just had this weird tour, things were a bit rocky, we weren't sure if we were going to stay together.' With renewed commitment, the band rented a space in Newcastle and put in six weeks of serious rehearsals. It was as though the tension surrounding the *Neon Ballroom* period had disappeared.

Established by Brazilian promoter Roberto Medina in 1985, Rock in Rio was far too ambitious an enterprise to hold annually. In fact, the 2001 event was only the third Rock in Rio. And it was coming at a particularly difficult time in rock festival history. Woodstock '99 was marred by riots, insufferable heat, violence and reports of rape in the moshpit. And Denmark's Roskilde Festival, where Silverchair had played in 1997, was still reeling from the fallout of the horrible surge during Pearl Jam's set in 2000, in which nine fans died. Even Australia's Big Day Out had paid a price, when 16-year-old Jessica Michalik died from a heart attack in January 2001 after being crushed during Limp Bizkit's show in Sydney.

The vibe at Rock in Rio, however, was uniformly positive. Sure, the Porta-Loos overflowed and most of the 250,000-per-day crowd — for seven days in the midst of a predictably sizzling Brazilian summer — headbanged ankle-deep in the mud created by high pressure water hoses that regularly sprayed the crowds. But this was an angst-free, good-natured rock & roll celebration. Patronised by Brazilian teenagers starved of live (Western) rock bands, it was a massive success, and raised around US$1.5 million for local educational charities. As for the crowd, they spraypainted their hair every colour of the rainbow and flaunted T-shirts that screamed 'Fuck me I'm famous'. Inflatable sharks bounced around the massive moshpit like beach balls at a Grateful Dead show.

The stage was a monumental piece of engineering. Forty metres high and 90 metres wide, it was built from 200 tonnes of steel. The bizarre stage set was cheekily described by *Rolling Stone* as having been modelled 'after a spiny mollusc or a female-pleasuring device'. Oasis's Noel Gallagher passed judgement on the stage setting, massive crowd and the entire event when he roared to a journalist, 'It's actually fucking genius. It's the most disgusting, brilliant, outrageous thing I've seen in my life.'

The festival's first six days were a musical rollercoaster ride. Axl Rose proved that Guns 'n' Roses were both alive and kicking with a memorable set (although, true to temperamental character, he insisted a punter wearing a 'Fuck Guns 'n' Roses' T-shirt be evicted). Rose even introduced into his band's Vegas rock act a samba outfit, who marched through the crowd while the band played on. On subsequent nights, ageless grunge godfather Neil Young kicked out the jams, Foo Fighters did it for the moshpit, and Britney Spears was booed, loudly, when the image of an American flag appeared behind her during the song 'Lucky'.

Silverchair were the penultimate act on the event's final night, proving just how big a drawcard they were. Only the Red Hot Chili Peppers — whose drummer, Chad Smith, revisited the good times of 1996 when he hooked up with the band the night before — were billed above the Newcastle three.

On the band bus heading to the show, Joannou summed up the band's feelings: 'It's beyond being nervous,' he said:

I mean, even 100,000 people is incomprehensible. I remember back to 1996 when we played the [Royal Sydney] Easter Show and that was like 25,000 people — and we were just there going, 'Wow.' So the prospect of over 250,000 just doesn't register.

Things got even more edgy when the band arrived at the site and were told there was a scheduling mistake — they didn't have two hours before showtime, they had exactly 45 minutes. From backstage, Joannou took a peek at the crowd and returned with his verdict. 'Oh my God,' he told the rest of the band, 'this is ridiculous.' A week before, he'd been chilling out on his couch at home on the Central Coast. Now 250,000 people were screaming for him and the band.

When they took the stage to a deafening roar, it was as if Johns's spangled coat had transformed him from Mr Introspection into the definitive rock star. The band opened their set with a blazing 'Israel's Son', Johns pulling off some wild rock moves. As the set progressed, the band mixed up the moods, playing the mellower 'Ana's Song' and 'Miss You Love' alongside the moshpit faves 'Pure Massacre' and 'Slave'. They also aired the new tracks 'Hollywood' and 'One Way Mule'. Being a one-off show, Johns seemed liberated; he had no concerns about playing the same songs for another crowd the next night. He playfully thanked the crowd in Portuguese and even made a strange aside about being a friend of Ronaldo, the Brazilian soccer star, which, naturally, no one believed. As the heat intensified, the water cannons were turned up, just a notch.

But that didn't stop a massive singalong during the opening verse of 'Anthem for the Year 2000'. It was so loud, in fact, that Johns stopped playing, clapping his hands above his head as 250,000 fans screamed his lyrics right back at him. The song had come to Johns in a dream about rocking a massive stadium crowd. Now that dream was coming to life before his stunned eyes.

The band closed the set with a screaming take on 'Freak', Joannou and Gillies bounding off stage as Johns drenched the audience in a spray of feedback. This time, post-gig, he didn't disappear; the three hung around for a time backstage with fans, posing for photos and scribbling autographs. Johns beamed. The band had played the biggest show of their lives. They'd even reconnected with Kevin Shirley, who mixed the band's live sound for the mammoth TV broadcast of the event (when he wasn't hanging out with Led Zep's Jimmy Page). When Johns headed back to their hotel, Joannou, Gillies and various members of the band's management and crew kicked on at a local strip club, where they witnessed the bizarre sight of a transvestite disrobing to Midnight Oil's 'Beds Are Burning'.

The next day, Johns's face was splashed all over the front page of the local newspaper, *O Globo*, which described their set as the 'surprise highlight of the day'. It left them wondering whether it was Silverchair or the Red Hot Chili Peppers who'd closed Rock in Rio III. Gillies summed it up when he declared: 'Rock in Rio was undoubtedly the most amazing experience we've ever had as a band. The crowd was incredible; I've never seen anything like it.' As for Johns, he was thankful that the lengthy flight home from Brazil gave him and his bandmates time to slowly return to earth. When he did, he remembered that he had a new album to write.

As cohesive as it sounds, *Diorama* was an album with a false start. The lengthy, exhausting *Neon Ballroom* tour had wrapped in December 1999, and Johns had started writing new songs during 2000 and early 2001. But he felt dissatisfied with the music he was making; the songs seemed too easy, too familiar, full of the crashing riffs and heavy feelings that had marked the band's first two albums, *Frogstomp* and *Freak Show*, and to a lesser extent *Neon Ballroom*.

Johns's frustration reached a peak in February 2001, soon after returning from South America. He spent two virtually sleepless weeks walking Merewether beach and fretting about whether he'd ever move forward with his songwriting. At the end of this period of uncertainty, he made a big decision. He erased the two hours worth of material he'd recorded so far. 'They just sounded too much like the last album,' he told me, when I covered the making of the album for *Rolling Stone*. 'I knew it was a risk, but I [also] knew if I kept them they'd be a safety net.'

Not surprisingly, the act was extremely liberating for Johns. And gradually, *Diorama*'s songs started to come. The elegant 'Luv Your Life', the sprawling 'Tuna in the Brine', the hook-heavy 'The Greatest View': these were all written after he'd scrubbed those early songs. Ignoring even his bandmates, Johns previewed the new tunes only to his brother, Heath, manager John Watson and Paul Mac.

Mac might have developed a rapport with Johns during the creation of their own EP, but he wasn't ready for the shock of the songs Johns was preparing for *Diorama*. 'I didn't get it,' Mac laughed when I asked him how he reacted to Johns's new music. 'Because he's not [musically] trained, here's this incredibly complicated stuff. I was going, "Fuck, what is this?"' Mac's new role was to act as musical translator, helping

Johns get on paper the music he was hearing in his head. Later on, Mac also contributed several piano parts to the album.

Mac's surprise at the new material was shared by Joannou and Gillies. Prior to the recording that was planned to begin in April, Gillies and Joannou got a call from Johns to visit him at home. For Johns, there was some of the same trepidation he had felt unveiling the *Neon Ballroom* songs. But this time around, he was more assured. He lit a joint, sat down at his grand piano and played 'Tuna in the Brine' to the Silver-pair. As he recalled later, 'Ben said, "How the fuck are we going to remember that?" It was great.'

'We sat around and he played them one by one for me,' the ever-amiable Gillies recalled, in September 2001. 'He said things like "This one sounds Beach Boys-y." It was very cool.' Joannou made a neat understatement when he commented that 'Some of the arrangements were quite complex.' Not only did Johns have the thumbs-up from Mac, his bandmates were on board with the new music he was writing.

It was just the encouragement he needed to keep going with these bold, cinematic pieces of music, songs that were the logical step forward from such *Neon Ballroom* tracks as 'Emotion Sickness' and 'Miss You Love'. But this time there was a key difference — he wasn't digging into his heart of darkness for themes. Johns was opening up to the world around him. It also helped that for the first time he was writing on piano and recording music on reliable home-recording gear (which Mac had helped install), instead of banging out demos on his guitar and recording them on cheap cassettes as he'd done in the past. Now he could experiment with vocal ideas and more complex arrangements before the band hit the studio proper. It was to have a major impact on *Diorama*.

Choosing a producer wasn't as easy for *Diorama* as for their first three albums. *Frogstomp*, *Freak Show* and *Neon Ballroom* were rock albums, in essence, so they needed a producer who could translate that raw rockin' energy to tape. Now the band needed someone different, someone who could understand where Johns was heading. This was an entirely different band to the rocking runts who blitzed the world with 'Tomorrow' six years earlier.

The band's new American label, Atlantic Records, proposed a shortlist of producers. Watson was keen for the band — especially Johns — to work with someone fresh, someone who would push him into the new directions his songwriting was taking. Launay wasn't on the shortlist, in part because he was too familiar to the band, but he listened to the demos, and put forward a couple of names as possible producers: Midnight Oil's Jim Moginie, who knew and understood the band and their work, having contributed various parts to *Neon Ballroom*; and Brian May, the guitarist for Queen. The epic scope of these songs reminded Launay of Queen's *A Night at the Opera* and he felt that May would connect with that. Both were first-rate ideas, but not what Atlantic and the band had in mind.

American Michael Beinhorn, who'd worked with nu-metal giants Korn, as well as Soundgarden and the Red Hot Chili Peppers, was the first producer agreed on by the band and Atlantic. While the trio fine-tuned the songs in three months of rehearsals, after returning from Rock in Rio, they waited for Beinhorn to finish Korn's latest album, *Untouchables*. But eventually they ran out of patience, and the deal fell through. In hindsight, this was fortunate, because Johns needed someone who could bring out what he would call the 'colours' and 'light' in his new songs; Beinhorn specialised in modern rock miserablists. Other contenders for the production job included Americans Bob Rock and Bob Ezrin, the latter a highly regarded veteran who'd produced albums for Lou Reed and Alice Cooper.

The nod eventually went to Canadian-born, British-based David Bottrill, a bookish type with a shaved skull, glasses and a thoughtful nature. He'd produced albums by skilled met-allers Tool, art-rockers King Crimson, baroque pop guy Peter Gabriel — even belter Toni Childs — so he'd proved his diversity. Bottrill's work with Tool proved he could handle heavy sounds, but his production work with Gabriel was just as impressive. The erstwhile Genesis frontman was a song-writer who shared Johns's anything-goes ambition.

After one meeting in LA, and several pricey phone conver-sations between Johns, Watson and Bottrill, band and producer first hooked up in June 2001, in the band's comfort zone of Newcastle. (The band had already thoroughly demoed the songs at Mangrove Studios in April.) Every morning at 10.30 they'd convene with Bottrill, work through the new songs, plot out their recordings, then disappear until the next day. Not since they were teenagers had the band made music in the morning. It wasn't done on a whim; Johns was making a very conscious effort not to replicate what he called the 'night ori-entated' vibe of *Neon Ballroom*. Instead he wanted an album that was all new sensations. Playing before lunch was one of these. 'I was trying to reverse things this time around,' Johns said, but added that 'it was really weird to play music' so early in the day.

'They're absolutely world class, without question,' Bottrill said of Silverchair, when I spoke with him in September 2001. 'Everybody in this band is of the highest quality I've ever worked with.' Clearly their producer didn't mind the early starts, either.

Sessions for *Diorama* began in July at Sydney's Studio 301, the ground zero for most well-budgeted local recordings of the past 10 years. (While Silverchair took over Studio One, the Whitlams and Midnight Oil were recording *Torch the Moon* and *Capricornia*, respectively, elsewhere in the complex.) Erecting the Silverchair table-tennis table was one of the first priorities for the band, as they settled into 301. As always, videographer Robert Hambling was everywhere, recording the making of the album for the 2002 DVD *Across the Night: The Creation of* Diorama. Engineer Anton Hagop was producer Bottrill's quietly spoken, super-efficient sidekick (and went on to win an ARIA for his work). Assistant engineer Matt 'Gizmo' Lovell helped out on the technical side, and then, at the close of business each day, would document the day's events for the band's website.

Basic tracks were recorded during July and August. Paul Mac chimed in on piano. Midnight Oil's Jim Moginie, who'd played on seven of *Neon Ballroom*'s tracks, added some keyboard squiggles to 'The Greatest View' and 'One Way Mule'. The latter was the only song Johns had saved from the tape he'd scrapped earlier in the year. Bassist Joannou and drummer Gillies spent a lot of time playing ping-pong with Watson, but Daniel Johns rarely left the control room. He was absorbed in the making of this record.

In late September 2001, the band (plus Bottrill, his two engineers and Johns's dog Sweep) had shifted camp to Mangrove Studios, the tranquil and very desirable musician's escape owned by INXS bassist Garry Gary Beers. Here they started to experiment with some of the songs, adding extra texture to the basic recordings laid down at 301. Johns's mood was up – the songs were coming together almost as he had planned them in his head. The only interruption was when a crew visited from cable station Channel [v] to announce that, even though they'd been the invisible men of rock during the past year, the band had won their fifth consecutive Viewer's Choice award. Johns, Gillies and Joannou laughed their way through the interview, which was aired at October's ARIA awards. 'We know other bands deserved it,' Johns mugged to the camera, 'but we're the 'Chair!'

By early October, the band was back in Sydney, at 301, confronting the most challenging — and costly — stage of the recording: the orchestration for six of the album's tracks. Johns co-composed the arrangements for three of these songs — 'The Greatest View', 'World Upon Your Shoulders' and 'My Favourite Thing' —with Larry Muhoberac, whose last encounter with Johns was when the singer, in his green beanie, had lain on the floor shouting out the notes to *Neon Ballroom*'s 'Emotion Sickness'. After this was the real glittering prize: a fortnight with the legendary Van Dyke Parks, who penned the orchestral arrangements for 'Across the Night', 'Tuna in the Brine' and 'Luv Your Life', writing parts for strings, woodwind, brass, harp and percussion.

The 60-something Parks is 24-carat rock & roll royalty. Born in Atlanta but based in California, he collaborated with Beach Boy Brian Wilson on his great lost album, *Smile*, and is often cited as the man who steered Wilson away from the more commercially orientated Beach Boys, freeing his music while helping to mess up his mind. Parks also co-wrote the classic 'Heroes and Villains' (and the not-so-classic 'Vegetables').

Described as 'some mad cross of Stephen Sondheim, Burt Bacharach, Cole Porter and Randy Newman' and the 'cult figure of all cult figures', Parks has worked his sonic alchemist's trick on albums from the Byrds, Fiona Apple, Ry

Cooder and U2. He's also spun some magic on his own hugely eccentric albums, recorded intermittently when he wasn't working with others. These records included 1968's *Song Cycle* and 1984's *Jump!*, which was a bizarre attempt to mould a pop opera out of the Uncle Remus tales of Chandler Harris (complete with all their very un-PC dialect).

Avuncular and often downright hilarious, Parks is a studio master, but not so self-obsessed that he couldn't recognise a spark in Johns that he recalled from his own musical youth. 'I see all the musical qualities in him I heard and saw in Brian Wilson,' he told me, during the only interview he granted while in Australia:

> [Daniel's] an undefeated romantic; an informed optimist. I know there's a lot of dark meat on that bird but lurking in there is the voice of the human spirit.

> When I got the new material, I was astounded by the musicality, the lyrics, brimming with enthusiasm and a life force that guarantees this group as a continuing major force in music.

Or as David Fricke put it:

> Van Dyke Parks doesn't work with clowns. He's got very high standards about music and musicality. The fact that he worked with them on *Diorama* is as much a tribute to what Daniel can do as a songwriter and the band can do as players as the fact that Van Dyke Parks has eclectic tastes. He doesn't just take a job for the sake of taking a job.

Mind you, Parks almost didn't make the trip at all. When Johns said he was hearing lush, cinematic arrangements for many of these new songs, Watson had put forward Parks's name, adding, 'but I think he's dead'. (Parks found the anecdote so funny that he now sometimes signs off his emails as 'the recently deceased Van Dyke Parks.') Johns wasn't familiar with Parks's work, but got very interested when Watson learned he was both alive and kicking (and still making music). Johns vividly recalls their first phone conversation: 'The first thing we heard was Van Dyke on the other end, playing the piano. I thought we were on hold before I realised. That was a good lesson: sometimes it's best to give yourself up musically rather than saying something.'

These phone conversations are hilariously documented on the *Across the Night* DVD, as Parks outlines his orchestral needs and dollar signs collect at the bottom of the screen. Even though the 9/11 terrorist attacks in New York delayed Parks's arrival by a fortnight, the connection between him and Johns was deep and true.

'I know a lot of talented guys, I've worked with them — I've almost made a career out of surrounding myself with talented people,' said Parks, in his unreasonably modest way, during a rare moment of downtime at Studio 301:

I've been very fortunate. I'm a musical grunt in LA, I work in the TV and film industry. This offer came out of the ether; it was a blessing.

When I looked into this work, immediately I wanted to weep. I thought the vocalist was in dead earnest; I liked that person, I wanted to know who he was.

And this beat seeing David Crosby in a jacuzzi. This is someone I wanted to know.

Silverchair's early music had been implanted in Parks's mind, almost subliminally – his children were big fans of the band's debut album, *Frogstomp*: 'It was throbbing through the walls, especially when they had guests. I got curious about it, but could never have imagined that I would be fortunate enough to work on a project of theirs.' Parks recognised that the music Johns was now writing was far more advanced than the simple riff and roar that won over his children. He also recognised that development as a mark of the musically gifted. 'All of the artists I like have a tendency to do that,' he figured, 'to leave me in shock. The artist has a special faculty for pulling along his or her audience and with difficulty they move forward with them. It can get kind of dull if the artist rests on their laurels.'

Johns would have loved more time to work with Parks, but they did conjure up some true musical magic in the two weeks. The orchestrations are signature Van Dyke Parks: epic, sweeping and dramatic, full of rich sonic detail and golden melodies. The best songs of Daniel Johns's life had been transformed into the band's best recordings and some of Parks's finest work. It said a lot about how rewarding it was for Johns to work with people he trusted and respected.

But by early December, the singer's mood had changed. He'd been in Los Angeles for a fortnight, mixing the album with Bottrill. Throughout the making of the album, the band's American record label, Atlantic Records, had liked what they were hearing, but they still hadn't heard that one song they felt would get the band airplay on the Rock and Modern Rock radio stations. These were the only radio formats that played Silverchair in North America. Atlantic's concerns reached a peak while Johns was absorbed with finishing the mix of the album. They expected him to pull a hit single out of his hat.

But writing a song to order wasn't Johns's specialty, especially when he had almost finished work on Silverchair's most accomplished and detailed record. When I met him in LA, briefly, he was moody and sullen, clearly distracted by the demands of Atlantic. In the past he'd been shielded, wisely, by Watson, from many of the machinations of the record industry — now he was coming face to face with the commercial expectations of a major label. This was a new and weird environment for him. Added to this was increasing pain in his knees, an early sign of his reactive arthritis.. Eventually, a compromise was reached when Johns wrote the song 'Ramble'. The last laugh was on the record company suits: this watered-down, by-the-numbers rocker ended up as a B-side for the 'Without You' single.

The first music to be released from *Diorama* was the defiant single 'The Greatest View', a very clear statement from Johns about the new, positive state of both his mind and his music. It debuted on Australian radio on December 21, 2001, the day after the video had been shot in Brisbane. When 'The Greatest View' was made available on chairpage before its official release, it rapidly became the most downloaded song in Australian music history. Ten thousand copies of the single were streamed, far outstripping the previous record holder, Paul Kelly, whose song 'Somewhere in the City' didn't even make it to a thousand downloads. It was another smart move on Silverchair's part — what better way to re-connect with your fans than by offering them a free song?

'The Greatest View' galloped into the Australian singles chart, debuting at Number One on February 4. Its timing was perfect, because the band had just completed a live return as part of the 2002 Big Day Out. Almost three years had slipped by since the release of *Neon Ballroom*, and the rock public were Silverchair-hungry. The successful launch was a great relief for the band, given that they'd spent so much time out of the spotlight, and during their period of reflection and recovery, Brisbane band Powderfinger had taken over as the country's favourite alternative rock band. Powderfinger's fourth album, *Odyssey Number Five*, sold 400,000 copies locally, a level Silverchair still haven't matched at home, and the band had scooped the ARIA awards in 2001. But their lush and tuneful songs didn't have that hint of obsessiveness heard in Johns's best songs, and their frontman, Bernard Fanning, couldn't match Johns in the enigma department.

In his first round of press for *Diorama*, Johns repeated the words 'light', 'energy' and 'positive' like a mantra. 'The Greatest View' encapsulated that; Johns described it to me as a song written for his parents, who have always watched over him, even when he was deep in depression at the end of the '90s. But that may not be the only interpretation, given the serious time Johns had spent in therapy. When a song opens with the line 'You're the analyst', it wouldn't be a stretch to think some of his on-couch experiences influenced the lyric.

Gillies echoed Johns's thoughts on the record, even if he expressed it in simpler terms:

We're really excited about it, it's really different. A lot of our stuff in the past has been kind of dark, so this is really quite uplifting. It's a happy album, which is cool.

If we were a band that kept doing the same thing over and over we'd get bored shitless with it. That's when people start fighting and generally bands break up. That's an advantage we've had, that we've always done things differently.

'It's not a record that is born out of misery, it's a record that is born out of optimism,' producer Bottrill told the *Sun Herald* in January 2002, describing Johns as 'much more into the positive aspects of life now. Misery is easier than joy, I think, but ultimately joy is more satisfying,' and confessing, 'It's rare that you get to the end of a project and you're not sick of each other, but this was more like a relationship that I didn't want to end. I miss them all.'

A lot had changed since the teen-angst-by-numbers of their first two albums, or the heavy neuroses of *Neon Ballroom*. *Diorama* was a synthesis — and a refinement — of everything Silverchair had recorded over the past eight years. Johns readily admitted that the three songs featuring the band's trademark grunt ('One Way Mule', 'The Lever' and 'Too Much of Not Enough') were included for the benefit of those long-term fans who had stuck with them since 1994. Yet to Johns they were afterthoughts, songs that didn't 'fill any holes in my soul'. But it was a compromise he was willing to make. Commercial suicide was not a step that would thrill the band's management or record company, who'd made a considerable financial investment in *Diorama*. Johns realised that his audience could only be coaxed along, step by step, into his new music.

'There's always an element of compromise,' he said:

You can't deny that. It's always there when you've got people who've supported you and bought your albums and gone to your shows, you have to say, 'Here's a song for you.' It's for the loyal people. Hopefully the other songs will challenge them.

It's hard for bands to make the transition and still be taken seriously. But we were fourteen and our fans were fourteen; we have to change. They've grown with our music, hopefully.

So while this trio of songs harked back to *Frogstomp* and *Freak Show*, such moodpieces as 'The Greatest View' and 'World Upon Your Shoulders' were natural steps forward from the rich melodies found on *Neon Ballroom*'s 'Paint Pastel Princess' and 'Ana's Song (Open Fire)'. But even though Johns still had some very dark days, he was pushing himself to generate a more positive, uplifting message with his songs. He was older, he was off anti-depressants, he was eating again, he was in love with Natalie Imbruglia, his occasional girlfriend since 1999, who was now becoming a stabilising influence on his life — and he was coming closer to realising the music he was hearing in his head. He didn't want to return from a lengthy break with *Neon Ballroom: the Sequel*.

While the combination of his music and words created more good vibrations than at any other point in the band's career, Johns's lyrics, when viewed in isolation, still made strange reading. But he was willing to defend them to the death. He stated that he preferred these lyrics to any others he'd written. 'It's really open to interpretation,' he accepted, 'but some of them are quite magical.' Sometimes, however, his 'feel good at any cost' message got lost in clunky prose. 'The Greatest View' opens with the couplet 'You're the analyst/ The fungus in my milk', which was almost as peculiar as 'There is no bathroom and there is no sink/ The water out of the tap is very hard to drink', from 'Tomorrow'. And there was a spooky, though clearly unintended prescience in the very Beach Boys-like opening track, 'Across the Night', in which Johns sings that he 'hugged a man's arthritic shoulder'.

But few rock lyrics stand up to this kind of English Lit 101 analysis; it's the combination of voice and music and emotion and electricity that makes for the best rock music. And that's where *Diorama* succeeds. At its core it is a complex, musically and emotionally rich and challenging album. Its moods shift between epic ('Tuna in the Brine', 'Luv Your Life'), aggressive ('One Way Mule', 'The Lever') and uplifting ('My Favourite Thing', 'The Greatest View'). And *Diorama* closes with the simple piano-and-voice ballad 'After All These Years'. Though it may have sounded like a comedown on first listen, the song is actually a message of hope for Johns's future. He'd endured a lot to get to this point of peace. 'After all these years/ Forget about the troubled times,' he sings, as the record waltzes to its finish. And he meant every word.

In the commercial scheme of things, *Diorama* was going to be a tough sell. There was no obvious hit single, not a lot of trademark guitar, and little of the angst or primal energy that had marked the band's earlier work. The response to *Diorama* took a fairly predictable course: first reaction was surprise, but once the music sank in, few critics thought it less than praise-worthy (apart from the British, but by now that was to be expected). In my lead review in the April 2002 edition of Australian *Rolling Stone* I wrote that by 'going light on the anti-depressant murkiness and heavy on surround-sound atmosphere, *Diorama* is one of the boldest statements ever made by an Australian rock band. Seriously.' It was granted a four-and-a-half star rating, almost a perfect score.

American *Rolling Stone*, also gushed: 'Johns and company have become genuine artists on their own terms. Heavy orchestration, unpredictable melodic shifts and a whimsical pop sensibility give *Diorama* the sweeping feel of the work of Brian Wilson or Todd Rundgren.' The reputable *All Music*

Guide seemed shocked that the band had made it through the 1990s and outlived grunge: 'Mostly this is a wonderful surprise from a band thought to have been finished in the late 1990s.'

There were naysayers, naturally. The British press had never thought much of *Frogstomp*, *Freak Show* or *Neon Ballroom*, nor did Silverchair sell many records in the UK, despite regular touring. Their European fanbase was on the continent, in Germany, France, Sweden and Holland, rather than the UK. The *NME* did its usual hatchet job on *Diorama*: 'They think they're making grand and mature musical state-ments,' they barked, 'but it just sounds like they're trying to impress their parents. Utter wank, but in a different way than before.' Canada had been a reliable market for the band — *Frogstomp* sold 204,000 copies there, *Freak Show* 183,000, *Neon Ballroom* 186,000. But Kerry Gold, writing in the Vancouver *Sun*, wasn't sold on *Diorama* either:

> The album is a meandering, highly ambitious odyssey that more often fails than it succeeds. It's either bravery or arro-gance that has driven Johns to think that he could ditch his formula for something that sounds at times like he's striv-ing for Elton John in Disney mode.

It didn't help the band's fortunes in Canada, either, when they found themselves entangled in a spat between their North American parent label, Warner Bros, and HMV record stores, over wholesale prices. Nevertheless, 'The Greatest View' made the Canadian Top Five, and the album debuted in the Top 30. A few negative reviews and a business hitch didn't seem to hurt.

Silverchair had shaken off their Nirvana-in-pyjamas legacy with an album that displayed Johns's songwriting gifts. The album debuted at Number One in Australia on April 7, going platinum in two weeks. It also set a new record — Silverchair became the only Australian band to have four albums debut at Number One. Not even INXS or Midnight Oil had done that.

Diorama's overseas release and promotion, however, was as big as any drama during the band's rollercoaster ride of a career. The release date was originally planned for July — preview shows scheduled for June in London and New York had sold out well in advance — but was rescheduled to August 27, 2002, after Johns was diagnosed with chronic reactive arthritis and cancelled all live appearances. It's a given in these times that you have to promote the hell out of an album — regardless of its merits — to rise above the hundreds of releases every week, but Johns was unable to do that. In fact, he couldn't even walk. Despite the favourable chart placings in Canada and Germany (the album was released in Europe on July 29), *Diorama* limped into the US charts at Number 91. Without the band's physical presence to talk it up, *Diorama* sank there soon after, despite Atlantic's innovative promotion plan — web chats, free downloads and streaming of earlier live shows, all on the band's official website — designed to cope with Johns's illness. There was even talk of a limited theatrical release for the *Across the Night* DVD. None of this, however, generated the kind of sales that typically follow a tour.

David Fricke perfectly summed up the fickle nature of the music industry, especially in America, when asked about the album's fortunes there:

> People don't measure the quality of their music or musical experience by quarterly earnings; corporations do that, not people. Because *Diorama* doesn't take off here in the first three months, it's like, 'Oh well, it's not happening.' But my take is that, well, it's not happening for you now, but that doesn't mean it'll never happen. To write them off now

makes no sense. They'll come back. The problem is that people here think that the music industry is America. The measure of what you achieve is whether someone recognises you when you walk down the street in New York.

Yet in Australia, by December 20, 2002, *Diorama* had gone triple platinum (210,000 copies) and become the band's fastest-selling album in their home territory. Six months after its release, record sales had received a second wind through some shrewd marketing. First there was Johns's 'comeback' performance at the 2002 ARIAs in October, where they collected five trophies. Then there was the season-ending episode of *Rove Live*, one of the few outlets on commercial TV for local bands to force-feed several million people their new music. Aware of the wide audience for the program, and keen to steer the band's music towards an even larger audience, Watson struck up a deal with the show's producers for an entire program dedicated to the band. It didn't seem to matter that the bulk of the show was lifted straight from the *Across the Night: The Creation of Diorama* DVD; the boost to album sales was remarkable. Not only had the band kept their loyal silver-fans — mainstream Australia was also snapping up *Diorama* as commercial stations such as Nova FM put their songs into high rotation for the first time.

The album — which had been floundering at the lower end of the Top 40 — raced back into the Top 10. Within days of the *Rove* show airing, every major label, aware of the kick-start that *Diorama* had received, was calling the producers of *Rove Live* suggesting a program dedicated to their own star of choice. A hefty TV advertising campaign and some high-profile Sunday news magazine stories — again, reaching a new audience for the band — didn't harm *Diorama*'s sales, either.

Johns appeared unfazed by the album's relative commercial failure outside of Australia. When we spoke in October 2002, he was more concerned about nailing *Diorama*'s songs for their Australian tour of March and April 2003. 'Providing we have adequate financial support, I want to do something that's larger than life,' he said, 'that's visually surreal as well. It's going to be a sensory overload.'

With some handy advance warning from chairpage, tickets for all eleven 'Across the Night' Australian shows sold out on December 4, the day they went on sale. Their first hometown show since they appeared as the Australian Silverchair Show in January 1999 sold out in six minutes. Tickets to the first Melbourne show were snapped up in nine minutes. By February 2003, with Johns's health very much improved, additional shows were announced to meet the frenzied demand for tickets — these six extra shows were sell-outs too. Virtually all the 7000 tickets for their Sydney Entertainment Centre show were sold on the first morning. Then there was more chairpage-assisted action when 1000 pre-sale tickets were snapped up for their shows at New York's Bowery Ballroom in June. Extra dates were added to their short tours of the UK and South America, to meet demand. Silverchair may have spent most of 2000 and 2001 out of view by choice, and had 2002 ruined by Johns's arthritis, but the band's fans still needed them. Badly.

Bibliography

Craig Mathieson. *Hi Fi Days: The Future of Australian Rock* 1996; 'I Can't Believe It's Not Rock' Australian *Rolling Stone*; November 2000; 'Backstage at Rock in Rio' Australian *Rolling Stone* April 2001; 'Grunge Glitter' *O Globo* 23/01/2001; 'Making of Diorama: The Resurrection of Daniel Johns' Australian *Rolling Stone* June 2002; 'The Uneasy Chair' Australian *Rolling Stone* September 2002; 'Silverchair's Greater View' Australian *Rolling Stone* April 2003; Australian *Rolling Stone* April 2002; 'Silver Polish' *Sun Herald* 27/01/2002; American *Rolling Stone* 08/08/2002; *All Music Guide* (Allmusic.com); Vancouver *Sun* 08/08/2002;

After All These Years:

an interview with Daniel Johns

The last time I spoke on the record with Daniel Johns was on January 14, 2003. He was in New York with his fiancée, Natalie Imbruglia, taking in four days of R&R before spending his last month in physio bootcamp in Los Angeles. Then he was due back in Australia for the 'Across the Night' tour, the band's sold-out return to playing live. After all of 2002's pain, Johns was in an upbeat frame of mind, talking about love, therapy, dreams, and the band's past and future.

You've finally announced your engagement. It must be a good time for you, after all you went through in 2002.

It's awesome, really good. It solidifies commitment and I think that's pretty important if you want stability — and that's basically what everyone wants. I haven't thought about having children or becoming an adult, but the wedding will happen at the end of the year. It'll be in Australia — maybe in my backyard. To scare off the paparazzi we could do it at [Newcastle's] Fort Scratchley and point the cannons at them.

Is this stability what you need, given that your life is pretty rootless?

It's a weird, strange lifestyle, but pretty exciting as well. Like anything in life, it has its advantages and disadvantages, but being in a rock band means there's more extremes. It's really great or really bad, all the time.

How do you juggle your audience's expectations with your own needs?

A lot of the people who want to hear 'Freak' and 'Anthem for the Year 2000' — well, they're not the songs I get the most satisfaction from playing. But I guess it's exciting in a different way now; when I'm playing songs I really want to play, that's exciting for me, it's like I'm playing for myself. When we're playing songs like 'Freak', they're not my favourite songs, but the enthusiasm and energy of the crowd is exciting. As long as there's a good energy exchange in the room, I'm up for it. But anyone expecting to hear 'Tomorrow' is going to come away disappointed. We could use it as the intro tape [laughs].

Diorama *has been your fastest selling album in Australia. Were you surprised by that, given that you haven't toured and have been out of action for much of 2002?*

I get updates, but I really can't believe it. It's crazy; I really don't understand it, to tell you the truth. Since we've were 14 we've always been told the importance and value of promotion, and we've gone 'bullshit'. Now all we did was turn up on *Rove Live* and sell all these fucking records! I guess people are more liberal in their spending around Christmas and are willing to take more risks. I've also bought a few thousand copies [laughs].

Will you look back at Diorama with mixed emotions: it was the best of times, it was the worst of times ...

I think I'll look back on it as a time of extremely conflicting emotions, rather than anything else. It's been the most emotionally turbulent experience of my life — the best moment of my life and the worst, in the course of one record. The best thing was having the confidence to do the kind of record I wanted to do and have the funding to do that. Now I look back and I'm really proud of it. Any other record, by this stage I'd be looking back, going 'Fuck, I don't like it any more.' And of course getting engaged — all the most amazing things I could imagine have happened during the course of this record. And also the worst: being hospitalised, in pain every day for eight months, having the American record company first not wanting to release it, then release it and not get behind it because radio refused to play it. It's been fucking weird.

Is the record effectively dead in America?

I'm told it's not, but I'm pretty confident it is. We're going to do a handful of shows: one in New York and one in LA, three shows in London, a week in Germany and dates in South America, and try to get on a film soundtrack in America. If something happens out of that, we'll tour more. But if nothing happens out of that, there's no point flogging a dead horse. Let it rest.

Everything's been contradictory. It's the only record I've made in my career that I'm really proud of, and it's the only one that's failed in America. I think it's a good indication of where my head is and where the American public's head is.

Changing the subject, is this physiotherapy a permanent fix?

I think so. There's no one who can give you sure answers that it [reactive arthritis] won't happen again in five years, but the doctor in LA is confident that she can fix all of this. Even if I have it in five years, if it's at the level it's at now, I'm not going to get too depressed about it, because I can manage it. It's not too bad. But six months ago, if someone had told me this is the way it's going to be for five years, I would have killed myself.

227

Have you been able to work on new songs during your downtime?

Ever since I got sick, I've had the longest bout of writer's block I've ever had in my life. I'm a little concerned about it, wondering if I can't write any more. I'm working on the same songs, trying to think of things to make them more interesting. I'm just finding it hard to write at the moment. It'll happen, though.

Could there be too much joy in your life?

Maybe, but it's not a theory I'm subscribing to at the moment. Maybe once I get married I'll just write forever.

Has bouncing between Australia and LA made writing more difficult than usual?

It still feels like I'm not ready to write. Even when I'm home for a couple of months, I still know that I'll be back in LA, hanging around medical centres every day, so I'm not very inspired. I think that has a lot to do with it. I think that once I'm through this treatment and play some shows and have this album out of my system, I'll be ready to write some stuff. I'm looking forward to it.

Is it true you're thinking about moving from Merewether to Sydney?

I don't know; we're thinking about living everywhere. Both me and Nat like to live in different places at different times. I'm definitely going to keep my place in Newcastle — I can't sell it, it has too many sentimental things. We're going to get a smaller place in Sydney, and Nat has a house in LA and a flat in London. We can move all over the place; it's good.

That's a very different outlook from the time you'd shut yourself off from the world, writing songs.

The whole thing with *Diorama* was to not experience real life — I didn't want to know what real life was, I wanted to be selfish and contained in my own head. So I just stayed in my house for months and wrote about the most fantastical side of human life that I could imagine. I exploited every fantasy that I had. Once you've done that you can either think of a whole new batch of fantasies and do it again or experience real life and try to interpret it and write a more real-life album.

'Real life' would be a fair description of Neon Ballroom.

Neon Ballroom was about one of the darkest points in my life. I guess I unconsciously write conceptually these days; everything's a variation on the one theme. The theme with *Diorama* was lyrical abstraction and escapism and exploring emotional colour spectrums. I guess the next time round I want to explore real life. But not just the dark side; I want to write a happy album that's real, rather than a happy album that is based around escapism.

The last year must have given you plenty of source material.

Definitely. I feel like there's lot to draw from. I always know when it's time to write, because I feel like my brain is a sponge; once it gets to the point where I feel like I'm going mad and have to go back to therapy, I know it's time to write, I need to get it out. I'm not quite there yet, but the sponge is growing, I can feel it.

Is therapy beneficial?

I think it's important for me. I don't go into therapy now and cry and moan about how hard my life is. I go every few months. It's the same guy that's helped me through everything; I just make sure that he keeps me in check. It's also good now that I've got a good relationship, a lot of the stuff that I went through when I was by myself, I can now speak about with my girlfriend-slash-fiancée. A lot of my therapy is just conversation; in the past I didn't have anyone to talk to that I trusted. Now I do.

Are you more trusting in general?

No. I think I'm becoming more trusting of the right people and knowing when not to trust people. I think the most fragile parts of my life are when I trusted everyone and that's when I got hurt the most. Now I just pick the right people.

Is Paul Mac one of those people?

He's amazing. He's one of my best, closest friends. He's just one of those people that when I'm with I'm just happy.

Is there any chance of you and him doing another I Can't Believe It's Not Rock?

Definitely. But next time it's not going to be called *I Can't Believe It's Not Rock*. Next time, I feel, it's going to be more important, more of an actual statement. For Paul, he felt like he'd needed to express himself artistically again after writing a very mainstream pop/dance record [*3000 Feet High*]. For me, I was going back into writing again and I felt like I needed a catalyst, something to get my internal fire burning again. We both did it for different reasons, but got the same satisfaction out of it. Next time it's going to be an actual album. We're going to come up with a name for the group and publicise it and let people know it exists.

What about other projects for you outside of Silverchair?

I'm not about to start writing for other people. If I wrote a song that I didn't really love but I thought could be a hit for someone else, I'd be too embarrassed to give it to them. And if I wrote a song I really loved, I'd want to do it myself. But I really love the idea of scoring films; that's what I'd want to be doing at 30, rather than being a rock star.

Any directors on a wishlist?

Baz Luhrmann. I'd also love to do a trippy, abstract animation, cult movie thing and write music for it — that'd be a lot of fun. I really love Paul Thomas Anderson, as well, I think he's an amazing director. I saw *Punch Drunk Love*; that was fucking phenomenal, one of the best scores I've ever heard in my life. But I didn't sit there thinking 'Fuck, I could have done that' — it was more, 'Fuck, I would have loved to have tried.'

I believe you've been listening to music by Brit folkie Nick Drake.

I don't listen to it very often, but I love it. It has a very profound effect on me. It was really encouraging: in a way, it gave me a whole new outlook on music. I always associated simplicity with being boring — I know Bob Dylan is a genius, but five minutes in I get bored. I'm not that lyrical as a person. I don't give a shit about lyrics unless the music's totally amazing. When I heard Nick Drake, I heard that minimalist music approach — which I've always found boring — but I found it so enthralling. It was the only time I've ever listened to that kind of music and wanted to keep hearing it.

Do you move through phases in your personal listening habits?

I'm back into Velvet Underground. I go through that phase three times a year, and I'm back in that phase now, especially being in New York. Last night I just wanted to be Andy Warhol. But I don't think Lou Reed would like me. Me a boy from Merewether, him a miserable git from New York.

What about the idea of self-producing the band's next album?

It's a possibility, but I'm also considering Jon Brion as a co-producer. And I'm thinking about a double album, producing one myself and one with someone else. Or four EPs, all containing six tracks. Seasonal albums, maybe, with different artwork and songs that encapsulate the different seasons.

Do you have a fundamental problem with playing live?

I just get bored really quickly. I know this next tour's going to be fun, because we haven't played for so long.

The trouble with playing live is playing the same songs — no matter how much you try to change them around, you just get bored really quickly. After three months of touring, I just want to stop and write another record. Live can be a really amazing experience, but it ceases to be amazing after three months, it just becomes fucking boring. I don't think we're going to have this problem with this record, though.

What about the idea of you just playing solo, with an acoustic guitar?

Maybe, but I don't think I'd be interesting enough, just sitting there with a guitar. I need tricks: loud drums, guitars. I don't think anyone in the world would be able to entertain me for an hour with just a guitar and their voice, not even John Lennon. I'd be bored, I'd need new things. What are you going to do after three songs? I'm sure Tim Rogers could do it, but even with him I'd be bored after half an hour.

It feels too earthy for me. I've been invited to things like that, but it's not pretentious enough for me [laughs].

The band's touring regime between 1995 and 1999 was gruelling. Do you have any regrets? Did it have a negative impact on you and the band?

I don't regret anything. The thing with that touring was that until '98 we were still in school — that was so fucking hectic. We'd go to school during the week, play shows on the weekend, and then tour during the holidays. Then we'd get back to school two weeks late after being tutored on the road. Then we'd have to catch up after school. None of us wanted to be dumb; we wanted to pass the HSC, we were trying our asses off. As soon as we ended school it became a thousand times harder; we found out that school was an escape. We didn't know it at the time, but I started to realise, 'Fuck, this is my life, this is all I've got.'

Why did Ben Gillies stop writing? He had co-writing credits on Frogstomp and Freak Show.

I think he's still writing. I think the problem is that we had totally different directions in what we wanted to do. The thing that has made this band work is that I've got a totally different vision to Ben. To keep this band working, I had these conceptual ideas that I had to do by myself. I can't share them with people. It was my dream. I wanted to do it in my own house and be totally selfish with it. Ben was cool with that. He just said that he loves playing in this band, and I guess he must like the songs that I write. I'm sure that he's writing at home.

Do you have any regrets that you didn't lean on Ben and Chris for support when you were coming apart as you wrote Neon Ballroom?

No, I don't, because anyone who's been through that kind of thing knows that it's a really intense, personal thing. It was much easier to share it with the universe than with my family and friends. That would have made it too personal, too much about me. I was trying to make it more about the problem, about helping loads of people and not just being about me.

A lot of people have said that Neon Ballroom **was a sort of emotional crutch for them, getting them through tough times.**

That was another thing that inspired the writing of *Diorama*. A lot of people told me how it affected them emotionally, so my whole approach with *Diorama* was to affect them emotionally but in the most amazing, positive way. Anyone that could relate to *Neon Ballroom* hopefully could relate to *Diorama*. They're totally different records, but are so easy to relate to if you're in that dark hole that everyone falls in. *Diorama* is good for people who are going through both good and bad stages in their life. It's total escapism.

How often have you thought about killing off the band?

I consider it every day of my whole life. Every day I wake up and think, 'This is the last day I'm going to be in a band,' then I go, 'Just one more day.' Then I write a song and go, 'This is the last fucking song I'm going to write for this band — OK, maybe one more.' *Freak Show* was the end for me; I'll never forget it. At the end of the tour, I said 'No more Silverchair!' Then I wrote *Neon Ballroom* and *Diorama* and said the same thing: 'No more Silverchair!' I don't know; it's not that I don't enjoy being in the band, I do. And I love those guys, because we have an amazing chemistry. But a lot of it is that attention-span thing: I get bored, I want to do other things.

Do you ever feel like a prisoner of Silverchair?

I did feel like a prisoner of Silverchair until *Diorama*. Then I realised that I could do exactly the same thing as having a solo career but have my favourite band playing with me. When I realised they were cool with that, that was a real important moment in getting my sanity back. I had all the advantages of being a solo artist — and being in a band. I wasn't selfish about it; I was very up front with Ben and Chris about it. I said that in order to be happy this is what I need, and if you're not OK with it, I totally understand. Because if I was presented with the same option, I'd be out of here. But they said, 'No, we just want to play, seriously.' Problem solved.

Have you, Ben and Chris grown apart over the past 10 years?

We've all moved, but in different directions. In a lot of ways that's good. I think a lot of the things I'm trying to do, Ben and Chris don't understand. I don't mean that as a judgement of their intelligence, but it's just that I can't even tell you how different we are as people.

If someone said to me, 'Pick two people who are your opposites,' it'd be Ben and Chris. When we started out, at 13 or 14, we were exactly the fucking same. But as we grew up and went through the same kind of experiences, it's interesting how it affected us and shaped our personalities. We went through the whole being-famous-and-going-through-adolescence thing together, and came out the other side complete opposites. I've no idea how it happened.

Do you spend much downtime with your bandmates?

Not really, to tell you the truth. Maybe in 10 years time we'll want to hang out together, you know, childhood friends hanging out and talking about the past. We still get along really well — we're the only band in history that never fights. It's never, ever happened. It's weird.

8

Tomorrow Never Knows

'I know I'm selfish, but I don't care.
I'm an indulgent bastard.'

—Daniel Johns

Daniel Johns has made it perfectly clear that he's not built for the standard album–tour–promotion grind that's crucial for selling albums at a time when perhaps too many records are released. Like such masters as the Beatles and REM — bands who've opted out of touring and focused all their attention on studiocraft — Johns is more interested in the band's recorded legacy. Talking to me in October 2002, he commented about touring, 'I understand it is an important part of maintaining a fanbase, which is what we need to get the money to make the kind of music I make. I'm more ambitious than ever, I want to write the best album ever. [But] I don't have a hunger for touring.'

This anti-touring attitude may eventually pull Johns away from his bandmates, Ben Gillies and Chris Joannou. As the songwriter, Johns receives the substantially larger royalty for each album sold; Gillies and Joannou are paid a smaller performing royalty. Johns understands that the pair therefore need to tour to make a living, but he doesn't fancy becoming their meal ticket. And given the thrills Johns gained from the *I Can't Believe It's Not Rock* side project, it's not unreasonable to assume he'll be involving himself in more non-Silverchair activities. He's got a hunger for writing soundtracks, too: 'I always feel external pressure from everyone,' he told me, when I asked whether he felt responsible for the livelihood of his bandmates, 'But, you know, if we're together as a band, their livelihood is more fruitful.'

Which, of course, isn't exactly saying that Silverchair is destined for a long future. Even in the band's private lives and musical tastes, the gulf between Gillies, Joannou and Johns is starting to show; they're drifting apart. While Johns has been tuning into acoustic-based artists such as Nick Drake, Gillies has been boning up on James Brown (even to the point of sporting a tattoo of the funk godfather on his upper left arm), and Joannou has been dipping back into old favourites such as Hendrix and Led Zeppelin, as well as producing tracks for Sydney garage rockers The Mess Hall, a first for the bassman.

Joannou and girlfriend Sarah McLeod live comfortably on the NSW Central Coast, where Joannou designs and makes the T-shirts his partner wears on stage. Gillies still lives in Merewether, where he spends time with his ballet dancer girl-friend, Hayley Alexander, whom he met in mid 2002. He's developed interests in yoga, astrology and chess, curious hob-bies for the man long considered Silverchair's party animal. He and Alexander have even taken salsa dancing lessons from Gillies's mother. And both Gillies and Joannou are quietly working away on music of their own. The three bandmates spend little time together. In contrast, as well-documented in the tabloids, Johns and fiancée Natalie Imbruglia have been spending a lot of their time away from Newcastle. In fact, they're quite the wanderers, drifting between Sydney and Imbruglia's homes in Los Angeles and London, where she was involved in a bizarre near-kidnapping in March 2003. It's a nomadic lifestyle Johns and Imbruglia have both said they prefer. 'You are at home with your loved ones,' Imbruglia said, 'and so when Daniel is with me, I feel at home. I'm a gypsy.'

Johns and Imbruglia are frequently seen in public in Sydney: the two were spotted at Brian Wilson's State Theatre show in Sydney in October 2002, and two days later Johns was watching Imbruglia perform at the Rumba popfest at the Olympic site in Homebush. He can't speak positively enough about Imbruglia, and her role in helping him recover from his chronic reactive arthritis. 'She's been amazing,' he told me. 'My family's always been there, but when there's someone you love, it's different. She's still fulfilling all the [promotional] obligations she has, but she's not taking anything else on board. I didn't ask for that, but I really appreciate it.'

But the more time Johns and Imbruglia spend in Sydney the more likelihood of their increased presence in the tabloids. Although he has been dealing with similar intrusions since he was 15, they still rile Johns, who typically goes out of his way to avoid confrontation. 'Yeah, it's fucking ridiculous,' he said, when I asked how it felt to be public property:

> You can get to a point where you become famous for being famous. That's why I'm not doing many interviews these days; I've already been all over the papers.

> You expect a fair bit of it going out with someone famous, but I'm not comfortable with it. You can't help who you fall in love with, though.

But for the moment, Johns's thoughts are on writing more music, most likely for Silverchair album number five.

Of the new songs he's recently written, he admits that two of them are even more cinematic than the songs on *Diorama*. 'I was originally thinking of doing something more minimalist, but I don't think I have it in me. I have to go bigger and better every time.' Ambition isn't something Daniel Johns scrimps on. But at the same time, he has no plans to write for an audience larger than himself, and readily admits that he writes mainly for personal satisfaction — and why not? The band has sold more than six million albums; Johns has his palatial Merewether home, investment properties and money in the bank. It's guaranteed that he won't go hungry for a long time, no matter how few records he sells in the future, or how few shows the band opt to perform. 'I know I'm selfish, but I don't care,' he told me, point blank, when I asked whether his audience's tastes impact on his songwriting. 'I'm an indulgent bastard. I'm a hundred per cent selfish when it comes to music. I do think about people when it's done, but not when I'm writing the music.'

Rolling Stone's David Fricke thinks Johns's potential is boundless:

> Daniel's still at an age where he can do whatever he wants. I never understood the phrase 'natural progression'. People do what they do when they're moved to do it. It's not like you're on a particular trajectory or path. I thought *Diorama* was quite good and has been very underrated.

John O'Donnell concurs: 'I think this hard year they've had will galvanise them. The resolve to stay in Silverchair — and what Silverchair means to them — is very strong. My hunch is that because of this last year they'll make more music as Silverchair than they might have otherwise.'

But it's not as if Johns is in a hurry to get back to recording. The fog of 1999's *Neon Ballroom*, and the reactive arthritis that kicked in while he was mixing *Diorama*, have, understandably, made him more than a little cautious about rushing back to the studio. Next time around, he wants the songs to come naturally — and he won't be writing to instructions from the record company. 'I think it's going to take me a long time to write the next album,' he said. 'I'm still not feeling the magic. I'm still just throwing things around and trying to get that feeling. It'll come.'

When 'Tomorrow' sprang out of nowhere in 1994, the good money was on Silverchair not lasting much longer than the song. Even the band weren't sure about their longevity. Joannou had contingency plans to become a mechanic, 'just in case the music thing doesn't work out'. Gillies was thinking about a career as an audio engineer. But John Lennon got it right when he sang that 'life is what happens to you when you're busy making other plans.' *Frogstomp* kept selling and selling, and the band — despite such nuisances as finishing high school and making it through puberty — went global in a way no other Australian band has since INXS.

And while *Freak Show*, *Neon Ballroom* and *Diorama* didn't explode commercially with quite the force of *Frogstomp*, they did cement the band's reputation as a creative rock & roll force. By 1997, Gillies was joking that, 'We could be doing this until we're bloody Aerosmith or something.' Johns — an enigmatic man, equal parts light and shade — is widely regarded as one of the most visionary songwriters of his time. And Silverchair's fans have remained loyal, despite the band's reduced touring. That was driven home with their 2003

'Across the Night' Australian tour, with tickets sold out almost immediately, and the demand for extra shows only tempered by concerns whether Johns's body could take more than eleven shows in four weeks. No other Australian band has such commercial firepower.

And they're still only 24, an age at which many musicians are just cutting their first album and learning how ruthless and fickle the music business can be. If Silverchair do nothing else in music for the rest of their lives, their legacy is established. They are one of the few bands to outgrow the grunge revolution and blossom into a creative force, true groundbreakers in Australian music. Oh, and they can rock like sons of bitches live, too. But I get the feeling that Silverchair have a few more thrills for us. After all, tomorrow never knows.

Bibliography

'Imbruglia Staying Put in England' *The Sun-Herald* 23/03/2003; 'Making of Diorama: The Resurrection of Daniel Johns' Australian *Rolling Stone* June 2002; 'The Uneasy Chair' Australian *Rolling Stone* September 2002; 'Silverchair's Greater View' Australian *Rolling Stone* April 2003

Discography

Albums

Release Date	High Point	Weeks in Chart	
27/03/95	1	86	*Frogstomp*
03/02/97	1	67	*Freak Show*
08/03/99	1	64	*Neon Ballroom*
13/11/00	16	85	*Best Of Volume 1* (CD + DVD)
31/03/02	1	50	*Diorama*
21/10/02	60	21	*Silverchair – The Best of Volume 1*
17/12/02	N/A		*Rarities 1994 – 1999*

Singles/EPs

Release Date	High Point	Weeks in Chart	
16/09/94	1	45	*Tomorrow* (EP)
13/01/95	2	22	*Pure Massacre* (S)
12/04/95	11	15	*Israel's Son* (S)
19/06/95	28	14	*Shade* (S)
13/11/95	N/A		*Findaway* (Fan club only)

Discography

Release Date	High Point	Weeks in Chart	
13/01/97	1	15	*Freak* (S)
24/03/97	9	29	*Abuse Me* (S)
30/06/97	5	21	*Cemetery* (S)
06/10/97	25	21	*The Door* (S)
15/02/99	3	35	*Anthem for the Year 2000* (S)
10/05/99	14	25	*Ana's Song* (Open Fire) (S)
06/09/99	17	31	*Miss You Love* (S)
Late '99	N/A		*Paint Pastel Princess* (Fan club only)
28/01/02	3	33	*The Greatest View* (S)
13/05/02	8	43	*Without You*
02/09/02	20	27	*Luv Your Life*
31/03/03	24	N/A	*Across the Night*

(Australia-only chart figures; courtesy of ARIA)

Collections

1997   *Freak Box* (Freak Show Singles Box Set)
2002   *Diorama Singles Box Set*

DVDs

2000   *Emotion Pictures*
2000   *Best Of Volume 1: Complete Videology DVD*
2002   *Across the Night*
2003   *Across the Night* DVD single

Soundtracks

Year	Track	Movie
1995	*Stoned*	*Mall Rats*
1996	*Blind*	*The Cable Guy*
1997	*Spawn*	*Spawn*
1998	*Untitled*	*Godzilla*
1998	*Freak* (Remix for Us Rejects)	*Head On*
2000	*Punk Song #2*	*Scary Movie*